PIERCED

HUSS McCLAIN

Copyright © 2018 by JA Huss and Johnathan McClain
ISBN: 978-1-944475-81-9

Edited by RJ Locksley
Cover Design by JA Huss

CHAPTER ONE

October in Colorado is spectacular. You don't get all the colors like you do back east. We just don't have trees like that here. You know, the kind that turn red and orange. We mostly have pine trees and they just stay green. But the air is crisp, and when you look west and notice that the mountains are now capped with snow, you can't help it. You sigh. You say, Finally. You say, Missed you, snow. And I'm gonna come visit this weekend for sure. See all those golden aspens and get giddy over the snowflakes falling as I holiday-shop in Vail Village.

But of course, that almost never happens. Getting up to the mountains on the weekends once summer is over is a freaking nightmare. Because the tourists pour in for skiing and they all have the same romantic idea.

I'm not really a romantic woman. I gave up on the idea of romance a long time ago. But I can appreciate the natural beauty of something and I have a nice view of the snowcaps from my office, so I find myself looking at them often these days.

Oh, did I mention I have an office now?

I do.

It's right next to my boss.

Pierce Chevalier. Owner of Le Man magazine, self-proclaimed king, and currently on my shit list.

Which is the whole reason I have the office.

After he wrongly accused me of being the Sexpert, publicly humiliated me in front of the entire world, and then came crawling back—begging my forgiveness and offering me a fat raise if I didn't quit—well, I decided to stay and make the most of things.

The office came a couple weeks later. After he hired Eden and Zoey to be his marketing consultants. I'm their liaison at the company, which was the justification for giving me the executive office that used to belong to Josh Washburn.

He took it well. Josh, I mean. Pierce… that's another story. He's still getting used to Valerie, his new executive assistant, who sits at my old desk manning the phones, and the appointments, and all the other shit I used to do, but don't anymore.

He even offered to share her with me.

So. Yeah. I came out ahead. I'm actually VP of social media. Pierce said he had to change my title because the raise he gave me put my salary a good twenty thousand dollars above Josh Washburn, who is the VP of advertising, and the accountants started asking questions about secret scandals.

I reminded him the scandal wasn't secret. It was very, very public.

So he said I could get a new desk, and did I need a new chair to go with it?

I sigh, spin my new two-thousand-dollar chair back to my computer, and begin scanning emails. I only have two new ones. One, a corporate reminder about the office Halloween party. And two, a mass email from the Tall, Dark, and Handsome Community Center saying they're looking for people to teach new classes and all ideas are welcome.

I hate this job now. Which really sucks because I used to love it. I used to love dominating Pierce's schedule and making people feel uncomfortable with my understated sexual innuendo. I mean, I eat my banana every morning like I used to, but Josh is all the way over by the printer room now. He can't even see me.

And I wear the thigh-high stockings and pretend to pull them up. Just like always. But now I'm stuck in this office, not blocking Pierce's door. So no one sees that either.

I can't even raise eyebrows by seductively sucking on my Starbucks straw.

Plus I have like… no work. VP of social media? Even if I did want to share an assistant with Pierce—and I don't. I'm not a girl who shares—there's nothing for her to do. Like… there's not even a social media department because Eden is gone. I mean, she comes in every Monday for a meeting. She's my only appointment today, so I'm gonna see her in like twenty minutes. But still, there are no donuts. There's no smiles. No daily greetings.

It's all… different.

I guess I could make Eden's old boss miserable. That would be fun. But Gretchen works down on forty-nine, so intimidating her is a production.

So I usually close my door and read erotic novels all day. Which, hey, I'm not really complaining about that part, but I'm all caught up on my TBR list. And Scarlett Savannah, my favorite dirty author, won't have another book out for six more weeks.

Six weeks is a long time to sit in an office and pretend you're busy.

I think I need another work-day hobby. Knitting is nice and quiet. Or I could buy one of those black velvet paint-by-number kits from Michael's and be artistic. Oh, I know. Scrapbooking! I wonder if the TDH Community Center has a scrapbooking class? I could get lost in twelve-by-twelve square paper and cute, die-cut thingamajigs. Or maybe I could—

"Knock, knock?"

I look up from my computer and see Pierce, standing in the doorway of my office.

"Can I come in?" he asks.

"You're the boss," I huff.

He smiles. Tightly. Like he's unsure how to proceed. It's just all so different.

"Uh… so how's things?'

"Things?" I ask, raising one perfect eyebrow. "Do you have a specific example of said things?"

"Well, no," he says, coming inside to take a seat in front of my desk. "Nothing specific. Just… wondering if you have time for a special project."

We both look at my desk. Which doesn't have a single file on it. Not even one sheet of paper. My Post-It pad is still crisp and every pencil in my little pencil can is sharp. I think it's pretty obvious that I do nothing in here all day.

But I'm still angry at him. So if he thinks I'm gonna be the first to admit I don't actually have a job to do and I'm just wasting corporate money, he's mistaken.

"I'm pretty busy," I say.

"Yeah," he says, sighing. "I know. And I don't want to take advantage or anything, but I could use your help."

I have my reading glasses on, so I do that head-tilt thing where you look down your nose at someone. "With what?"

He looks around. Plucks a pencil out of the pencil jar. Taps it to his head as he thinks.

He doesn't have a project for me. He just wanted to come in here and feel me out.

We both know this.

But then he gets an idea. I swear I can see the little light bulb go off in his head. "The Halloween party."

"What about it?"

"We… need… well…"

"Pierce?"

"What?"

"You don't have a project for me. And I don't even have a job here."

"Of course you do! You're the VP—"

"Of social media, I know. The little plaque outside my office says so. But we both know there's no social media department. Not to mention, I'm not even on social media and have no idea how it even works."

"You don't have socials? How did I not know that?"

"Well, you did think I was the Sexpert. So I'm just going to assume you don't actually know anything about me."

"How can you still be pissed at me? It's been months! I gave you a promotion, and an office, and—"

"Again," I say, putting up a hand to cut him off, "I do realize all that. And once again, it's all meaningless. You don't even know what a social media department does."

"It's not meaningless." He tugs on his suit coat. "And

7

I'm well-versed in socials. I was Snapchatting just last night."

"With who?"

"Uh…" He looks over his shoulder, like he needs a second to think, then says, "Valerie. She's my chat friend now."

"You know I can tell when you lie, right? Your left eye does this little wink thing every time."

He huffs, then leans forward in his chair. "How long will you continue to do this?"

"Do what?"

"Punish me."

I laugh. Stop. Then laugh again. It's a little bit of a guffaw with a healthy dose of maniacal thrown in for good measure. "This is not me trying to punish you, Pierce. This is me biding my time."

He lifts up one eyebrow. "Biding your time until… what?"

"Until I have the perfect diabolical plan to pay you back."

He sits back in his chair, breathes deep. "So that's what you need? Payback?"

"I was publicly humiliated. A woman doesn't just get over it, Pierce."

He winces when I snarl his name. "You hate me."

"People look at me funny now, you do realize that?"

"Look at you funny how?"

"Like I'm hiding some secret sexual fetish side."

"Aren't you?"

"What do you want?"

"I mean, you do come off as… kind of a…"

"A what?"

"You know. Like you're into the whole Red Room

spanking thing, right?"

"Anastasia Steele? You're comparing me to Anastasia Steele? Please."

"Well, you wear those tight pencil skirts… and those sexy secretary glasses. Plus, I know you read that smut in here. You don't even use an eReader. Everyone can see the covers. I used to have little Christian Grey fantasies when you used to look at me. Before… ya know, you decided to hate me."

I laugh. And it's not even maniacal. It's real.

"Why is that funny?"

"My dearest Pierce," I say, still chuckling, "you are no Christian Grey. If anyone is Mr. Grey in this relationship, it's me."

Now he laughs.

"Is that funny?"

"Uh, well. No. Well, kinda. I mean, it's sorta accurate, actually. Which makes it funny." He clears his throat. "So I laughed."

"Why are you here again?"

"Yes," he says, standing up and buttoning his coat. "The Halloween party. You're in charge."

"No." I laugh again, then get deadly serious. "I do not. Do. Halloween."

"Are you sure?" he asks, a little twinkle in his eye. "Because I could've sworn you'd be into it."

"Into… what? Handing out carbohydrates to sticky-faced children?" How could this man ever think I'd be into Halloween?

"No," he says, lowering his voice. "You know. Costumes and… roleplaying." He waggles his eyebrows at me.

Which makes me squint at him.

9

"So yeah. Beth used to do it, but she quit last month. So you're in charge. Better make it good, Myrtle. I've got a special edition of the magazine coming out the first week of December called Inside Le Man and I'm counting on it to launch us into the holiday advertising season. We need to sell two million dollars in ads before January first or none of us will have jobs in the new year."

I'm just about to open my mouth to protest, tell him where he can shove his Halloween party, when a shadow appears in my doorway.

"Knock, knock!" Eden says. "I had to make the rounds and pass out donuts, so I'm early." She looks at me, realizes she's interrupting an argument, and shrugs. "Sorry. Should I come back?"

"I was just leaving," Pierce says. "Myrtle will fill you in on the Halloween project. Should be right up your alley, Eden. Sugar and sexy. The two things you do best."

He walks out with a huff. Eden and I both watch him disappear, then she closes the door and says, "What was that all about?"

"He thinks I'm in charge of the Halloween party."

"Fun!"

"I hate Halloween."

"Oh. Well, I love it."

"Of course you do."

"So I'll help."

"Wonderful."

"Jesus, Myrtle. What's wrong with you these days? You used to be so... sexy and mysterious. And now you're always hiding here in your office like a wallflower."

"I'm not a wallflower!"

Eden recoils because I just sorta yelled that last part.

"Sorry," I say, pointing to the chair Pierce just

10

vacated. "Sit. Let's catch up. I miss you, Eden. So much. I wish you were still here."

She scrunches up her face. "Are you sure you miss me—"

"Of course."

"—and not your old job as Pierce's dom?"

I laugh for the third time in ten minutes. And this time it makes me happy. "I told him I was the top!"

"You so are. Did he deny it?"

"Tried. But we know who ran his life. Valerie couldn't boss him if her life depended on it. And she doesn't. She's a meek little mouse when it comes to Pierce. And you know what the worst part is?"

"What?"

"He likes it. He actually beams every time she says, 'Yes, Mr. Chevalier! Right away, Mr. Chevalier! I'm on it, Mr. Chevalier!' That's probably why he moved me to this stupid job."

"You're a VP, Myrtle. I don't think that's what he was thinking when he gave you a fifty-thousand-dollar raise."

"I'm so bored, Eden." I'm whining now. I know it. But I can't stop. "The world does not need another black-velvet Elvis and if I have to knit Christmas sweaters and scrapbook this stupid Halloween party, I might as well just die of humiliation right now!"

"OK," Eden says. "We're getting out of here. Right now. You need a field trip."

"To where? And to do what? I'm not throwing this stupid Halloween party, Eden."

"I'll do everything. Just… get your purse. We're going shopping."

CHAPTER TWO

*"**Please, come on in.** Make yourself at home,"* Andrew says as I walk into his office and sit on the sofa facing his desk. I assume he's being sarcastic, as I have already let myself in. And I make myself at home wherever I am, so, yes, sarcasm.

Historically, I'm not much of a gnawing-on-my-nails kind of a person, but lately, in the wake of all this Myrtle nonsense, I find myself doing it unconsciously. It's become so unconscious that if Andrew didn't say...

"Hey. Please stop spitting your nails on my sofa."

... I don't know if I'd notice that I was doing it right now.

"Merde!" I might yell as I stand and tug at my waistcoat.

He sighs. He does that a lot. Or at least he does it a lot when I'm around. I have to assume he does it a lot in general. That worries me.

"Do you need to see a doctor?" I ask him.

"...Why would I need to see a doctor?"

"I'm worried about your lung capacity."

"What? Why—?"

"You don't wanna be climbing a mountain or some shit and have your lungs give out, do you?"

"What are you talking about?"

"Myrtle!" I exclaim.

"Wha—? Why—? Who—? What? What does Myrtle have to do with my lungs?"

"Nothing. What are you talking about?"

"What? What are you talking about?"

We kind of stare at each other for a moment. Then he says, "Let's start again. Please, come on in. Make yourself at home."

"She won't let me off the hook, man," I tell him. "I've done everything I can think to do and she's still holding it all over my head."

"Have you apologized?"

"Define 'apology.'"

"Dude—"

"Of course I've apologized! It was the first, second, fifth, eighth, and like seventeenth thing I did. In between giving her raises, promoting her, and telling her she smells nice all the time."

"Think that last one is actually just sexual harassment."

"I don't know what she wants. I mean, I'm playing it cool. Not letting her know that it's getting to me."

He raises an eyebrow at me.

"What?" That's moi.

"I'm just..." He stops himself short.

"Spit it out, man!"

"OK. I mean, I'm sure that you are playing it cool. For you. Buuuuut…"

"Buuuuut what? What are you saying? Are you saying I can't play cool? I can play cool, mon ami. I am Mista motherfucking Cool!" I flop back down on the sofa to make my point. But my goddamn waistcoat bunches up again. It drives me crazy when it does that. I try to tug it down. It won't sit right. So I stand again, straighten my jacket and vest, and lean casually on the arm of the sofa.

To show how fucking cool I am.

Andrew stares at me the whole time. He might blink once.

"Mista motherfuckin' Cool," I reiterate. For effect.

He comes around the side of his desk, walks over to me, and takes me by the hand.

"What are you doing? Why are you doing that? Don't do that. What are you doing?" I ask, as he draws me down next to him on the sofa.

"Bro," he says, like you talk to someone standing on the edge of a building to keep them from jumping. "Maybe you need to take some time off."

"Time off from what?"

"Um… all of it. Work. It's been a rough few months. You might be a little burned out."

"I don't get burned out," I tell him, trying to stand. But he pulls me back down. He's really strong. That rock-climbing shit must work.

"I know, I know," he says, patting me. (I hate being patted.) "But you've had a lot on you with the whole Eden thing. And what that did to the whole Myrtle thing. Hey!" he says, with a clap. "Have you even been to Paris this year? I don't think you have. You should go to Paris. Isn't it always grounding for you?"

"Why do you say that?"

"Because… you've told me it's… always… grounding. For you."

I manage to pull free from his grip and stand. I look at him sitting there.

"Gotta be honest… I came down to my best friend's office to chat about an employee problem and shit is starting to feel like an intervention, man."

He nods. Sighs again. (Seriously, I'm worried about him.) And then he says, "Well, couple things. One, Myrtle is not an 'employee.'"

"She isn't?"

"I mean, she is, but she's more than that."

That catches me by surprise. Because he's right. But I have tried to keep it to myself. So I don't know how he knows that.

"How do you know that?" I ask. Obviously.

"C'mon, man," he says, standing up as well. "I saw how she looked at you. And how you looked at her. Before…"

He doesn't finish the sentence with, Before you falsely accused her of trying to ruin your company and publicly humiliated her, but I assume it's implied.

"Do you remember when you had that team-building thing?" he asks.

I pause, remembering. "Which team-building thing?"

He doesn't so much sigh now as he blows out through his lips. I'm going to get him to see a pulmonologist I know.

"At the rock-climbing gym? The one you had to try to ferret out who the Sexpert was? You gave a big speech? Any of this ringing a bell?"

"Dude, I give lots of speeches and do lots of things."

"It was the day you told me you thought Myrtle was the Sexpert!"

"Oh. Oh, the day she was wearing the leggings with the cutouts and the tube-top. I think she also had on pink climbing shoes. Her hair was pinned back with a brass hair pin. Nails were fire-engine red. That day?"

"Yes!" he says, way too excited if you ask me, pointing his finger and kind of jumping.

"Jesus, man. Calm down. Maybe you need the holiday."

"No, dumbass! Right there. That thing you just did."

"What did I do?"

"You don't bother to remember anything. About anyone. Ever."

"That's not true."

"What's my middle name?"

I don't know what this game is that we're playing right now, but I find it intensely unfair. "Um…"

"You've known me for almost thirteen years. You're my best friend. I moved my company to the ridiculously-named TDH because you asked me to. I would lie down in traffic for you and I love you like a brother… What's my middle name?"

I can feel my jaw tightening. My fingers twitch. I want to chew on them. That's weird. "Crans… fan… dimmel… berg…?"

Fuck. I have no idea what Andrew's middle name is. Huh.

He shakes his head, "Andrew Cransfandimmelberg Hawthorne. That's my name? How does that even—?" He shakes his head again. Harder. Like he's shaking something out of his brain. "Fuck it. Look, my point is that you don't know anything about anyone. Because you're selfish."

"Thanks."

"Hey, everybody's selfish to one degree or another. You've just elevated it to an art form, but as an artist, I have to admire that. But my point is, dude, it took you being introduced to Eden like six times to remember who she was. But you just described what Myrtle was wearing four months ago. To the letter."

I pause, considering this. "It might have been silver. The hairpin."

"Jesus, man," he says. "That. That's how I know that she's more than an employee."

Touché, Andrew Cransfandimmelberg Hawthorne. Touché.

"She thinks I don't know anything about her," I tell him. I think a little poutily.

"Why do you say that?"

"She said it to me. Like ten minutes ago. She said, 'I'm going to assume you don't know anything about me.'"

He bows his head and looks up at me. "Is that actually what's got you so upset? That she thinks you think of her—or don't think of her—like everybody else?"

I shrug. Then, "Yeah, OK," I say. "What's the other thing?"

"What?"

"When I said this was starting to sound like an intervention, you said, 'Couple things. One. Myrtle is not an 'employee.' What's the other thing?"

"Oh. Yeah. This is an intervention."

I knew it.

"And what are you intervening in?" I ask.

"Your sanity. Your wellbeing. Your fucking lifespan, man. As in, I'm trying to help you extend it."

"I'm never gonna die. I don't like the idea of it."

"Yeah, well… that right there is the problem."

I glance out the window for some reason. Something about the mountains outside catches my eye. The view from Andrew's office is different than it is from mine even though it's just two floors lower. I never noticed that before.

"Sorry?" I ask.

"I said," he says, "that's your problem."

"What is?"

"You hold onto everything so tightly. Or you try to. You can't control everything, man. You know what rock climbing teaches you?"

"Oh, Jesus, please don't with the whole 'rock climbing is a teacher of life' bullshit."

"Can't help it. It is. And one of the things it teaches is that you have to be pliant."

"Pliant?"

"Pliable."

"OK."

You can't actually grip shit too tightly. It's about communing with the rocks. Finding harmony with them. Realizing that they are more powerful than you and learning to submit. It's about finding compromise within yourself."

"Right. And after you do all that shit, you tighten your knuckles around those stones and you hold on for dear life."

He wanders around behind his desk and sits. He looks tired. Maybe I need to get him to a cardiologist too.

And he's worried about me.

"Dude," he says, flopping into his chair, "what can I do to help? When I got to Denver you were obsessing about the whole Sexpert thing, and I thought when that got sorted out you'd mellow a little. Isn't your dad happy with how things have turned around for the magazine?"

"He's thrilled."

"That's great."

"Yeah. He's talking to me more, becoming more involved with what I'm doing…"

"Really? Good. That's good, right?"

"I'll be honest. I don't hate it. And it looks like we're maybe going to turn what was looking like a nosedive around and maybe even beat our total revenue from last year."

"That's amazing!"

"Yeah… it is. Hm." I kind of frown.

He notices. I know he does because he asks, "So, what's wrong?"

"I just told Myrtle that if we don't sell two million in ad revenue before December that we'll all be out of a job."

"What? Why?" He kind of moans the second word. It's hard to tell if it's an actual moan because he has his hands over his face.

"I dunno! I'm trying to, like, engage her or something. Get her to feel excited. Or connected to… something. Me. Or whatever. I don't fuckin' know! I run a men's magazine, not Psychology Today!"

He spins his chair around so that his back is to me. I look outside at the mountains again. Yep. Still there.

He rolls the chair back around. Slowly. "You know another way you could try to engage with her?" he asks.

"How?"

"Engage with her. Like, I'm saying… don't just say you're sorry. Show her you're sorry. I'm saying, like, swallow your fuckin' pride, man. Prostrate yourself a little bit."

I have never once, in my entire life, had it suggested to me that I prostrate any part of myself to anyone or anything. I'm not even really sure I know what the word means. "Is that like… bow?"

"No, that's 'genuflect.' Which is what you expect people to do to you, your highness."

"I do not."

"Bro… there's a throne in your office. Literally, it means to lay yourself flat. To completely abdicate the pretense of power and give over to another. I've done it. With Eden."

"I'll bet you have. Sicko."

He doesn't laugh at my joke. Fuck him. I know it was funny.

He goes on, "When I realized that I had been unfair to her. When I held her responsible for my feelings. I had to earn her trust somehow. Had to. So I just admitted my failings and basically threw myself at her mercy. And, finally, she forgave me. Because she could see I was cowed."

He lets that hang in the air. Then follows up with…

"And you know who told me to do that?"

"… Myrtle?"

"Myrtle? Dude, I'm terrified of Myrtle. I wouldn't be in a room with her alone long enough for her to give me directions, much less life advice. No, man. It was you."

I am rarely speechless. I am now. I work out one word. "Me?"

21

"Yeah. I mean not in so many words, but that was what you encouraged me to do. Just to be... repentant. And I was. And it worked. Whatever. I know you're not in a thing with Myrtle exactly, not like I was with the Lady Presley, but she clearly means something to you, so you just have to decide how much that something is."

I take a moment to digest this. I just came down to blow off some steam. I wasn't ready for my man to go full-on Dr. Phil on me.

"But," I say, haltingly, "I'm not you. And Myrtle isn't Eden."

"Yeah, no shit," he says—kinda harshly, if I'm being honest. Then he catches himself. "No, I know. But, still, people are people, and if you want to move past whatever this is to... whatever you want it to be... you gotta do something, mon frère."

It's so cute when Andrew speaks French.

My eyes dart around the room, taking everything in. To what end, I have no idea, but I think I'm looking for something that's actually inside my brain.

"OK. Thanks. I gotta go." I start to leave.

"I'm serious, man. Submit. Go to Paris. Stop lying to Myrtle about the magazine to... whatever you're trying to do. Honestly, that part confuses the shit out of me, but you do you."

I nod. Not in acknowledgement. I actually have no idea what he just said. I wasn't listening. But I do it as a reflex, and my hand is on the door to leave when Andrew's developer kid—um, Declan, I think... no. That's Scottish. The kid is Indian. Nepalese? No, I think for sure Indian.

Anyway, he walks in. "What's up, Pierce?" the kid says.

"Hey... man," I say.

"You dunno my name, do you?" he asks.

"I—" I don't even feel like trying right now. "Declan?"

"Seriously? It's Dev."

"Ah! Yes! I knew it started with a 'D.'"

The kid rolls his eyes. He's precocious.

I'm just about out the door when, for some reason, I turn to ask, "Hey, Dev?" He turns to me. "Do you know Andrew's middle name?"

"Cransfandimmelberg," he says. "Isn't it, Andrew?"

It takes me a moment before… "You guys working on a new eavesdropping app?"

"Government contracts are government contracts," Andrew says.

"Andrew?" He looks at me, inscrutable. "Does it hurt?"

"What?"

"Prostrating yourself."

He pauses and then says, "Yeah, but in a good way. If you do it right."

And off that bit of what I assume is foreshadowing, I'm gone.

CHAPTER THREE

Outside the TDH is bustling with people and food trucks. Eden and I stop at one to grab coffee, and then we start strolling. This part of the TDH is mostly office buildings, but a little further north there are tons of shops. All of them remind us that it's a new season and the holidays are right around the corner.

"So…" Eden says. "The Halloween party. Last year it was stupid. Hardly anyone dressed up. I came as Harley Quinn. God, that part was fun! I wish I was dating Andrew last year. He could've been Joker."

"I have no idea. I take Halloween off every year. Pierce knows this. And yet he came into my office thinking this would get me engaged? Just… God, he infuriates me!"

"Come on." Eden snorts. "Pierce doesn't know anything. He pretty much bumbles around from minute to minute like a dog looking for squirrels."

"True," I mutter, my attention now on the woman

25

outside the TDH Community Center who is thrusting fliers at unsuspecting pedestrians. That scrapbooking class pops back into my head like a bad acid-trip flashback. I walk faster to get away from her. "But I've been his assistant for seven years, Eden. Which means he's had seven chances to notice. I feel like... like it was all a waste of time."

"It wasn't. And he loves you. Everyone can tell."

"Loves me? How could a man who thinks I'm into Halloween have any feelings for me at all? It makes no sense."

"Are you sure you're not into Halloween?"

I huff. "Positive. I hate all holidays. I don't do Christmas, or Valentine's Day, or St. Patrick's Day parades."

"New Year's?" she asks.

"No. That stupid midnight kiss. It's all fake. And even if it wasn't a new year, I'd despise any day that proclaimed itself dungeon master of resolutions."

Eden stops walking and squints at me. "Dungeon master?"

"Never mind. Why did we stop?"

"We're here."

I look at the shop we're standing in front of. It's one of those pop-up seasonal stores with the Grim Reaper painted on the window. He's holding a sign that says, 'Party Central.' "No," I say.

"Yes," Eden says, gripping my coat sleeve and tugging me towards the door. "We need to get you into the spirit, so you're choosing a costume. Besides, we need new decorations. And a theme. We need to pick a theme."

"Isn't the theme Halloween? Like what more is there?"

"Oh." Eden laughs. "Just wait." She pulls the door open and waves me inside.

I'm just about to make a run for it when the community center lady says, "Classes start soon!" as she thrusts her flier at me.

I go inside before that scrapbooking idea can take root.

"All who enter will die, muah-ha-ha-ha-ha..." the mechanical Dracula spits as I clear a path through fake cobwebs.

"We need one of those," Eden says.

"Dracula? No. There will be no Draculas at this party. There will be no witches, or goblins, or mummies, either. I do not do haunted houses."

"Myrtle," Eden says. "That's what Halloween is. We have to make it spooky."

"No," I say again. "I don't do spooky either."

"It has to be! Scaring people is the whole point!"

"You don't need silly monsters to scare people. Two minutes ago I didn't realize Halloween parties had a theme, but I do now. And the only black at my party will be the tuxedoes."

"Tux... what? That's not how you do Halloween."

"It is now. Come on," I say. "There's nothing here for us. We're going to that event planner place across from the art gallery. I've got a corporate credit card. If we're going to throw a party to entice advertisers, we're going to do it up right."

Ten minutes later we're standing inside "Corporate

Affairs" speaking to Maggie, my new personal party planner, about what we're looking for.

"I don't understand," Maggie says.

"What's confusing about it?" I ask back.

"You want a Halloween party with no Halloween decorations?"

"I want an event, Maggie." I look at her over the top of my eyeglasses. "One worthy of the Le Man name. Something visually stunning that will photograph well."

"O-kay."

"I want… I want people who match."

"Match?" she asks.

"Yeah, what do you mean?" Eden says. "We need people dressed up in costumes, pretty orange and black streamers, pumpkin spice cupcakes, and hard apple cider."

"No," I say, pointing my perfectly manicured red fingernail in her direction. "That is the opposite of what we need. Our theme is not Halloween."

"It isn't?" poor, confused Maggie says.

"No. It's… I mean, I don't really know what it is. It's just not that. We need sophisticated. And mysterious. We need—"

"Oh!" Maggie says. "I know! A masquerade!"

"Yes!" Eden says. "A masquerade ball! That's brilliant!"

"Thank you," I say, polishing my fingernails on my Victoria Beckham coat. Maggie shoots me the stink-eye, because I suppose it was technically her idea. But if I hadn't come in here insisting on something… chic instead of cheap, she'd never have had that idea in the first place. "I am a fountain of inspiration. So listen, Maggie," I say, getting out my credit card. "I've got an expense account like you wouldn't believe. I want every man in a tux, every woman in a little black dress, and I want masks. I want tables set like we're hosting royalty. I want mysterious, I want seductive, I want a night these people will never forget."

"Of course! Of course! When is the party?"

"Halloween," I say.

"On Halloween?"

"Isn't that when most people have Halloween parties?"

"But that's a Monday this year. And people sometimes have children to take out trick-or-treating. Is this a family party?"

"Of course not."

"Then we should have it the Saturday before. Which gives me less than two weeks."

"Yes," I say. "It's tight. Eden, we'll have to split up for this. You take care of Maggie here, I'm going over to the printers to see about invitations."

"Paper invitations?" Eden asks. "We could just send e-vites."

I laugh. As if. "Meet me at the office when you're done and we'll go over all the details."

I leave and head back toward the printer's. I'm eyeballing that community center lady a block away, but there's no way to avoid her. The printer is right next to the dry cleaners, which is right next to the community center.

"Classes start—"

"I know," I say, brushing past her to make for the printer's door. "All ideas are welcome."

"You got our email!" She beams, stepping forward to block my way.

"Yes, I got your spam. Now if you'll excuse me—"

"Have you ever thought about giving a class?"

"I don't scrapbook, I'm sorry."

"Not scrapbooking." She laughs. "This is the TDH, ma'am. No one is scrapbooking at our community center."

"No?"

"No."

"Then what do you do in there?"

"Well." She shrugs, pulling her coat tight around her body. The wind is biting today. They must be really hard up for new classes if she's being forced to solicit people outside in the cold. "We have pole dancing, belly dancing, tantric yoga—"

"Really?" I ask.

"Yes. We're a very progressive community center. We're looking for new, innovative ideas. Something worthy of the young professional types around here. We had a woman sign up last week to teach submission."

"Sub... like..." I lean forward and whisper, "BDSM?"

"Yes," the bright-eyed do-gooder says. "Exactly like that. It's called Subs for Hubs and it's almost sold out."

"Sold out? People want to do that?" I ask. "Cow down to a man?"

"Lots of people. Yes."

"Hmmm." I chuckle. "Interesting."

"Do you want to take it?"

"Me? Submit?" I laugh. So much laughing today. "No. I do not submit to anyone."

"Oh, right. I'm totally getting that vibe. Maybe you need a dominatrix class then?"

"Honey, I could teach the dominatrix class."

"Great idea! Oh, that's perfect. Wanna go inside and talk about a lesson plan?"

She just wants to get out of the cold, I get it. But... there's some small, nostalgic part of me that kinda wants to go with her.

"No," I say, refocusing on my task. "I'm planning a party and I've got a lot to do. Have a nice day."

Inside the printer, Jeremy, the salesperson at the counter, is confused. "A Halloween invitation that has no Halloween elements? And something that says 'masquerade' but no gaudy Mardi Gras colors?"

"Why is this so hard? Yes. More like a wedding. Classy, you know."

"Ah... right. Where is this party?"

"It's a private affair, I'm sorry."

"Oh, I just wanted to make sure I wouldn't go by mistake."

"Jeremy," I say, losing patience with everyone right now. "Just get me some classy samples." I would walk out and go somewhere else, but this is the only printer that doesn't involve a car.

He leaves in a huff and it occurs to me—the people of the TDH are so damn judge-y. And what I'm doing is not insane. Those community center classes, now that's insane. How is that normal but a black-tie affair for Halloween isn't?

A book plops down on the counter and Jeremy opens it to reveal stunning silver and white handmade papers.

"Yes," I say. "This is my Halloween vision."

"If you say so, lady."

There are so many exquisite options I take the book over to the table and get lost. More than an hour later I'm pulled out of the fantasy ball I'm planning when my phone rings.

"Yes," I say. Curtly, because it's Pierce.

"Where did you go?"

"I'm at the printer choosing invitations for the Halloween party."

"Invitations? Is that really necessary? Can't we just send an email?"

"Who's planning this party, Pierce?"

"Who's the boss, Myrtle?" he snaps back. It's an uncharacteristic response from him, but not altogether unpleasant. At least he's not placating me.

"I thought we discussed this already, Anastasia?"

I hear him huff through the phone, but I can't tell if it's a laugh or a snarl. "Eden is here waiting for you."

"And?"

"And she's talking my ear off and I feel compelled to listen since, you know, she's practically my sister-in-law now."

"God, you're such a baby. Tell her I'll be there in fifteen minutes and then we can go to lunch and discuss what she and the event planner came up with."

"Event planner? For a Halloween party? Myrtle, it's a potluck. All they have to do is bring a bag of chips and dress in a costume."

"Surely you jest."

"No. I do not. This is the extent of the Halloween party. You should know, you've been to seven of them."

"Have I?"

He hesitates. Like he can see my perfectly-groomed eyebrow rising up on my forehead. Like this is a trap. Like he took a wrong turn and he's not sure when that happened. "Haven't you?"

"I'll be there in fifteen minutes." And then I end the call, look at the four options in front of me, and choose the one that looks like lace. I fill out the form with all the pertinent information, and take my choice up to Jeremy, who has been side-eyeing me the entire time.

"This," I say "With this printed on them."

He picks up my sample, fingers lingering on the cut-paper filigree lace that folds over the front like a door, and then reads my slip. "You're sure?"

"Jeremy, do I look like a woman who second-guesses herself?"

"Uh... no, I guess not."

"Good. Then place the order. I need them in five days."

"That's, well... that's gonna cost you."

I plunk down my platinum American Express corporate card and say, "Make it happen."

Outside it's even colder than when I came in. And that perky community center lady is still doing her thing.

"Think about it!" she calls as I briskly pass her by. "I could totally see you bossing around some lucky man! You'd make a great mistress!"

I stop in my tracks, consider this, then turn to her beaming face. "I would, wouldn't I?"

"So great!" she says, her words blowing out in a puff of steam.

"And that would be the whole point, right? To boss a man."

"Yup. It's perfect. All the subs would get their hubs to take it! You'd sell out too!"

I think about it. Picture it in my head.

"You've done this before, haven't you?"

"I'm sorry, I'm not allowed to discuss my qualifications. Legal restrictions. So if you need that in order for me to sign up as an instructor—"

"No, no! We don't. This is a community center. If you have a lesson plan and can commit to the time, you're in."

I take a moment to formulate what might turn out to be the diabolical plan I was looking for. And then I smile and say, "I'll be in later with my course syllabus." Because I just came up with a delicious way to get back at Pierce. Something that will drive him so much crazier than Eden's cupcake fiasco this past summer.

CHAPTER FOUR

*"**Monsieur Chevalier**, your Vichyssoise,"* the server says, as she places my soup in front of me. I only like to eat Vichyssoise in colder temperatures. I don't know why. Normally, one would prefer to eat a cold soup in the summer, I suppose. But for me, there's something inversely comforting about cold and cold. I've never been comfortable being too comfortable. Not sure what that's about. I just like Vichyssoise in the cold.

Colette is the server's name. She's been working here almost as long as I've been coming here. And I've been coming here since it opened. I feel a little like they should have a plaque with my name on it somewhere around. I'm not an official investor, but it was struggling a bit when it first opened its doors and I made sure I ate here every day. Sometimes twice a day. And I'd have business meetings here, and tell people about it, and essentially just stamped it with my imprimatur. And, slowly but surely, it became the spot in the TDH.

I know who I am.

Which is to say, I know the influence I have. I have a fair amount of influence everywhere because of who my father is, but here, in this little corner of the world—the TDH neighborhood of Denver, Colorado—I have an exceptional amount.

I try not to abuse it. I really do. I know Andrew thinks that I have a monarch complex, but I don't. Or, at least, I don't think I do.

And even if I do, I'm a beneficent ruler. I'm more like Louis XIV and less like Marie Antoinette. I would never dismissively tell someone to eat cake.

I would have Eden's dad bake everyone a cake and then I would deliver it to them personally.

Okay, so maybe I do have a monarch complex. But whatever. It's not easy being the boss and I'm a very generous ruler.

"Anything else, monsieur?" Colette asks it with bedroom eyes. I know she's coming onto me. She's been coming onto me since the first time we met.

It's also possible she just has bedroomy eyes. She always kind of licks her lips when she asks if I need anything else, so I have to assume that the combo of the two is her making a pass.

"No, thanks, Colette. I'm good."

Suddenly, her bedroom eyes turn dark. They're still bedroomy, but now they're bedroomy and angry. She takes a step back. "Gabrielle."

"Sorry?"

"Gabrielle, Monsieur Chevalier. C'est mon nom. Pas Colette."

Really? Her name is Gabrielle? I wasn't even close.

I start to say, "Je suis désolé," but she walks off in a

very Parisian huff before I get a chance. I have to say, that is one of the things about this place I like best. Its authenticity.

I'm eating alone. I like to do that occasionally. It gives me a chance to just... be. I rev at a pretty high idle a lot of the time, and being alone, in a place that feels familiar, it lets me power down a bit. And I need that every once in a while.

Again, I know who I am.

But just as I'm about to lift a spoonful of cold soup to my lips, I look up from the table to see Myrtle walk through the door.

She looks incredible.

She's wearing that black blouse she has with the lace patterns on it. It's sheer and covered at once. I remember when she bought it. She wore it the day she came to help me pick out new upholstery for my office furniture and I told her that I wanted something like that in my office. It was a double entendre. I know she got the joke because she rolled her eyes at me the way she does.

Did.

The way she used to.

She still rolls her eyes at me, but it's different. It has something like contempt in it now when she does it.

And, if I'm being honest, that makes me fucking sad. In my entire life, I've known only two people I can trust completely. Andrew is one. The other one is standing in the entrance of this restaurant, wearing a semi-sheer blouse with lace patterns on it and a skirt so tight that even after having seen her maneuver around in ones just like it for the last several years... I still don't know how she does it.

The real tragedy of this whole thing is that I still feel

I can trust her completely. She just knows she can't trust me anymore at all.

I'd give just about anything to have her trust back again.

Sacre motherfucking bleu.

She's looking around like maybe she's meeting someone. There are a bunch of assholes wearing Rolexes over by the bar. It's a beautiful bar. Deep, rich oak accented by a brass railing and runner. Too bad it has to be cheapened by idiots who think that wearing a fancy watch makes you a gentleman.

I glance down at my Breguet Grande Complication Tourbillon to see that it's eight o'clock.

A little early for a date. I can't imagine she'd be meeting one of the assholes. They're all laughing and patting each other on the back. She'd eat any one of them alive. I wonder who she's here to see.

I'm also a little surprised that I'm so curious and, dare I say, possessive.

"Hey!" I almost look around to see who's shouting, until I realize it's me.

Myrtle, along with much of the restaurant and bar, turns my direction. I wave her over to join me. She doesn't move, lowers her head, and stares at me instead.

I stand. Wave her over again. Again, she doesn't move in my direction, and continues staring, her head lowered, her eyes reminiscent of the angry bedroom eyes on Colette.

I place my napkin on the table and head in her direction. She stays in place, but her upper body moves back and away. She twists her neck.

"What are you doing here?" I ask upon arriving.

"I'm sorry?" It's not an apology. Nor do I think she

didn't hear the question. But I ask a different question. The one I suppose I actually mean to ask.

"Are you meeting someone?"

"Pierce—"

"It's not one of those Rolex idiots, is it? You remember what I told you about the last Rolex guy you went out with. If you have to broadcast how well you're doing, you're not doing that well."

"Pierce. You're wearing a half-million-dollar watch."

"Six hundred thousand. But that's the point. You wouldn't know it to look at it."

"Pierce—"

"You're saying my name a lot. Wanna sit?" I gesture to my table, I believe invitingly.

"No. I don't want to sit."

I nod a bit. We stand there saying nothing for what is probably less time than it feels like, but more time than two people who have known each other as long as we have should.

Finally, she says, "Your food is going to get cold."

"It's Vichyssoise."

"Then it's going to come to room temperature."

I lower my voice. "What do I have to do to get you to stop being pissed at me?"

"I dunno. What would it take for you to stop being pissed at someone who publicly humiliated you while at the same time questioning your loyalty, integrity, and character?"

I try to think of an answer that isn't total bullshit. "Um... a raise and a promotion?"

She starts to walk past. I take her arm. She looks at my hand. "Anastasia, you need to let go of me. Right. Now."

I shake my head, release my grip, and say, "This is fucking ridiculous. You're full of shit."

"I'm full of shit?"

"You. Yes. You are. If you were really so upset, you wouldn't still be working for me."

"No? You don't think that it makes infinitely more sense for me to take your money, a cushy job, the liberty to do whatever I want, whenever I want, secure in the knowledge that you can't do a goddamn thing to me? Because if you suddenly got it in your head to fire me, I'd rain down an unlawful termination suit on you that would fuck. Your. World?"

She says that last three words in a really breathy, sexy way while stepping in very close. I have a sudden urge to bite my nails, but just tug at my vest instead. Dignified.

I say the only thing I can think to say. "Why are you talking to an event planner about a Halloween party?" I do not know why it is what manifests in my brain, but there it is.

"Don't worry about it. You want me to do something special? Help create a special spread for the magazine? I'm doing something special. I'm helping create a special spread for the magazine." She gets even closer now. Her lips right by my ear. Her warm breath on my neck. In all the time I've known her, I don't think she's ever been this close to me. It is both weird and pretty... um... great. "Why?" she whispers. "Don't you trust me?"

I'm not a stammerer. I don't stammer. Or at least I didn't before about half a second ago. I start to work out my reply when a woman walks in and comes over to where we stand.

"Myrtle?" she says.

"Oh, hi, Pearl."

Pearl?

"Sorry I'm late," the person apparently named Pearl says.

"No problem," says Myrtle. "I just wanted to make sure we go over everything in detail. Make sure it's all fine by community standards."

"Well, as I said, it is the TDH. What's standard elsewhere doesn't really apply here, but happy to go over everything. I love this place. Oh, hi, Gabrielle!" she says to Colette, who happens to be passing by.

"What are you going over in detail?" I ask. "Who's this?"

"Hi," Pearl says, extending her hand. "I'm Pearl."

"Pearl. I'm—" I stick out my hand in return, but Myrtle interrupts our shake.

"Are you hungry, Pearl? I'm starving."

And at that, she whisks Pearl away toward a booth in the back.

As I watch them walk away, I think about what Andrew said to me. That I need to make a profound apology. That I need to, somehow, prostrate myself.

I've never done that in my life. I've been taught, trained, and conditioned not to. Which is three ways of saying the same thing, but the point is that it's been drilled into me to never bow. I don't know if I even know how to.

I wish I did. Because it's Myrtle. And for Myrtle, I'd—

"Monsieur Chevalier? Will you be returning to your table?" an approaching busboy asks.

I glance at where Myrtle and... what's her name... are taking a seat. My table faces them directly. I could sit there and stare at them. Or stare at her. I could try to get her to pay attention to me. Not because I need the attention, but because… because… because…

"Monsieur? Your table? Will you be returning to finish your meal?"

"No, no. I think I'm done."

CHAPTER FIVE

"By the way, I haven't told you yet, but I love your name."

"Oh." I smile at Pearl. "Well, thank you. Yours is exquisite as well."

"When I was a kid I hated my name. It was so awful. People called me Grandma all the time. I suppose you got that too."

"I'm sorry? What?"

"People, you know. Making fun of your stuffy name?"

I pause, honestly considering this. "No. Never. I didn't have friends. Or enemies, for that matter. I grew up in a Quaker boarding school in Pennsylvania. Just outside Philadelphia. My mother was the school librarian."

"Of course she was," Pearl laughs. "That makes total sense."

"Does it?" I ask.

"Yes, well, you have a… librarian thing going on,

right?"

I look down at my sheer lace blouse. "This doesn't say 'librarian'."

"No," Pearl says. "It's not your clothes. Well, it kinda is. It's your hair, maybe. The bun."

I pat my head. "It's a French twist."

"Right," Pearl says. "Sorry, of course it is. But the pencil skirts—"

"Not librarian. My mother never wore a pencil skirt."

"No, you're right. I'm trying to tell you that you're... you know. Sexy. In that sexy-librarian-slash-secretary way."

I raise my chin and then give her one nod. "OK. I'll accept that."

And then she winks and says, "Dominatrix way too."

"Exactly," I say, smiling. "That is the look I'm going for, so I'm very happy you picked up on it."

"Myrtle, everyone is picking up on it. You're going to rock this class so hard, the whole TDH will think we're having an earthquake. By the way, who was that man you were talking to? One of your subs?" She winks at me.

"Not yet," I say, glancing over where Pierce was standing. "But he will be."

Pearl snickers.

"He's my boss."

"What?"

"Yes. And he owes me. So he's decided to take my class. In fact," I say, pulling my brilliant revenge plan into something more coherent. Something more diabolical. I like Pearl. I could get used to her being around. And I'm OK with community center classes too. But only as a vehicle to deliver my revenge on Pierce.

That thought is so delicious, I almost snicker.

"He's my beta tester," I continue. "I need to test this whole class thing out first, Pearl. To make sure the Hubs for Subs understand what they're getting into when they enter the lifestyle."

"Oh, my God. You just gave me chills. You're the real deal, aren't you? I mean, the woman teaching Subs for Hubs seems to know her stuff, but you, Myrtle. You have expert stamped all over you."

"Thank you again. But as I've already stated, I'm not allowed to discuss my qualifications due to legal restrictions."

"Right, right, right," she says. "No problem. But... OK. Beta testing?"

"Yes," I say. I can see she is not pleased with this, but I'm really not into teaching a class on how to be a dominatrix. I just want to make Pierce uncomfortable. Oh, hell. Who am I kidding? I want to humiliate him the way he humiliated me. And he can't even bitch about it because it'll be private. The exact opposite of what I experienced. "You see, Pearl, the BDSM lifestyle is serious business. I've got a few techniques I need to test before I can unleash them out into the world. It's the responsible thing to do."

"Mmmm-hmmm," she says, tight-lipped. "I get that. I do. And of course, if you say you need it, then we must. But..." She taps her tablet and holds it up. "Let's set the class up now. Get it all on the books."

"Do you get a bonus for this?"

"What?"

"Well, you were standing outside in the cold this morning soliciting people to teach. And you did spam me. Is there like... a bonus for signing people up?"

Pearl deflates a little. "It's that obvious?"

45

"Well, something is obvious. I don't know the details. The bonus was just a guess."

"Listen," she says, leaning over the table. "I shouldn't be talking about this, but the people who own the community center don't think it's cost-effective."

"It's a community center," I deadpan. "It's not supposed to make a profit."

"Right? I know! But... the land."

"Oh," I say. "I get it. They want to turn it into condos, right?"

"Worse," she says. And now she's frowning severely. "They've already turned part of it into election headquarters for Chad Walter and if he wins... well, the entire TDH will lose."

"What are you talking about?"

"You haven't heard? The TDH wants to split off and become its own city. Chad Walter's family actually owns the community center land. Now he's running for mayor and if he wins there's gonna be a special election in December to section off the TDH into a new electoral district and then his family is going to sell the community center to the new city and turn it into city hall."

"Huh," I say. "And you think... BDSM classes will save it?"

Pearl sighs. "I know it's stupid. But there's a ton of land over on the south end of the TDH. Why can't they put the stinkin' city hall down there?"

"True," I say. "They could do that."

But why bother when you already have this place in the perfect location?

"Please, Myrtle? I need your help."

God, am I really going get roped into this? All I want is simple, satisfying revenge. I don't want to teach a real class, for fuck's sake. So I say, "Well, I mean... I don't think the whole sexy community center thing will save it, Pearl."

"It could," she insists. "It could. The Subs for Hubs is so popular, Myrtle. You don't understand. It really could turn it around. These husbands are pretty excited about their wives wearing collars."

I roll my eyes. That makes me want to gag. "Well, those men won't be interested in my class. It's two different things."

"I get it," Pearl says. "But they will be interested in you, Myrtle. You're... you're... fascinating. You really could save the community center."

Jesus Christ. What have I gotten myself into?

I walk to the parking garage after dinner with Pearl and think about Pierce the whole time. God, he infuriates me. And he used to be so fun. I really did love running his life. And maybe Eden was right. Part of my problem is that I miss being his assistant?

I certainly did a better job than Valerie is doing.

And I was kind of the boss. Everyone had to get through me to get to him. And he liked it. He did. He liked me.

Didn't he?

I sigh as I get into my Tesla, then make my way down the garage ramp and out into the crisp Colorado night. I live about fifteen minutes east of TDH on a sixty-acre plot of land. It was actually my father's house before he moved up north to be closer to work.

Even though I grew up with the boarding-school Quakers in Pennsylvania with my mother, Colorado was where I spent my vacations as a child. My father has always lived here. He met my mother when she was in college, but it was one of those whirlwind romances with lots of sex, an unplanned pregnancy, and no commitments once it was over.

My father was not going to give up his job to settle down back East and my mother was never going to travel with him for his work.

So she moved home, got a job at the school, and just kind of settled into being a spinster.

My father was way too wild at heart to be contained like that. So... they went their separate ways. Amicably, I suppose. I never heard them fight. She never complained that the child support was late. I always had a plane ticket waiting for me when it was time for a school break.

I lived a double life. During the school year I was shy, skinny Myrtle with the librarian mother. But during breaks I was... wild. Just like my father.

And it occurs to me now that no one from work knows who I am. Not even Pierce. And I didn't even plan it that way. I have just always lived a double life. It's just part of me now.

There's a gate at the end of my driveway and the twelve-foot wrought-iron fence that surrounds the property is imposing. I greet Samantha with a wave as I pull up to the security station, and wait for her to let me in.

She waves back through the window, then points at her book. Smiling and nodding enthusiastically.

It's the last Scarlett Savannah novel I read. She borrows them when I'm done. Some people might wonder why I let my security people read while they're on duty, but… the gate isn't here to keep people out. It's to keep things in.

I smile back, feeling satisfied that she and I share a love for dirty books, and ease forward down the long, winding driveway to the house.

The road goes on past the house, but I know everything down that way has been buttoned up tight for the night. And it's late, so I don't go down to check on things or hang out with the on-site employees, I just pull my car into the garage, get out, plug it in, and go inside.

The growling from the corner of the dark kitchen is expected. I should've been home hours ago, but dinner with Pearl kept me longer than I thought it would.

And when I flick on the kitchen light Dave hurls himself at me, teeth bared, ears back.

I catch him in my arms and he immediately begins to purr like a kitten.

Which makes me laugh. Because kitten he is not.

Meanwhile, Betty, Dave's better half, is rubbing up against my legs, getting hair all over my stockings.

"I'm not that late," I protest. They mew and growl back at me, disagreeing. "Dinner's coming."

But I'm still distracted by Pierce and my new revenge scheme. Could I really entice him to be my sub?

I laugh under my breath as I get the chicken out of the fridge and start preparing it for Betty and Dave. They sit at my feet swishing their tails, trying their best to be patient. A few minutes later I put their dishes on the floor, pet them both on the head as they eat, and then make my way to the back of the house to change.

But I stop at the basement stairs. Hesitating. I haven't really been down there since I moved in a few years ago.

Never even unpacked the boxes.

I sigh again. How did I get roped into this?

You didn't really say yes yet, the inner monologue starts.

But I didn't say no, either. In fact, I nodded my head the whole time Pearl was going over what I'd need to get started.

And it would be the perfect way to get back at him.

You could just let him off the hook, inner monologue continues.

"Yeah, right," I huff. And then the door to the basement is open and I'm going down to check things out.

Because I am Myrtle Rothschild.

And I made a pact with myself the minute I stepped out of that stupid Quaker school when I was seventeen and started a new life at the University of Denver.

No one gets to humiliate me in front of the entire world ever again.

I flick on the light when I get to the bottom of the steps and take in all the crates and boxes that represent the old me. Not the old me. Not the wallflower girl with the thick glasses and too-skinny legs, and the librarian mother.

The old me that came after that.

The one who wore latex, and corsets. The one who cracked the whip like she was born to use it. The one no one in their right mind would ever call meek, or dull, or plain.

I admit, I kinda miss the old me.

And once I start unpacking wardrobes, once I find the costumes, once I pull on the boots, and once I get that whip in my hand...

Well. I've made up my mind.

I will make Pierce Chevalier my bitch.

So I spend the rest of the night looking through boxes, prying crates open with a crowbar, and setting up Myrtle's room of pain and pleasure.

And then I sit down at my computer and start typing.

When I go back upstairs it's nearly three AM. But I don't even feel tired. I feel... refreshed. Because tomorrow morning I'm going to give Pierce an ultimatum.

Either he meets my demands.... or I quit.

And when he says yes, because he will say yes, I will bring him into my room of pain and pleasure.

I will make him wear a collar.

I will put him in a cage.

I will humiliate him the way he humiliated me.

CHAPTER SIX

"*That is a bullshit* contract and there's no way, I'm signing it, Derek!" I'm on the phone with my attorney, Derek. He's a good guy. I'm lucky he's on my team. "And there's a million other lawyers who could negotiate a better deal, so either become one of them or I'll find one of them!"

"Pierce. Please—"

But that's all I hear him say before I take the nine iron that I'm holding and smash 'end' on the speakerphone on my desk. Which, I probably should have been able to foretell, also smashes the speakerphone itself. Damn.

"Valerie!"

I have to yell extra loud because the speakerphone is also my intercom, which I can't use, because it is now broken. Because I smashed it with a nine iron. For fuck's…

I take a breath, finding myself extra-stressed today. In fact, I've felt particularly worked up since leaving the restaurant last night.

I'm sure the two things are unrelated.

"Yes, Mr. Chevalier?" the meek voice that lives inside the meek body of Valerie says, as her meek head pokes its way through the glass door that accesses the glass wall that comprises my office. Once upon a time I thought that I might feel self-conscious having a completely translucent office, but then I remembered... I like it when people can see what I'm doing. Shows I have nothing to hide. Which isn't exactly true, but image is everything.

In any case...

"Two things," I say, "One: I'm going to need a new speakerphone."

"Yes, sir," she says, writing it down.

"And two: Call my massage therapist. I need a treatment."

"Yes sir," she says, again. Also writing it down.

I observe her. She's so nervous. So eager to please. So unassuming.

I really, really miss Myrtle.

"Oh, Mr. Chevalier?" she says.

"Yeah?"

"Ms. Rothschild is here to see you."

Huh. I just manifested that shit out of that.

"Yeah? About what?"

"She didn't say. She just started to head in on her own but then she kind of, um, saw you, well, smash your..." She points at my broken phone. "And then heard you yell and... and she kind of smiled, and sort of licked her lips, and adjusted her stockings, and then told me to tell you she needs to see you."

One thing about Valerie, she's specific when she relays information.

"She did, huh? Yeah, okay. Send her in." I slide my nine iron back into its place in the canister I keep by my desk, straighten my tie, pull my vest down, and when I turn back around, Myrtle is standing there. Knee-length tube dress and tiny matching blazer taunting me with the memory that this is what I used to see every day sitting in the seat where sweet, scared Valerie now sits.

In addition to her too-sexy-for-most-jobs outfit, Myrtle wears a smirk.

"What was all that about?" she asks.

"What was what about?"

"The smashy and the yelly. Was that Derek on the phone?"

"How'd you know?" I ask, making myself comfortable in my office throne. That's interesting. I never before realized how weird the phrase office throne sounds. Huh.

Anyway…

"Because you were yelling, 'I'm not signing it, Derek.'" She tilts her head at me. "What aren't you signing?"

"Oh, nothing," I say, twisting my neck out. "There's a chance to take over a new building in Paris. Finally open a Parisian office like I've been wanting to do forever. But the deal they want to make is bullshit. I know when I'm being fucked on real estate. I've fucked people on real estate deals dozens of times, so, y'know, you can't pull that shit on me. I'm the fucker. Not the fuck-ee." That didn't come out quite like I wanted it to, but whatever. "In any case, I'm not signing it. What?"

That last part is in reference to the way she's looking at me. Which is with a dollop of skepticism topped with a soupçon of curiosity.

"Why would you be taking over a new building?"

"Why wouldn't I?"

"Because the magazine continues to be in trouble, I thought. Which is why I'm in charge of this party for this special edition, and blah, blah, blah."

Fuck. I forgot all about that. Goddamn it. Women remember everything.

"Whatever. Don't worry about it. What's that?" Now I'm referring to a piece of paper she's holding in her hand. I just noticed it. It is the least interesting thing about her.

"Oh," she says, "This? This is what I'm here to see you about."

She… saunters? No. Myrtle doesn't really saunter. Prowls is maybe more like it. She prowls over to my desk and takes a seat behind it.

"You just gonna plop yourself in the CEO's chair without asking?" I ask.

"What're you gonna do? Fire me?"

"Touché. What's the paper?"

"Well," she says, taking in a deep breath and adjusting her blazer over her unreasonably effervescent breasts. "Speaking of contracts… I have one for you to look over."

"Jesus. What now?" I stand from my throne and walk over to look. Before I can pick it up, she snatches it back.

"This," she says, withdrawing it from my view, "is how you can help make things right. You wanna make things right? You wanna be let off the hook? This is how you can do that."

She licks her lips, puts her finger to her teeth, checks the tip of her finger for lipstick, then lifts her chin, tips her head to the side, and looks at me with the eyes of a sleepy tiger. I've never actually seen a sleepy tiger, but I have no other way of describing it. Sleepy tigers are the most dangerous in my mind. They look docile but next thing you know they go all tiger. Goddamn sleepy tigers.

"What are you talking about?"

"Well, you know the woman I had dinner with last night?"

"Pepper?"

"Pearl."

"Sure."

"Pearl and I were talking about something and it gave me an idea."

"Who is she?"

"Who?"

"Penny."

"Pearl."

"Whatever! You've got an idea that'll make things right? What is it?" I ask with curiosity and more than a little anxiety.

"This contract," she says, placing it back on my desk and splaying her hand out across it, "is your key to being forgiven. You have asked what you can do that will make me forget and forgive what happened?" She points one long red nail down at the piece of paper. "The answer is on this page."

I shake my head slightly and then look around the room to find the goddamn hidden cameras. Because I feel completely confident that I'm being punked.

"Okay," I say, slowly. "May I see it? Please?"

I really draw out the please. I want to make it a sincere question. I really do. I just don't know how one does that. Oh, well.

She gets a glint in her eye and then pushes the paper to the edge of the desk. My desk. I'm not sure how the tables got turned with her sitting in the boss's chair and me asking her questions that conclude with 'please,' but here we are.

I take the paper up, involuntarily making a smacking sound with my teeth and tongue as I do, and read. Here is what I see:

In consideration of injurious wrongs committed against one Myrtle Astrid Rothschild as perpetrated by one Pierce Constantine Chevalier...

I look away from the page to glance at Myrtle, who gives me a 'go on' look.

Wrongs that so damaged her reputation and standing as to cause permanent harm...

"Permanent harm? I gave you a promotion and a raise! How the fuck—"

"Keep reading," she says.

I turn my attention back to the page once more.

Mr. Chevalier agrees to make psychic reparations ("psychic reparations?") in the form of personal subjugation at the hands of Ms. Rothschild.

"What. The. Fuck?"

She nods. "Go on."

And whereas Ms. Rothschild's humiliation was a public affair, with respect to Mr. Chevalier's own public profile, Ms. Rothschild agrees to maintain silence in regard to all activities executed in the privacy of Ms. Rothschild's... "Dungeon? What the fuck are you—?"

She rolls her index finger in a 'keep reading' gesture.

In exchange for his agreement to assume the role of SUBMISSIVE TO MS. ROTHSCHILD...

"This is fucking insane. Okay? Let's just... This is fucking insane."

But, for whatever reason, I keep reading.

... Mr. Chevalier will be pardoned and forgiven for

all injuries inflicted and wrongs committed and at the conclusion of the endeavor, Ms. Rothschild agrees to never speak of it again. Agreed to and signed...

I glance over the rest of the half-baked legalese, feeling my eyes grow wider with every word I read, and finally I place the paper back on the desk, take a deep breath, and say as calmly as I can, "Are you out of your fucking mind? What the fuck is this?"

From over my shoulder, I hear the mousy voice of Valerie say, "Sir?"

"Val—What do you want?"

"Did you call for me?"

"No! I didn't! Will you please get the hell out?"

She nods her head like she's bowing in a Japanese tea house and ducks away. When I look back at Myrtle she's sporting a full-on Cheshire Cat grin.

"What," I begin, slowly, "the fuck is this?"

"Your penance," she says. "You say you want forgiveness? You want to pay penance? Here's your chance. I look at it like this," she says, standing and rounding the desk to face me directly. "You publicly humiliated me." I find myself backing up as she walks toward me, even though I don't mean to. "You want to find a way for me to forgive you." I'm bumping into my throne now. "I want to be able to feel like we're even." I fall into the seat, as she leans over me and whispers in my ear. "And this is a way for me to get what I want, you to get what you want, and nobody. Ever. Has. To know. And gee, won't that be nice?"

Her hot breath on my ear causes my dick to jump. Which takes me by surprise and causes me to jump. I leap out of the seat and march past her.

"You're fuckin' bonkers, lady. You know that? You're

out of your goddamn tête!"

She just lowers her chin and smirks. Again. "Pierce… honestly? I feel like you're getting off easy. I'm offering to sign a legally binding contract that says no one will find out about what happens between us. That's a far greater courtesy than you gave me."

"Jesus Christ. You really think you are Christian Grey, don't you?"

"Do I?"

"Sure as fuck seems like it! I mean, this idea of yours is as bizarre, incoherent, ludicrous, and derivative as that Fifty Shades shit!"

"Derivative?"

"You took this idea from that book, and the woman who wrote it took the idea from those Twilight books, didn't she?"

"You really read Fifty Shades?"

"Everybody read Fifty Shades!"

This is insane. I find myself breathing heavily, in and out, through my nose. Stalking my office like a panther. Or a caged tiger. Or maybe a cheetah. I dunno which animal I feel like I am exactly, but it's something dangerous and supple. That I feel certain of.

And then, quite suddenly, I hear Andrew's voice in my head. Telling me I need to prostrate myself. To lay myself at Myrtle's feet. If that's what I want. If I want her to forgive me. If I want to genuinely and truly apologize and make it right.

And then I hear my father's voice telling me to never supplicate myself. To maintain my power at all times. To always retain my dominance. And those two voices, competing in my brain, are giving me a fucking headache.

I turn to say something to her. I don't know what

exactly. Just something. To yell or to... I dunno. But when I spin and see her standing there...

I've known her for seven years. For seven years she has been my one constant. The most important woman in my life. I've not had another woman enter my world for more than a few weeks. At most. But Myrtle has remained.

And she still remains. She doesn't have to be here. I'd like to pretend that it's the money and the promotion, but I don't think she cares about those things. Not really. I just don't think it's a guiding force for her.

I know what is. I think I've always known.

It's her sense of self. Her sense of ownership over who she is. Pride in the person that she wants to be and that she unashamedly shows the world.

And I stripped her of that. I tore that from her and no amount of money or promotions or even saying I'm sorry can make up for it. Can repay it.

She is my rock. Like Andrew likes to talk about the mountains he climbs as sturdy, reliable, unshakable... that's what Myrtle is to me.

Fuck. Is this what people mean when they talk about having a "conscience?" Because if so, this blows.

I breeze past her to the desk. I look at the paper there. Words jump off the page at me: Dominant. Submissive. Safe word. Ball gag.

Ball gag? Oh, Pierce, what the fuck are you doing?

Shit. I dunno. But I'm doing it.

I pat my jacket. I normally have one on me, but I don't just at present. And so, without looking back, I thrust my hand out behind me and say to Myrtle...

"Gimme a pen."

CHAPTER SEVEN

I have no memory of walking out of Pierce's office. I don't know how I got back into my office. I don't know how I got behind my desk, or sat in my chair, or any of it.

Because all I know is that Pierce signed on the dotted line.

I'm breathing heavy, I realize. My heart is racing, my pulse pounding in my head. My vision narrows down to a tunnel, my eyes fixed on the closed door of my office as I swallow hard, and for a second I think, Holy shit, something's wrong with me. I have low blood sugar, or I'm gonna faint, or maybe I'm having a panic attack?

Because it's been years since my body reacted this way. Years.

It's unfamiliar and frightening, but neither of those feelings are altogether unwelcome.

What am I doing?

You're getting even, the little voice in my head says. And Pierce is getting what he deserves.

Yes, that part makes all the sense. It's the other part that doesn't.

The part where I dress up in those boots and corset. The part where I put the blindfold over his eyes and hold the whip in my hand.

I think I'm having a panic attack. Because my heart is fluttering like... like... like a girl who owns a whip, and a pair of latex boots, and dresses up in a corset.

I suddenly have an urge to tell someone about this. I need to discuss it. I need a trusted friend to confide in. And not the typical trusted friend, either. The... lifestyle kind.

And the really shitty thing about that realization is the fact that I don't have anyone. Not one person.

I moved away from the old me. Not the old, old me, who was also left behind. The last old me.

Mistress Myrtle.

I made a decision years ago to walk away. To walk out on all the people I'd normally turn to and so now, in the one moment when I need that support system, I'm left with no one.

God, what am I doing?

This time that inner voice doesn't chime in. There's no way to rationalize this. At all.

I just offered my boss a sexual ultimatum.

I'm insane. Totally insane. I'm going to get fired and probably sued.

My desk phone rings, making me jump in my chair. I pick it up automatically and say, "Myrtle Rothschild, how can I help you?"

"Oh, hey, Myrtle. It's Larry down in maintenance."

"Yes," I say, trying to breathe normally. "What can I do for you, Larry?"

"Eden called this morning and told me you need the second floor for an event."

"Yes, the Halloween party. That's right."

"OK, but she said the party is on a Saturday?"

"Yes. Apparently Halloween parties don't always happen on Halloween."

"Sure, sure," he says. "I get it. But we gotta pay people to, you know, run it. So we need to invoice purchasing and—"

"Oh, yes, of course. Sorry, I'm a little distracted. So we need—wait staff?"

"Yup.

"And security, I presume?"

"Mandatory, since it's off hours."

"What else? We've got an expense account to spend, Larry. Tell me what you need."

"Should I make a list and send it up to you?"

"That would be great, thank you." I purr out that last part, starting to feel more like my new self now. "And you're invited, of course. So I hope you don't have plans. I expect you to show up and have a good time."

"Oh," he says, chuckling. I can almost picture him blushing. "Well, thank you, Myrtle. The wife and I would love to come to your... party."

"Wonderful," I say. But what was that hesitation? It was weird, right? But he doesn't offer up anything else, so I just say, "I'll email you Maggie's contact information. She's my event planner. She'll handle all the party details from here."

"Got it."

I set the phone down and look at the tall, skinny window next to my office door, then squeak out a small gasp in surprise. Because Pierce is peeking through it.

"What are you doing?" I demand, standing up, walking over to the door, and pulling it open. "Why are you spying on me?"

Pierce looks over his shoulder at Valerie, then back at me, then he pushes forward into my office—into me, actually, since I'm blocking his way—forcing me to step aside.

"Anastasia, this is not appropriate behavior. You were not invited in."

"I'm the boss. I don't need an invitation." So he keeps going, walks around my desk, takes a seat in my chair, and props his feet right up next to my computer.

"What the hell are you doing?" I ask.

"Close the door. We're not done with this negotiation."

"Aren't we?" I laugh.

"Close. The door. Myrtle."

I look over at Valerie again. Is she taking notes? I close the door, turn, plant my hands on my hips, and glare at him with the appropriate amount of dissatisfaction. "So you've changed your mind. I knew you would."

And I kinda did, didn't I? I mean, that has to be the reason I came up with this ridiculous plan in the first place, right? I knew he'd say no and then I wouldn't have to do it.

"No, I didn't change my mind." He takes his feet off my desk, leans forward, and whispers, "But I want an addendum to the contract, Ms. Grey."

I laugh again. It's haughty this time. Slightly contemptuous.

"I told you I read the book. I know there's room for negotiation, so that's what this is. Renegotiation."

I smile, even though I don't want to give him the

wrong impression. Because picturing Pierce reading the Ana-Christian sex contract negotiation is just fun. "So..." I say in my low, throaty Mistress Myrtle voice. I kinda missed that voice. I wonder if Andrew needs a new Sultry Siren? Because that's what Mistress Myrtle sounds like and it's a helluva lot better than the one he's currently using. "You fancy yourself an expert."

"I am the boss," he says. Is he using his Master Pierce voice on me? "So I could make the rules up as I go."

"Whoa," I say, putting up a hand. "That's not—"

"But I won't. I just want something of my own added to the contract." He pulls the folded paper out of his inside suitcoat pocket and flattens it out on the desk.

"Oh," I say, getting it. "You're afraid I'm going to sue you for sexual harassment."

"What?" He screws up his face, like this was not what he was thinking at all. "No. I just want a date."

"A date?"

"Yeah. A date. With you. One that doesn't involve the Red Room of Pain."

"Pleasure," I correct him. "My room is about pleasure." I purr that last part so smooth, he blinks. And if that desk wasn't hiding his groin, I'd probably see his cock jump.

He clears his throat. "A date. A weekend, actually. We're going to the mountains. The magazine owns a place up in Vail and—"

"Hold on," I say, putting up a hand. "You want to take me away for a ridiculous romantic weekend?"

"That's right. And it's a deal-breaker. So if you say no, I say no. I'll rip this contract up, walk out of this office, and have expectations, Myrtle. Job performance expectations."

"Oh." I laugh again. It's loud too. "Is that so?"

"Yup. Take it or leave it."

"I don't think you understand what this is."

"I understand," Pierce says. "Perfectly. You want to humiliate me like I humiliated you."

"That's not exactly it," I say, feeling defensive.

"Sure it is. And I'm fine with it. I probably deserve it. But it's not going to be fun for me. So I want some perks. I want the new car and the new computer. I want the glider ride and the helicopter tour. I want you to work for it."

"Oh, my God. You really did read the book." I have to cover my mouth to hide my smile.

"So we're going on a date to Vail and I'm gonna give you the Christian Grey experience."

"You're not Christian," I say. "I am. So technically I should be giving you the—"

"Sign it," he says, thrusting the paper at me.

I glance down at the paper, which is filled with the red marks of new demands, and then reach for my glasses that hang on a chain around my neck, and put them on with one hand as I reach for the contract with my other.

Pierce's hand clutches mine before I can do that, and I look at him, realizing I'm half bent over the desk and this is not at all a position of dominance.

I snatch the paper away and turn my back to him. Scanning the new details.

"Share a bed?" I ask, looking over my shoulder.

He shrugs.

"Breakfast in bed?"

He smiles at me.

"You want to eat sushi off my breasts?"

"Sign it."

I turn my head back around so he can't see my

reaction. "This is your idea of a helicopter tour, Anastasia?"

"Sign it. Or deal's off."

I'm breathing heavy again. My heart is racing—fluttering, really. My pulse pounding in my head as my vision once again narrows down to a tunnel.

Only this time... I'm angry.

Who the hell does he think he is? To make demands of me? I'm the mistress, he's the sub, not the other way around. And I do not do romance. I just... do not do romance. Picturing myself sitting across from Pierce with candles between us makes me itch.

Calm down, Myrtle. You've handled men like him before. You know what to do.

Yes. I do, don't I?

"OK," I say, turning back to face him. "This is acceptable. But today is Tuesday. So, starting tonight, you're mine. I get what I want before you get what you want." I reach for a pen, sign the amended document, and then toss it onto the desk. It flutters slowly, back and forth in the air, and finally settles in front of him. "I'll email you instructions by four o'clock today."

"Perfect," he says, folding the contract back up and sliding it into his hidden suitcoat pocket. "Or not perfect, but... whatever. From Friday night to Sunday afternoon, you're mine. Got it?"

Oh, I'm going to spank that arrogant smile right off his face tonight. He has no idea what he's getting into. "We'll see about that."

He gets up, walks out, and closes the door behind him

I take a seat, the chair still warm, reminding me of his presence. And I squirm a little, my confidence fading slightly.

I don't do weekends away. I don't do any of those things he asked for. Breakfast in bed? Sleeping together like we're a... a couple? Like this is some romantic getaway?

Just. No.

The only interesting thing on that list was the sushi. Because that's kinky.

I do kinky. I do kinky quite well.

I don't do romantic. I don't use candles for atmospheric lighting. I use them for dripping wax. I don't wear a corset to please men, I wear it to intimidate them. The handcuffs, and the blindfold, and the paddle are all the tools of my trade and they have nothing to do with romance.

And he's going to figure that out tonight.

I spend the rest of the day making my plan, and when four o'clock rolls around I send him instructions.

Then I leave early. I go home to get ready, thanking my lucky stars I was already down in the basement last night.

I am Mistress Myrtle and this class I'm planning for Pierce is not for beginners.

CHAPTER EIGHT

Fuck am I doing?

Rhetorical question.

I am driving to my former assistant's home under the premise that in order to make up for my horrible mistake in falsely accusing her of something she didn't do, she should be allowed to do some freaky submissive sex shit to me.

Jesus. When you say it all together at once like that...

The real question, of course, is why am I doing this?

Also kind of rhetorical.

Because regardless of what people think of me—and to be fair to "people," they think of me the way they do because I ask them to—I'm not a bad guy.

I'm not a nice guy.

But I'm not a bad guy.

I know what bad guys look like. I've been around them my whole life. Rolex-wearing knuckle-draggers. Guys who will do whatever it takes to get ahead and who will fuck over anyone in the process.

I've never presumed to be a saint. I'm certainly not as fundamentally decent as someone like Andrew. But I'd like to think I'm a reasonable distance apart from those other nut-sucklers.

Sure, I've had a good time in my day, but I've never hurt anyone on purpose. I've never fucked anyone over intentionally. And I've always treated the women I've been with with respect. My single mother taught me that and I take it seriously.

The fact that after I went to the Denver Women's March, I wound up sleeping with two of the women I met there was not my fault. I'd like to think it's because they just saw me as a thoughtful, progressive, forward-thinking, sensitive dude who looks like he's good at fucking.

And really, isn't that the way we all want to be seen?

But that's beside the point. The point is that I may be a self-absorbed, sometimes clueless, fundamentally flawed owner of a men's magazine, and possibly afflicted with an Oedipal complex, but who isn't?

I'm not making any sense.

But none of this makes sense.

Agreeing to some weird dom/sub thing doesn't make sense. Inviting her to come with me to Vail this weekend doesn't make sense. Treating this thing like she and I are in a relationship doesn't make sense.

I was never in a relationship with Myrtle. Well... I mean, I was. Of course I was. Just not a romantic relationship.

It was actually somewhat more than that. It was the longest lasting, most deeply personal, and frankly, most intimate relationship of my life. I came to depend on her. In all ways. She was almost like the other part of me. More than half the time she was able to anticipate the things I'd want before I'd even thought to want them. And now that part of our relationship is over, and…

Hold on. Wait a minute. I'm thinking about this like she and I were a couple or some shit. That is not what this has been. I am her boss and she is my employee. Period. End of story. And I did something shitty, as her boss, and, as her boss, I'm not above making amends.

I mean… I gave her a raise, a promotion, and apologized like a hundred times, but that doesn't seem to have been enough for her. So here I find myself. And, of equal importance, if she wants to do this thing—play this game, whatever—I'll go along. But I'm not going to let her shame me. Because no one else can shame you. Shame is something you feel or don't feel. And I refuse to feel ashamed.

And after this week is over and we're up in Vail, I'm going to treat her like she's never been treated before. I'm going to give her the weekend of her life. And she's going to feel so goddamn guilty for everything—all of it—that the universe will have righted itself and she and I will be balanced in a new normal and everything will make sense again between us.

This all makes sense.

It one million percent does.

I'm sure of it.

I wheel my McLaren to the west as the GPS instructs me to do. It occurs to me, quite suddenly, that I've got no idea where Myrtle lives. In all the years she's worked for me, I've never been to her house. I guess I always just kind of assumed she lived in the TDH. If I had stopped to think about it, I would've imagined her living in a cute condo around the corner from Le Man—decorated in nouveau goth chic or something—and maybe having a cat. Maybe two. There's a fine line between sexy cat lady and crazy cat lady, but Myrtle strikes me as the type of person who knows where to draw that distinction.

In any case, as I pull up to a long driveway that ends at what can only be described as an imposing looking wrought-iron fence, I can feel my brows rise and my eyes widen with the very sudden awareness that I may not know Myrtle at all.

As I roll forward, slowly, I look down at the GPS and back up at the house. Down at the GPS and back up at the house. Down at the GPS... I press the brake and sit there.

If this really is Myrtle's place, then I was right to have thought she didn't initially come to work for me for the money. And she sure as hell didn't stay for the promotion and a measly fifty-thousand-dollar raise. Good lord.

After a moment, a door to a guard shack by the main gate opens and a head pops out. A woman's head. Early thirties, attractive. Then the rest of her body pops out. She's wearing a guard's uniform.

I draw the sharply deductive conclusion that she's a guard.

She makes her way down the driveway to where I'm idling. She's carrying a clipboard and a well-worn paperback. She reaches the car door and I roll the window down.

"May I help you, sir?" she asks.

"Uh, I'm here to see Myrtle Rothschild? Am I in the right place?"

"This is the Rothschild residence," she responds. "What is your name, please?" She glances at her clipboard. I notice it only has one name on it.

"I'm Pierce Chevalier."

She looks at the clipboard. Which I find silly. Then she looks back at me and says, "I'm sorry. I don't have that name here."

"What? What do you mean?"

"I mean, sir, there is no Pierce Chevalier on the drive-on list."

"What? I can see the sheet. It only has one name on it."

"Yes, sir. And Pierce Chevalier isn't it."

"Well, can you, like, call up to the house and tell Myrtle I'm here?"

"Ms. Rothschild has left specific instructions that she is only to be alerted when the person whose name is on this list arrives."

I close my eyes, feel my jaw tighten, and do my best not to yell. "There's only one name! I'd hardly call that a fuckin' list!"

I did my best.

"Sir," she says, placing her hand on a nightstick she has attached to her utility belt, "I'll ask you to take a different tone, please."

I take a deep, deep breath. Let it out.

"Fine. Look… I'm here to see Ms. Rothschild. We have a scheduled… thing. My name is Pierce Chevalier. I am her boss. I own Le Man magazine. Surely you know who I am."

"Your name is not on the list, sir."

Fuck this shit.

"OK. Fine," I say, throwing the car into reverse and starting to back up.

"Perhaps it would be under another name…?" she half says, half asks. Pointedly.

"Excuse me?"

"Ms. Rothschild is a very private individual. Discretion is a priority. Perhaps, sir, for both your privacy and hers, your arrival is anticipated under a different name?" She raises an eyebrow at me.

My face feels like it's a mixture of confusion and annoyance, but then those feelings are replaced by a dawning disbelief. I know she reads my sudden realization because she fights to conceal a small smile.

I sigh, close my eyes, gnash my incisors together, and work out, "Anastasia Steele?"

The small smile on her lips blossoms into a delighted grin and she says, "Welcome, Ms. Steele. I'll buzz you in."

As she walks away from me toward the guard house, I have to fight the impulse to back out of here down the driveway and flee as fast as I can. But... a deal is a deal. A contract is a contract. And if I'm being totally honest, now I'm just really fucking curious.

The massive iron gates swing inward, like a giant, metallic mouth opening to consume me, and I roll forward toward the Twilight Zone. As I pass the guard woman, she continues smiling and says, "Have a pleasant evening."

I don't think I like her.

The driveway is a roundabout. I take notice that in the setting sun, what during the day probably looks like a beautiful, stately manor, will—in a matter of moments, once it becomes night—look like Dracula's fucking castle.

But at the same time, for whatever reason, I'm weirdly comforted. Because it kind of resembles the house in Marseilles where we lived when I was very young. My dad's house. I've only been back twice in the last two decades. And even though I definitely don't have the fondest memories of leaving there as a child, there's something about the feeling of coming home that feels like… coming home.

Which is the most uselessly tautological thought I've ever had, but, y'know, wherever you go, there you are, so…

I step out of my car and slam the door shut, taking a moment to stare up at the house and the darkening Colorado sky. It's big. I am struck, occasionally, by just how big this world is. And now is one of those moments.

I step to the front door and ring the bell. The door opens, revealing yet another attractive woman in her early thirties. This one is dressed in the smart attire of an estate manager. Most people would probably not immediately identify the woman's smart attire as that of an estate manager, but when you've seen as many estate managers as I have in my time, you learn to pick them out pretty quickly.

"Mr. Chevalier," she says, "Welcome. I'm Katherine, the sanctuary operations manager."

Can't put one past me. Although… "Sanctuary?"

"Myrtle will be with you shortly. Please, come in."

She extends her hand. We shake. I wait for her to turn into a vampire bat. She doesn't. I enter.

Inside, the castle vibe fades away into something more… elegant and refined. Her décor looks more downtown TDH penthouse than country estate. Very RH Modern with metal, geometric-inspired tables, subtle shades of gray, and couches and chairs in the next room that give the impression of being just a little too low to the ground. It's almost like Myrtle delights in confusing people. Giving them the exact opposite of what they expect, then doing that again and again until you finally give up and stop trying to figure her out.

Down a hallway, I can see few blonde women dressed in gray uniforms exiting out the back door. "G'night, Kristy, night, Claudette, night, Melody," says Katherine. The women all smile and wave good night in return.

I don't know what's got me more off kilter. The fact that nothing about this looks like anything I expected, or the fact that thus far I have seen no men wandering around here, which leads me to only one logical conclusion:

There are dead bodies in the backyard and I'm probably going to be murdered tonight.

"Um, what is this place?" I ask.

Again, Kate ignores me (Kate? Katy? Kelly? Shit.) and says, "Myrtle asked that you wait for her in the great room. You wanna follow me?"

"Sure. This all feels completely normal."

She smiles, politely, and walks in the direction of a large room with a wall-sized painting of what I think is an abstract white tiger. I follow, obediently, supposing that's something I should get prepared for.

"Can I get you anything?" she asks.

"No. I'm good. Thanks." I tug at my vest out of habit and wander around the space taking in the art and decorations, all of which are similarly abstract and modern and seem to have a tiger theme, but it could just be my overactive imagination and irrational fear that Myrtle is going to morph into a man-eater tonight and I'm on the menu. I turn to ask more questions of… what's her name… but she's gone.

This is it. I'm here. I'm doing this crazy shit. And I have to make a choice right this second. Stay and go through with this insanity. Or risk pissing off Myrtle again, fully endowed with the understanding that if I do, she is gone. In the wind. Vapor. I will never see her again. In my gut, I know that it's either go through with this or face the wrath of a Myrtle scorned.

I'm weighing this decision, trying to conclude what to do, when suddenly I hear something from behind me. A… meowing. Sort of. It's more of a purr/meow/growl kind of thing. At least I was right about one thing: Myrtle is a cat person and those paintings are of tigers.

And that's when I turn to see…

What. The fuck. Is that?

Is that…? What the…?

Is that a fucking leopard?

Jesus Christ! What the fuck is happening right now?

That's it. I'm fucking out of here.

But as I make for the exit, another fucking leopard, or hyena, or whatever the hell it is, rounds the corner. And they start walking toward me. No. Not walking. Stalking. Holy shit, they move just like Myrtle. I'm freaking out.

Oh, my God. Myrtle's a witch. That's what this is. Holy shit. Maybe one of these is Myrtle! Maybe they both are! Maybe Myrtle is actually twins! Or triplets! What the fuck is happening?

And just as my head is about to spin right off my shoulders, I hear a loud crack.

I snap my neck to the left and there, standing in another doorway, is… Myrtle.

Her hair is pulled back into a severe ponytail and she's wearing the tightest dress I've ever seen. Cinched at the waist to make her look like an actual hourglass, it comes to about mid-thigh. And then I can see the slightest hint of skin before black latex boots pick up the theme and run the blackness the rest of the way down to the stiletto heels that click-clack on the wooden floor.

She also has on gloves.

It's a lot of look.

"Betty. Dave. Come here."

The two cheetah/leopard/hyena/bears do as they're told and turn their attention from me to her. They walk over, and she kneels down to pet them. And suddenly they don't look as scary as they did a moment ago. Neither does she for that matter. She looks happy and giddy in a way that I've never seen her. Ever. Not once. And I smile in spite of myself.

She looks up and sees me smiling, and suddenly her demeanor changes. She stands, says, "Go, sit," to the two animals that were just licking at her cheeks, they do, and then she cracks the whip she's holding once again, and I know my own smile drops away pretty fuckin' fast when she says...

"Let's get started, bitch."

CHAPTER NINE

I have never seen Pierce cower. And he doesn't cower now. But it's something related to cowering. He steps back, turns his head to the side, looking at me from the corner of his eye, and says, "What the fuck is happening?"

I crack the whip. It's very long and it has never, ever been used on a lion. But Pierce doesn't need to know that. The tip snaps one of his expensive shoes and leaves a mark.

I smile. But only because he can't see me do it. He's too busy looking at the mark I left on the toe of his shoe. And by the time he looks back up at me, my smile is gone. "Did I give you permission to speak?"

He opens his mouth to say something. Probably something snarky and rude. But then he just runs his fingers through his hair and sighs.

"Good choice," I say, circling him. He spins with me, half looking over his shoulder where Betty and Dave are both now sitting. Watching.

"So you're what? A lion tamer? What the hell is up with the cats?"

"Not cats," I say, slowly stalking toward him. I crack the whip again, and this time it catches the edge of his leg.

He hops back a step. "Jesus! Stop doing that!"

I continue circling, the heels of my thigh-high latex boots clicking on the floor. "We need a safe word before we get started. Because if you tell me to stop again, I'll stop. And then this will be over and the deal is off."

"I think the deal is off," he says, trying to side-eye me, Betty, and Dave at the same time.

"Does it scare you, Pierce? Or just make you uncomfortable?"

"Uh... Yeah. Everything about this is making me uncomfortable. The gate, the house, the... where does one even buy a whip like that?"

I look at the whip in my hand. I have gloves on, so I can't feel the well-worn leather handle, but I don't need to feel it to know what it feels like. "This," I say, "is actually a family heirloom."

Pierce just looks at me. "Who are you?"

I smile and walk forward. Get close to him, still circling. He stays still now, because I'm pressing my lips up to the back of his neck. I breathe softly on his skin and feel a thrill when it prickles up with chills. "You're about to find out."

He shrugs his shoulders up to his ears like he's trying to make that chill go away, and then steps back. "You're crazy. I mean, everyone knows you're weird. Your little act you put on at work—"

I snap the whip again and his words fall away. "Is it an act?" I ask.

He points his finger in my face. "I knew you had a secret fetish side."

I turn my back to him and walk across the room. "Follow me. Or don't. Up to you."

I catch Katherine staring at me from around a corner. She smiles one of those big, fat smiles that are nothing but teeth and then turns away to hide the laughing fit that is surely coming.

Katherine has been the manager out here at the sanctuary since I moved in. We're not what you'd call friends, or anything. We don't go out for drinks. We're more like sisters. She lives here on the property. And when she saw me come down the stairs to wait for Pierce all dressed up like Mistress Myrtle, she made it very clear she wasn't walking down the hill to her little carriage house until she saw his reaction.

"Shoo," I whisper in her direction. And she's just about to protest when we both hear the clicking of Pierce's shoes as he crosses the living room.

Following, just the way he was meant to.

She ducks away and disappears.

I lead him through the mansion, taking the long way to the basement on purpose, to confuse him. Make him second- and third-guess his decision to come tonight. Make him question everything he thought he knew about me. And when we finally stop in front of the door that leads down into the basement, I can tell he's breathing hard.

Poor, poor Pierce. He has no idea what he's getting into.

Ten minutes from now he'll be in his car driving away as fast as his McLaren can take him.

Then I'll have gotten my revenge, have had a good

laugh, and be let off the hook for this stupid romantic weekend idea he pulled out of nowhere this morning. I might even grab a bottle of wine and trot down to Katherine's house so we can giggle over it.

I pull the basement door open slowly. It squeaks. Loudly. Like a door in a creepy movie.

And then I turn to him. "Are you ready?" I purr.

He swallows. Looks down the dark steps. Then at me. "It's down there, huh? In the basement?"

"That's where most dungeons live."

He hesitates.

"What's wrong?" I ask. "Losing interest in my secret fetish side?"

"You know… we could just… do this another way?"

"Another way?"

"Yeah, you know." He waggles his eyebrows at me, trying to pretend he's cool. Like he's in control here. Like this is just some fantastic joke. "My way."

If I wasn't in character, and if I didn't take this character seriously, I'd laugh. "I'm going to punish you for that."

"For what?"

"Every moment of my time that you waste comes with consequences." He squints his eyes at me. "Every time you make me say something twice, I will punish you twice as hard."

"Fuck it," he huffs. "Fine. I'm going. See?" He starts down the stairs. Quick, at first. Then slower. "Are there lights? Or is me breaking my neck just part of being dominated?"

"I'm going to gag you first," I say. "To make you stop asking questions." Which makes him hesitate, but he recovers and continues until he's at the bottom looking up at me.

I flash him one last smile and then I close the door and the darkness is complete.

"For fuck's sake," he says. "Could you be any more dramatic?"

Oh, yes. Yes, I can. Just give me a moment.

My heels click on the stairs. One. At. A. Time as I descend. When I get to the bottom I lean into him, so close I press my lips to the outer shell of his ear, and say, "Come with me."

"Lights? This isn't a haunted house... is it?"

I take his hand in mine and walk forward, weaving through the various contraptions that have been placed throughout the room, and ignore him.

"In due time, my little pet," I say.

He mutters curse words under his breath and I'm glad it's dark. Because I can't stop the smile.

"How can you even see where you're going?" he asks.

I don't answer this time. I just drop his hand and walk away.

The only sound in the room are my heels on the bare concrete and his long, tired sigh.

"Stay where you are," I say. "Something might jump out and bite you."

"That's not funny."

"Before we go any further, I want you to pick a safe word. A word you can use if things go too far, too fast, or get too uncomfortable for you. Pick."

"Any word?"

"Any word."

"And if I say it—?"

"I stop whatever I'm doing."

He's silent for a moment. I can almost hear him

thinking. Then, finally, he says...

"Sacrebleu."

"Sacrebleu?"

"Yeah. It's a French expression."

"I know. Are you sure?"

"Yeah. I think so. No. Wait. I'm not sure. It could be good or bad. I don't want to accidentally shout it out if I like something and have you stop inadvertently."

I'm starting to get the feeling he's stalling. "Pierce—"

"Sacapuntas!" he exclaims.

"Saca... what?"

"Sacapuntas. It's Spanish for 'pencil sharpener.' That's my safe word."

Well... I don't suppose there's any chance he'll shout that by accident.

"But I doubt I'll use it," he goes on, adding, arrogantly, "I can take whatever you dish out."

And that's when the growling starts. It's low, throaty, and even though I'm the one who set this all up, I get the chills too.

"Sacrebleu!" he shouts. Unbelievable. "Please tell me that was a recording."

"Don't move," I say. "Or you'll find out."

"Myrtle?"

I walk over to the cage, feel around until I find the lock, pull the pin out of the safety and open the door.

It creaks. Just like the door to the basement.

The growling gets louder.

"Myrtle? What the fuck is that?"

"Shhh," I say. "Just take off your clothes."

"What? No fucking way. Is there an animal in here? Turn the damn lights on!"

The roaring gets louder and I sense Pierce go utterly still. Three seconds pass. "Myrtle?" he whispers.

I say nothing.

"Myrtle!" He whisper-screams it this time. "That isn't real! I'm not falling for your scare tactics and woe be unto you when I get out of this crazy-ass haunted house fake dungeon—"

The growling settles down to a low, threatening rumble.

"Turn the lights on."

"Take off your clothes, crawl over here on your hands and knees, and get in the cage."

"Fuck that!"

I crack the whip.

"No. I'm not doing it. Not until you turn the lights on."

"You don't make the rules, I do. That's the whole reason you came over here tonight."

"So you can put me in a cage?"

"Would you rather go on the rack? I can handcuff you to the wall and spank you until your pretty ass is bright red."

He laughs.

"That's OK," I say. "You can laugh. But I'm dead serious."

"OK, hold on. Because some of that sounds... fun, but—"

I crack the whip again. "Do it. Or leave. Those are your choices."

"Is there a goddamn tiger in here?"

I start walking toward him, the sound of my heels on the floor too loud in the silence. When I reach him, I slide my hands inside his suit coat and press my whole body up to his. "Do you think there's a tiger in here?"

His head turns, like maybe his eyes have adjusted to the darkness and he can see shadows. "Why wouldn't I? You have two cheetahs so—"

"Servals," I say. "They're servals. And they're not down here. Do you want me to help you?" I ask, pulling his suit coat down his arms.

"Myrtle—"

"Shhh," I say, dropping the coat on the floor and starting on his shirt buttons. "The first lesson you need to learn is trust," I purr. "Tonight is all about trust."

He stammers out a few unintelligible words but when I reach the bottom button on his shirt, he sucks in a breath.

I really didn't think he'd get this far, so when my fingertips brush up against the bare skin of his stomach as I remove his shirt, I have to wonder how far I'll go.

Am I really going to strip my boss naked and put him in a cage?

Oh, you betcha.

I might not have a job tomorrow, but one thing's for sure. Pierce Chevalier will never humiliate me again.

"Myrtle," he says, hands gripping mine when I reach for his belt.

"Yes," I whisper.

"There isn't actually a tiger in here, right?"

"Where would I get a tiger?"

"Fuck if I know. You have those… cats upstairs. And the gate. The security. And—"

"Do you want me to stop?" I ask. "All you have to say is…"

"Sacapuntas?"

"Mm-hm."

But before he has a chance to say anything more, I drag my fingernails down his chest, making chills run through his body.

"Because I will. Stop. If you want. And you can walk out of here and pretend this never happened."

"No. No," he says, breathy, the feel of my nails on his skin given voice by the sound of his languid protest. "No. I don't wanna stop."

The growling starts again.

"OK. Fuck. Seriously? I think you have a tiger in here."

"Maybe it's a recording?"

"Maybe it's not."

I unbuckle his belt. Release his trouser button. Pull his zipper down. "Take them off," I say.

I have no idea what's going through his head right now. I can't even begin to imagine. But I don't have time to wonder because he kicks off his shoes and drops his pants.

"This isn't fair," he says.

"Now get down," I say. "And crawl. I'll lead you over to the cage, don't worry."

"Ten minutes," he says. "I'm staying ten minutes and then this is over."

"This is over whenever you want it to be."

I know how frustrating it is. Believe me, I get it. There is nothing worse than being in charge of your own submission. Being the one who has all the power but gives it up willingly.

It's hard.

But Pierce doubles down. He drops to the floor and my fingertips thread through his hair. I fist it, gripping tight, and then pull him along as I walk over to the cage.

"It's directly in front of you," I say. "Just crawl in and wait."

"Wait for what?"

"Oh," I say. "Hold on. I almost forgot the gag."

CHAPTER TEN

Good morning, Pierce. What did you do last night?

It doesn't matter who asks that question tomorrow. Nobody is getting a fucking answer.

The most unpleasant thing for me at the moment is how cold the floor is. My boxer briefs are thin and this concrete and metal is goddamn chilly. But all of the sudden, out of seemingly nowhere, I am struck with this thought: I'm not going to complain.

I'm not going to whine. I'm not going to bitch. I'm going to take everything that's coming my way. Because allowing Myrtle to get her wrong-headed revenge is one thing, but taking it on as my own servility is something else entirely.

So when she comes at me with the ball gag, which I can barely see in the dimness of the room, I don't protest or balk at it. I simply open my mouth as wide as I can.

"Aim for the teeth," I tell her. "I just had them whitened."

And then I champ them together in a flashy grin and once again open wide. She hitches back for a second. My guess is that my apparent and fresh eagerness is throwing her off guard. Good.

She places the gag in my mouth and her breasts are suddenly dangerously close to my face. They've never been this close before. She smells pretty wonderful. I don't know how a person can smell like beauty and punishment, but Myrtle does.

Once she has the gag securely placed in my mouth, I ask, "Cooiguadrnkowtrfust?"

"What?"

"Cooiguadrnkowtrfust?"

"Jesus," she says as she unfastens the strap, pulling the gag free. "What?" she asks again.

I spit a couple of pieces of plastic-y tasting ball gag from my lips. "I said, 'Could I get a drink of water first?' I'm thirsty and I don't know how long we'll be down here."

"Are you fucking serious?"

"No." I grin. Then I open my mouth again and say, "Proceed."

I can't see well enough to actually observe her frustration with me, but I can feel it.

"Pierce?" she whispers into my ear, leaning in close.

"Yeah?"

"This is not a game."

"Oh, really? It's not? Then what the fuck do you call it?"

"I call it retribution. I call it an agreement. I call it punishment. And right now, you need to shut the fuck up and take it."

And at that, she slaps me across the face.

There's a tense moment in which the air seems to stop moving. I can feel her holding her breath. I know I'm holding mine. The only sound is the low growl and padding steps of what is either an actual tiger somewhere down here, or an exceptionally realistic sound system.

I continue to have a lot of questions.

And then the most unexpected thing happens...

I feel the lingering burn of her hand across my cheek. The sting of her fingers making contact with my six-thirty shadow. The jolt of adrenaline that came of being touched so violently, from out of nowhere, and the flush of blood that accompanied it.

I don't think I've ever been hit before. Ever. In my life. This is the first time I've ever been struck. By anyone. Ever.

I think I love it.

"Again," I say, the heavy breathing of either her or the phantom tiger the only sound other than my half-yearning voice requesting another smack.

"What?" she asks.

"Do it again."

"Pierce?"

"Slap me. Again."

We look at each other for a moment. I can see the whites of her eyes, staring at me. I know she can see mine. I wonder if she can see the gleam in them. After several protracted breaths, she rears her hand back and does it again. She slaps me across the face. Harder this time.

But it's not enough.

"Harder," I say.

"Pierce..."

"Put the gag back in and do it harder."

Even in the dark with her dark clothes covering her, I can see her chest heaving.

"Let's go, Christian. Let's do this shit."

And then the energy inside my little cage shifts. She no longer seems uncertain, like she just was, or playfully mistress-like, as she was before that. Her energy now is all business. Like she's been challenged and she's readying herself to respond to the challenge in front of her.

She grabs me by the hair and yanks my head backward. With her other hand, she picks up the previously set-aside ball gag and places it in her own mouth. Then she squeezes my cheeks, hard, forcing my mouth to open like a fish's might.

And now she brings her mouth to mine and presses the ball into my open 'O.' Her lips touch mine. Our teeth grind against each other's. And then, with her tongue, she forces the ball forward until it's resting once again in my stretched maw, and she straddles me. Her skirt rises up her thighs and now she is pressing the warmth of her pussy into my hardening cock.

And it is hardening. It is hardening at an alarming rate.

The sticky warmth of her crotch against mine and the softness of her breasts against my chest as she fastens the gag tightly around the back of my head is making me throb.

It seems to take her a bit off guard, because she draws back, lifts herself off me, crawls back out of the cage, stands, and straightens her dress down her hips. She stares at me. I don't move. Just sit there in my underwear, ball gag in mouth, legs stretched out in front, waiting for whatever is going to happen next.

I'm prepared. I'm prepared for anything. I am Pierce fuckin' Chevalier and I can take whatever Myrtle goddamn Rothschild can dish out. She can spank me, whip me, burn me, choke me, I can take it all. And when she's gotten whatever it is that she hopes to get from this experience, I will have my turn to show her who I really am. Because she thinks she knows me. But she doesn't.

Hell, I'm learning more about myself right now than I even knew. I've just discovered that even when I'm not in control, I'm still in control. My aura is too strong. My chi is too powerful. Even stripped and gagged, I am the master of my domain. I am the king of my jungle, and there is no one and nothing that can—

OH MY HOLY FUCK, FUCK ME IN MY ASSHOLE, MYRTLE JUST LIT A CANDLE AND THERE IS, IN FACT, A TIGER IN THE CAGE NEXT TO ME WITH ITS FACE UP AGAINST THE BARS! AND IT'S DROOLING ON MY DICK!

Um... OK... This was not in the book...

CHAPTER ELEVEN

The sound he makes comes out like, "Thewuhnaanunduhboot!!"

"Sorry? What was that? You thought we were… knocking boots?"

He shakes his head. Hard. "Thi. Wah. Nah. Ii. Da. Boot."

"Oooooh." I realize what he's trying to say. "Yeah, no, you're right. This was not in any book. Because you're not in a fiction now, Anastasia. This is real life."

Pierce stares at me, candlelight flickering off his wide eyes. And then he reaches around and pulls the gag off.

I smirk. I can't help it. Because I called it, didn't I? It's probably been a little more than ten minutes since he stepped through the door, but not much. He's going to run out of here and in two minutes I'll be making my way down the hill to Katherine's house to enjoy a bottle of wine through fits of laughter.

"This is crazy. This is weird! What are you doing?

97

Where did you get this tiger? What the hell is going on and when the hell can I leave?"

"You can leave right now, Anastasia. You're the one in control, remember?"

"Myrtle," he says, teeth clenched, his voice low and angry.

"Pierce."

"Are you going to explain?"

"I thought I did."

"You didn't." And that's when Sebastian roars. So loud even I jump a little. He's a true kitty cat. And he's almost twenty years old. True, he's never been in a situation like this, but he's been in some weird situations in his life, so that roar was really more of a yawn. His way of saying, Let's get this show on the road.

Plus, he's not even in the same cage as Pierce. I'm not worried about Sebastian. Pierce, on the other hand—let's just say I hope he doesn't have a heart condition. Because he scoots away to the farthest side of his cage, back pressed up against the bars, and yells, "Get me the fuck out of here!"

I feel obligated to put up a fight. Make a big deal about him quitting. So I do that. "Are you sure?" I say. "Just say the word. The word you chose. But be sure. Because once you say it, once you quit, you quit for good. And this wasn't enough to erase your debt to me."

"What do you want from me?"

"Submission," I deadpan. "And don't tell me I didn't make that clear, because I did."

"This is a wild animal," he says, pointing to Sebastian. "You never said anything about being eaten by tigers!"

"Don't be dramatic. The whole point of submission is to trust that your mistress will take care of you. How would letting my tiger eat you build trust?"

"You say that like owning a tiger is normal!"

He's losing control now. There are about thirty seconds until he grabs his clothes and runs to his car, and I want to make the most of those moments. I want him to think about my words as he's driving home, tomorrow as he gets ready for breakfast, and all the days that come after when I'm no longer in his life because he fired me for stripping him down to his underwear, stuffing a ball gag in his mouth, and putting him in a cage.

It's sad, really. That this is how my seven years of servitude to Pierce and Le Man magazine will end. But that's the way it has to be. Because I cannot go on working for him as the VP of Social Media.

I just can't.

"It is normal, Pierce. Because this is who I am."

"You're a crazy tiger lady!"

"No," I say, voice even and low. "I'm a sane tiger lady."

"Oh, well," he huffs. "That explains everything!" He takes a deep breath, side-eyes Sebastian the way he did Dave and Betty upstairs, and then looks at me and says, "I always knew you were... different. But this is... this is..."

"This is what?" I ask, truly interested in whatever new opinion he's forming about me.

He blows out a long breath of air and stays silent.

"You think I'm into Halloween. You think I'm motivated by money. By a new title and a big office. You think you can buy my forgiveness with expensive furniture. But your most egregious sin was that you thought I was the Sexpert."

Sebastian gets up, prowls the length of his large cage, and then flops down on the other end. Bored.

But all Pierce sees is the wild animal. He sees teeth, and claws, and stripes. He's imagining all the ways this living, breathing death-machine can hurt him.

"But you're so sexy," he finally says. "I don't understand why you'd be offended by it. I mean, it was a clever-as-hell idea."

"Oh, it's not the idea of the Sexpert that offended me."

"Then what's the problem? I don't get it!"

"I know," I say, suddenly sad. "That's the problem."

"Would you stop talking in circles and just... explain?"

"I thought you were leaving?"

"Well, I'm not. OK? I'm not. I'm not leaving."

"I'm going to tell you the truth now. And the truth is..." I pause. "You don't get to know me, Pierce. You don't get to understand what's happening. Because I've worked for you for seven years. And the reason you're confused right now—the reason you think I'm into Halloween—is because you don't know me. I realized that as I was dragged out of the auditorium when you told the whole world I... lied to you."

"What?"

"You thought I lied to you. You thought I was keeping secrets from you."

"Well, obviously you are! Why the hell do you have a tiger?"

"This has nothing to do with the tiger. Or this place. Or any of that. None of this is secret. My problem with you is that you don't trust me. After seven years of me having your back, seven years of me running interference on your behalf, seven years of taking your side in every way I could possibly think of, you thought I was lying. You thought I was trying to screw you over. And that… that is a sin that might not be forgivable. So why don't I just do the grown-up thing here and quit so you don't have to fire me tomorrow?"

"Quit?" he yells. "You are not quitting, lady! I didn't come all the way out to your… your… your jungle castle, strip myself down to my skivvies, and crawl into a cage so you could quit on me! No! I'm here. I'm present. I'm invested, OK? So do whatever you have to do to set this right. I'm not leaving and you're not quitting!"

He crosses his arms like a little kid. Makes a stern face that says he's serious. And for a moment my heart beats fast. Panic, I realize. "What do you mean you're not leaving?"

"I'm not leaving. Look," he says, picking up the ball gag and pulling the strap back around his head. "Imf. Nof. Leafing. Lefs fuffing wo tis shik."

But… he has to leave. He has to. That was the plan. If he stays… Jesus Christ. If he stays, I'll have to actually do this! I'll have to dominate him, and smack his ass, and handcuff him! My boss will have to submit to me and I'll have to dom the fuck out of him! Because that was the promise I made. That's the whole point. And if I don't do all that then… then I lose again!

I thought for sure he'd run when he saw Sebastian. And hell, that was being generous. I really thought he'd run the moment he saw Dave and Betty.

But the cats aren't enough.

So now what?

How do I scare him out of this? How do I hand in my resignation as the winner?

Because that was always the end game. I have no future at Le Man as a VP. I don't even want to be a VP. I don't even need the fucking money. I stay there for him. It's always been for him. And this stupid job is... well, stupid. I can't go on working there as Myrtle Rothschild, VP of Social Media. I just can't.

And I refuse to leave with my tail tucked between my legs. If I'm walking out on Pierce Chevalier, then I'm walking out on my terms, not because I lost playing this stupid game.

Pierce drags the gag down his face. "Myrtle?"

"What?" I whisper.

"Are you going to show me?"

"Show you what?" I ask, turning away from him. Because I suddenly have no idea what I'm doing. What the fuck was I thinking? Inviting my boss down here? He's in a cage, for fuck's sake!

"Who you are."

I press my lips together and shake my head. "No. That's not why you're here, Pierce."

"Well... I am here. So you better deal with it. Because I'm not leaving."

Get your shit together, Myrtle. You have to do something and you have to do it now.

I reach into the top of my corset and pull out a lighter and I start lighting candles. Because I have no clue what's happening right now. This started out as a joke. A way to get even. A way to get out of this stupid relationship. Which is also stupid, because it's not a relationship. I thought it was at least a friendship, but I was wrong about that too.

So I just light the candles. There are dozens of them around the room. Tall candelabras with thick pillars on top. Two on each side of my... equipment.

And when I'm done, I turn back to him, his face

flickering with the soft glow of candlelight. He stares back at me, then slips the gag back in place and nods his head.

"First," I say, walking over to a table. There's various paddles, whips, and devices neatly laid out on top of crushed red velvet. Other things too. Hoods, and collars, and spreader bars. I make a selection, still unsure of how this night went so spectacularly wrong, walk back over to him, open the cage, and say, "Give me your wrists. I'm going to handcuff you now."

He does this. Willingly. And I can't help but be a little impressed. My first trip down to a dungeon certainly didn't go this way. I was scared to death. And maybe he is scared? Maybe he's just better at hiding it than I was.

But he doesn't look scared. Not when I lock the cuffs around his wrists and not when I fasten them to the bars of the cage. Not even when Sebastian walks over to the side of the cage next to Pierce, flops down, and begins to chuff—that weird half-purr, half-growl thing only tigers do.

Pierce just looks at him and huffs some air out his nose. As if they're sharing a moment. Some kind of caged-animal camaraderie.

I lock the cage back up and walk over to the first piece of equipment. Then I clear my throat and say, "OK. Welcome to BDSM 101. I'm your mistress and this is what you can expect."

I start with the most daunting piece of dungeon furniture.

"This is the stockade," I say, picking up a candle so he can get a good look at it. "Your wrists will go in here. Your ankles are fastened down here." I point to the bar between those two parts. "And you bend over this. Any questions?"

He smiles through the ball gag and shakes his head.

"This," I say, walking on to the next piece of furniture, "is the punishment bench. Extreme deluxe version. I think it's self-explanatory."

I walk on, stopping again. "This is the lock-down system. I call it the rack, but it's not for stretching you out like the torture device of the same name, just... immobilizing you in an upright position."

I move on, going over each piece of furniture, then make my way to the table and start picking up the smaller things. "This is a spreader. I don't think I'll use it on you, but I like to have it just in case. This is a cock cage. This is a thigh sling. This is a..." It goes on like that for several minutes. I look back at him after each explanation, trying to decipher his thoughts.

But I have no idea what Pierce is thinking right now. None.

All I know is that he nods. He just... agrees.

When I'm done explaining things I walk back over to the cage, open the door, and uncuff him, leaving the restraints attached to the bar. I grab him by the hair, fist it, gripping tight, and pull him forward until he understands that I want him out of the cage.

He crawls, looking up at me.

God, my heart is beating so fast.

"You may stand," I say.

He does.

I remove the ball gag and drop it onto the tray set aside for used items. "Any questions?" I ask.

"When do we start?" he says, smiling.

"We're done for tonight."

"What?" He laughs. "You're kidding."

"Your mistress does not joke when she's in the

dungeon."

"But..." He looks down. Which makes me look down. He's hard. There's no way to miss it.

"Not tonight," I say, forcing my eyes back up. "Now put your clothes back on and leave."

I want to die right now. Because tomorrow morning I have to walk into work and see this man outside of my pleasure room. And that is not how this game is usually played. Things are kept separate. The lifestyle never meets real life. Not when I play.

God, I did not think this through. At all.

I walk over to a red velvet couch and sit down, crossing my long legs seductively because Pierce is watching.

I watch him back.

I watch him pull on his pants. Shrug on his shirt. Button all those expensive little buttons. I watch him fasten his belt, and put on his shoes, and pick up his coat. And when he's all put back together he smiles at me. "So. Same time tomorrow?"

"Same time tomorrow," I reply back. "Now leave."

He turns to go, but then he turns back. "Myrtle?"

"What?"

"Can I ask you one thing?"

"What?"

"What is this place?"

"My dungeon."

"No. This house."

"Oh," I say, looking at him. He seems... at ease now. All traces of panic and fear gone. God, did I ever get him wrong. "It's a big cat sanctuary," I say. "My father was a lion tamer in the circus before I was born. Then he trained tigers and lions for movies. Then he opened up the main

105

sanctuary up north. That's where most of them go. The ones people get for pets and then decide they're not really pet material when they eat the family dog. But this is our family estate. He turned it into a retirement center for the older performing cats so they could live out their days being pampered. Sebastian was never going to eat you. He's as tame as they come."

Pierce chuckles a little as he turns to the stairs, slowly walking up. But he stops halfway and says, "I know."

I got dominated last night, dude."

I know I thought that I would never tell someone what I did last night if they asked, but Andrew didn't ask. I just find myself unexpectedly excited to share the news with my old friend.

"What?" he asks, mouth full of breakfast burrito.

"Jesus, chew, man. Were you raised in a barn?"

"Yeah," he says.

Oh right. He grew up on a horse farm. Forgot that. In any case... "Dude, last night... man."

I plop down in the chair facing his desk. He begins to speak. I wave my finger at him, forcing him to swallow before he speaks again. Once the bite has cleared his gullet, he says, "What the hell are you talking about?"

I lean in close, lower my voice. I don't know why I do it. There's no one else here. But I do. "Last night..." I look around for a reason I can't identify. "Last night, I went to Myrtle's house."

"O-kay."

"And she stripped me down to my underwear, put me in a cage with a lion, shoved a ball gag in my mouth, slapped me, showed me her torture toys, gave me a hard-on, and then sent me away. Dude… it was fucking awesome."

I lean back in my chair and smile. He stares at me for a second, picks up his napkin, wipes his mouth, throws the napkin and the rest of the burrito in the trash can, nods, and says, "Come again?"

"I know. I know. You were right, man. I needed to prostrate myself. But what we didn't consider is that I didn't just need to prostrate myself for her. I needed to do it for me."

He pinches the place between his eyebrows. Shit. Now I feel like I need to get him to a neurologist too.

"Lemme… lemme see if I can parse through what you're saying." He takes a breath. "Are you saying that when I suggested you needed to cow yourself before Myrtle, you took that literally? I mean, are you saying that you went to Myrtle's place to do some kind of BDSM thing? Is that what you're saying? 'Cause it sounds like that's what you're saying."

"Yeah. That's what I'm saying. It was great." I pop my shirt cuffs and tweak my cufflinks because… I dunno. Because I think it looks cool.

"Dude…"

"Hey, listen, do me a favor. Don't tell anybody. OK?"

"Who'm I gonna tell?"

"Um, your girlfriend?"

"Dude. C'mon. You know me a little. There's no way I would—"

"I'm sorry, what did you do, exactly?" Eden asks as

she barrels into the room. Declan, Andrew's development guy, is on her tail.

"Andrew, I'm sorry, I'm sorry," says Declan, "she stopped by my desk on her way to see you and I was showing her what we're working on and I just opened the app on your phone remotely, and… shit. Sorry. Hey, Pierce."

"Declan."

"Dev."

"Sure."

"What did you do?" Eden asks again.

"Honey," Andrew starts, but Eden throws up a 'talk to the hand' hand and he backs off.

"OK!" says Dev. "Feels like my work is done here! See ya!" And he takes off. Can't believe I forgot that Andrew has a developer called Dev. Funny.

What's not funny is the way Eden is looking at me. She has her hands on her hips and is staring at me, hard. Her glasses are down at the tip of her nose and she's looking at me over the tops of the rims. She's breathing a little hard. Not like she's out of breath, but almost like she's kind of pissed. And even though millions of people have seen her cupcakes millions of times, I'm trying not to stare at the rising and falling of her chest because she's Andrew's lady friend and because I'm classy like that.

"I have no idea what you're talking about," I tell her.

"I'm talking about what exactly you did to my friend, Myrtle. What did you do?"

I look at her. I look at Andrew. In return he looks at me with a combination 'sorry/what do you want from me' expression. I close my eyes, take a long inhale, and say, "I did exactly what Andrew told me to do."

"What?" Andrew leaps forward. "Babe," he says, "I

109

didn't. I mean, I did not."

"He told me to make myself unctuous."

"What? I never used the word 'unctuous.'"

"Doesn't 'unctuous' mean 'servile?'"

"Sort of. It also means 'oily.'"

"Oh. Well, it's possible I'm going to wind up being that too."

"Shut! Up!" I've never heard Eden yell before. Just like everything about her, it comes across as kind of sweet. But I don't tell her that. I just shut up, as she demands. "Start over," she says. "Explain what the hell happened."

And so I do.

I tell them both about the fact that I can't seem to get over Myrtle's continuing resentment towards me. I tell them about the fact that, unlike usual, I can't just seem to let it go and move on. I tell them that I told Myrtle that I'd do what I had to to make it right between us. I explain about the contract and the whole Fifty Shades stuff. (I leave out the part where somehow I have gotten nicknamed Anastasia.) I tell them about the house and the dungeon and the tiger and the stuff that Myrtle did to me. And the stuff she didn't do. I tell them that in return for letting Myrtle dominate me, she's coming to Vail with me for the weekend.

And when I'm done telling them everything, I once again flop into a chair and pop my cufflinks. Again, because it's super cool.

Eden looks at me, looks at Andrew, and then back at me. And says, "You have got to be the stupidest smart person I have ever met."

"I... Thanks?"

"Jesus," she says, coming to sit in the chair beside me. "Why are you doing this to her?"

"Me? Doing…? What? What are you talking about? What am I doing? She's the one doing things. I'm the one getting drooled on by tigers and shit."

Andrew rounds his desk and sits on the edge, facing me as well. "She's right, man. I'm not sure you should be playing this game."

"What are you talking about?"

"Man, c'mon. She could sue you, or—"

"Oh. My. God!" That's Eden again. "No wonder you two are best friends. Oblivious geniuses are so out of fashion, you guys. C'mon! Get it together!"

Both of us look at her, obliviously. Like the geniuses we are.

"Honey," Andrew says, "What're you—?"

"Myrtle is in love with you, Pierce! She has been for a long time! And you making her do this… this… thing with you, it's mean. It's some kind of weird power game. And it's mean."

"OK," I say, slowly. "First of all, she's not in love with me. I don't know if Myrtle's the kind of person who falls in love. And regardless, she kind of hates me these days."

"Yeah, dummy! Because she's in love with you and you hurt her. Are you really that self-involved that you can't get that?"

Shit. I'm not sure I heard what Eden just asked. I was thinking about Myrtle's crotch on top of my crotch last night. "What?"

She huffs. "Love and hate are sides of a coin, Pierce. Yeah, she hates you because of what you did to her. But that's only because she loved you. Probably still does."

"There's no—"

"And you love her."

111

Whoa. What? Wait a minute.

"Whoa! What? Wait a minute," I say.

"C'mon, you totally do. I mean, it's been obvious since the first day I started work at Le Man."

"Obvious how?" I ask.

"Like, uh, you would pay attention to her? You'd say nice things to her? You remembered her name." I look at Andrew, who raises his eyebrows. "I mean," she goes on, "on anybody else, stuff like that would just be basic courtesy, but coming from you? You might as well have been freakin' proposing to her."

I can feel that my mouth is a tiny bit agape, but I can't seem to find the resolve to close it. So, after a moment, I just stand up. "That's ridiculous," I say, popping my cuffs and adjusting the knot in my tie. "Absurd. Don't you have some dirty videos to make or something?"

"Don't be a dick just because you don't wanna face the fact that I'm right," she says.

"Hey," I tell her, "I don't need a reason to be a dick," and I start to leave.

I'm just about at the door when I hear, "Pierce?"

I turn back to see the two of them standing side by side. A unified front. A team. I mean, she's clearly the captain, but still... a team.

"Yeah?" I say.

"Myrtle's a really, really good person. She has the exterior she has, but underneath it, she's... she's soft. Just, whatever it is that you think you're going to get out of this, don't puncture her again. OK? I don't think she'll stick around if you hurt her again."

Yeah. No shit.

"Don't worry, mes amis," I tell them with a wink as I open the door. "I got this."

I so totally do not got this.

Is it possible that Eden is right? Could Myrtle have an actual thing for me? Could I have a thing for her? That's crazy talk. Yeah? I mean, I know what I feel about things. Don't I?

Don't I?

To be fair, last night I learned more about myself than I've learned in probably a dozen years, so…

But no. There's no way Myrtle could've had a thing for me—like, a real thing—and I wouldn't have noticed. I mean, it's not possible.

Is it?

Is it possible that I'm really that blind to shit going on around me?

"Oh, hell, I'm sorry. I didn't see you coming," I say to Valerie as I bump into her in the hallway next to my office.

"Oh, no, sir, that's all right. I'm sorry. My fault." I wish she wouldn't do that. It wasn't her fault. If I had accidentally bumped into Myrtle like that, she would've said something like, 'That's OK, I love being manhandled.' Or something equally disconcerting and probably needing to be reported to HR. "I was just coming to find you," Valerie continues. "Ms. Rothschild is waiting for you in your office."

"She is?" Valerie nods. "OK. Great. I'll, uh…" And then I kind of lose myself for a second.

Valerie's voice brings me back. "Sir?"

"Uh, yeah. Great. Thanks, Val." She smiles and nods, and heads off. I look up at the ceiling for reasons passing understanding, and then continue on into my office where I do, indeed, find Myrtle waiting. She's once again sitting behind my desk, legs crossed. She's eating a Twizzler. Jesus fuckin'—

"Help you with something?" I ask.

"I need to push your time to eight tonight."

"My time?"

"Your expected arrival time. I need to push to eight o'clock. That is if you're still planning on showing up."

"Oh, yeah. I'll be there. Wouldn't miss it for the world."

She eyes me. "Yeah?"

"Yeah."

I nod. She rolls her tongue around her Twizzler and then bites it, aggressively.

"Good," she says.

"Good."

"OK."

"OK."

"So," she says, standing. "I'll see you then."

"Believe it."

She crosses to stand directly in front of me, takes another bite of her Twizzler, and chews in my face. I tilt my head, watch her, and try as hard as I can not to blink first.

"See ya," she finally says, as she brushes past me and the smell of her that I caught last night finds its way into my nostrils again.

Just as she's almost at the door, unexpectedly and out of impulse, I say, "Myrtle…?"

She turns, one eyebrow lifted, Twizzler… twizzling… in her mouth, and says, "Hm?"

I squint. I don't know why. It's not like I can't see her. But I don't know if I actually do.

"Yes?" she says. "What? What is it?" The question is

freighted. There's a low-level anxiety inside the asking. Like maybe she's not sure if I'm just going to pull the plug right here and now. Or fire her after all. Or…

"Can I bring anything?" I ask. I immediately regret the lameness of the question, but it was the best cover I could come up with when I decided that I didn't want to ask any of the more real questions I have swimming around in my head.

She looks puzzled for a moment and then she shoves the last bit of Twizzler in her mouth, and as she chews it, she says, "See ya at eight."

Damn.

Suddenly I really want a Twizzler.

That's probably something we could work into tonight.

CHAPTER THIRTEEN

When I round the corner to my office, Eden is waiting for me. "Did we have a meeting?" I ask. My phone begins to ring.

"Um... no," she says. "I just need to talk to you about something." Then she stares at my ringing phone. "You can get that. I'll wait."

"It can't be anything important," I say. "I don't actually do anything here." Then I chuckle under my breath. Last night was weird at the end. Hell, who am I kidding? The whole thing was weird. But the end. I dunno. I felt kinda... off. A little bit sad. I've been thinking about it all morning but I can't place my finger on the precise thing that bothers me.

I sit down at my desk, punch the blinking light on the phone, and say, "Ms. Rothschild, how may I help you?"

"Myrtle, it's Pearl. From the community center?"

"Yes," I say, picking up the handset to take it off speakerphone. I smile at Eden and hold up one finger.

"What can I do for you, Pearl?"

"Well, I'm just really anxious to get your class on the calendar. We're in such a time crunch, you know?"

"Are we?" I ask. Eden is squinting her eyes at me in a weird way. It's distracting.

"Yes, the election is coming up. And we need to make a big impression."

"Ooooooh. Yes. I remember."

"So can we maybe meet for lunch today?"

"Lunch today, well—" And I'm just about to say OK, but Eden is shaking her head, mouthing the words, No. I'm taking you to lunch today. "I can't do lunch, I'm sorry."

"Oh. OK, how about dinner?"

"Ooooh," I say, my lips making a tiny 'o.' "Well, tonight is not good either. I have... things I need to prepare for."

"Tomorrow?" she asks, her voice filled with hope.

"This week is just tight, Pearl. I don't think I can do it. How about Monday? Can we do Monday?"

"Monday..." She is clearly unhappy about Monday. "OK. I guess. I mean, I know you're really busy and I'm so, so, so appreciative that you're doing this, so yes." She has talked herself into Monday. "Do you want to meet at the restaurant?"

"Sounds perfect," I say. "I'll see you at noon!" I place the handset back down before Pearl can object because now I'm positive Eden is looking at me weirdly. "What?" I say. "Why are you looking at me that way?"

She turns, closes my door, and then takes a deep breath. "Did you... and Pierce... do anything interesting last night?"

"He told you?"

"Yes. Well, no. Not exactly. I walked in on him telling Andrew."

I smile a classic Mistress Myrtle smile. "Why, yes. We did have a fascinating evening."

"What are you doing? Are you crazy?"

"I might be. But I don't care anymore, Eden. I mean. This place"—I wave my hand around to indicate my office, but it's not my office. It's the whole magazine—"I don't want to stay here. So hell, why not go out teaching Pierce a lesson, right?"

"No," she says.

"No what?"

"You're not quitting. You can't quit on Pierce. That's just so... so wrong."

"It's actually not," I say, leaning back in my expensive leather chair to cross my legs. "I have no duties here. I have no purpose."

"Your purpose is the same as it always was."

"Wholly untrue. I don't even have a job description. How can I run a social media department when you, the only person we had in social media, left?"

"I'm still here. And you're still in charge of me. We're planning a really big event at the moment. You have purpose!"

"So what?" I scoff. "The party is just a façade. The whole position is just a façade. It has no meaning at all."

"You told me that the magazine is in trouble. That Pierce is counting on this December spread to raise two million dollars in advertising."

"Right. There's that. And I'm sure the photographs we get from the party will be super interesting. But I'm not in charge of advertising, Josh is. He's taking care of it. I'm in charge of decorations, Eden. How does that give me purpose?"

"It's... gonna be... social and we're gonna... media the fuck out of it!" She stammers out that entire ridiculous sentence.

But I don't laugh at her. Because Eden is sweet and she's trying hard. "You don't get it," I say.

"I do get it! You feel adrift. And it's because your job used to be supporting Pierce and now you feel like Valerie has taken your place."

"Valerie," I sneer. "She could work here a hundred years and never replace me."

"Exactly!"

"Exactly," I agree. "And yet there she is. Sitting at my desk outside Pierce's office."

"You have this desk now. And this office and—"

"Eden," I say, holding up my hand to make her stop. "I'm done here, OK? There's nothing you can say or do to change my mind."

"So why are you and Pierce playing this little sex game then, huh?"

"So I can humiliate him the way he humiliated me, and then walk out."

She purses her lips and shakes her head. "You're as cliché as the romance novels you hide in your desk drawer, Myrtle."

I laugh. "Obviously you and I don't read the same books. My story is not cliché and neither is my smut."

"You're pretending you don't love him when you do."

"Bullshit. Love? Please. I do not love that man. I admire him. I respect him. Or I did. Before—"

"Jesus, just let it go! He made a mistake, so what?"

"A mistake?" I say, standing up. "It wasn't just a

mistake. A mistake is something done by accident. He planned that morning, Eden. Planned it."

"Believe me," she says. "I know that better than anyone because my boyfriend helped. He planned it to humiliate me, not you."

"And yet..." I say, pausing because I'm about to say something I shouldn't. I know I shouldn't, but I want to. And sometimes 'I want' wins. "And yet you do not have a job cobbled together to make you feel important when you're clearly not. You have a new business. You have clients. You have a whole future in front of you. You won, Eden. You got everything you wanted. I didn't. I lost everything that was important to me here at Le Man."

"So tell him! Just tell him that!"

"I've tried," I say, sitting back down in my chair. "I have. But he's not listening to me. He still thinks moving me into this office and throwing money and perks at me is the answer. And I can't do it anymore, OK? I can't. I'm done. I'm going to see this little game through to the end and next week I'll be gone. That's the only outcome that makes sense to me."

"Well... well, then you're stupid."

I lift an eyebrow up at her.

"You are. Because he loves you and you love him and—"

"Whoa." I laugh. "He does not love me. He doesn't even miss me! He thinks Valerie is my replacement! Just what the fuck is that, Eden? It's so insulting!"

"You're just misunderstanding his intentions!"

I sigh. "OK, listen. I'll give you the benefit of the doubt and agree that maybe this office and these new perks are his way of making it up to me. Maybe they are genuine." She smiles. "But only as a hypothetical so you'll

121

hear me out. Because my perception of this situation makes sense. OK? It does. So one," I say, holding up a finger. "We were a team. A team, Eden. The perfect team. We were synced up, and in tune, and on the same page. I was part of him, and he was part of me, and it was perfect. And then suddenly, out of nowhere and through no fault of my own, we… weren't."

"I understand that, but—"

"Two," I say, ticking off another finger. "He didn't even consult me. He never once asked me if I was the Sexpert. Not once. And I have always been honest and upfront with him. Always. And I thought he was being honest and upfront with me too. There was trust there, Eden. And he threw that away like it was last week's garbage."

"I get it, but—"

"And three," I say, holding up my last finger. "He hired Valerie."

She just stares at me. Like there's more to that.

But there isn't.

Valerie.

"She's not out to replace you, Myrtle."

"I'm sure she's a perfectly nice woman. I'm sure she's competent in her own way. But Valerie, Eden? Just what the everloving fuck was he thinking? Is that how he saw me? As just another Valerie?"

She frowns. Because now she gets it.

"She's… she's…" But this, I think, is the reason I'm sad. "She's so… ordinary. She is the epitome of every other executive assistant out there. Is that all I was here? Was that all I was to him? A Valerie?"

"You know that's not all you were."

"Do I? Because I don't get it. She gets my job. She

gets my status. She gets everything I had—"

"Then why did you take the job as VP? Why didn't you just tell him no? He wasn't going to force you into a promotion."

"It wasn't a promotion. It was... a payoff. That's all."

She crosses her arms and scowls. "You are the one who accepted the position."

"Yes, because I didn't understand who he thought I was. I thought he'd hire another me. Not a Valerie."

"There is no other you, Myrtle. Anywhere."

"That might be true," I say. "But he's satisfied with her. He might even be happy with her. So then I have to ask myself... am I just a joke around here? Was I just sexy Myrtle who sits in front of Pierce's door? He obviously doesn't need me. He's never needed me, Eden. He just needed a Valerie. And it's not fair," I say. That sad feeling is back, only much, much sadder. "It's not fair because... because..."

"Because you needed him," Eden finishes.

I nod. Tears are actually stinging my eyes. "I needed him. And I know it's naïve, but I really saw us together forever. And now it's over and I can't." I shake my head and force those tears back. "I can't stay here and watch what I thought was the perfect relationship just... fall away into something as ordinary as Valerie. It wasn't love, OK? It has nothing to do with love. It was mutual respect. It was a partnership. It was something he and I built together and yeah, maybe we got a little comfortable. Maybe I got a little comfortable. But it was all I had. And now I have nothing. Valerie is the new Myrtle. Do you know I actually heard someone say that the other day? I wanted to die of humiliation all over again. There is nothing left for me here. Nothing at all. And there's nothing I can do about it because now I'm not Myrtle, Pierce's erotic and scary gatekeeper. I'm Myrtle, that weird woman who does nothing all day and gets paid more than Josh Washburn."

She sighs. It's long and sad. After several seconds of silence she says, "Do you want to go to lunch with me?"

I nod. "Can we go right now?"

She laughs. Because it's barely ten thirty. "For sure. Let's go."

I don't go back to work after I'm done hanging out with Eden. I wander down to Corporate Affairs and chat with Maggie about the party. I'll stay at Le Man through the party, I decide. I started this, so I have to finish it. I owe Pierce that much.

But after I finish with Maggie I can't make myself go back to work. I can't face those people.

Everyone knows what I know. Everyone sees what I see.

Everyone but Pierce.

So I just drive home and start getting ready for Pierce's visit tonight. I grab a bottle of wine and a glass, go down into the dungeon, and throw myself into preparations. And when that's complete, and I'm satisfied with the sequence of events that will occur, I go upstairs to my bedroom, walk into my closet, and carefully choose my outfit.

Pierce Chevalier is going to get the full Mistress Myrtle treatment.

I'm going to make him see me. I'm going to make him

regret all his bad decisions.

I'm going to show him what he'll be missing when I'm gone.

CHAPTER FOURTEEN

It's already dark when I pull up to the guard shack. Colorado's vast, almost blue-seeming night sky stretches to infinity. The same guard from last night sits inside the guard station, reading a paperback. I roll down the window and say, "Anastasia Steele to see Ms. Rothschild."

She grins, slightly. She looks down at her list of one name and says, "Ah, yes. Welcome, Ms. Steele."

I roll my eyes. Perfect. "Hey. What's your name?" I ask her. She looks taken aback by the question.

"Um. Samantha," she says.

"Samantha what?"

She cocks her head. "Crabtree."

"Samantha Crabtree. OK. Sure. So, whatcha reading there, Samantha Crabtree?"

Her eyes narrow, sizing me up. "A novel."

"I see that. What novel?"

She takes a breath and says, "You can go through, Ms. Steele."

Ah. She's not interested in my usual charming, get-to-know you banter. OK. That's fine. I can appreciate a person who doesn't trust me. Hell, I may appreciate them more than a person who does.

"Cool," I say, smiling. "Catch you on the flip, Crabapple."

"Crabtree."

"If you say so."

The huge gates swing open and I roll through. My heart speeds up a little bit as I make my way around the drive. I've never felt this way before. I'm almost a bit lightheaded. I've been sober for pretty much my whole life, so I don't know entirely what it feels like to be drunk, but I've certainly seen it. And in my recollection from the one or two times I have been tippled, it was a little like this. Buzzy. That's how I feel. I'm buzzy.

I've spent part of the day wrestling the thoughts that Eden put in my head earlier. The notion that somehow Myrtle has feelings for me. Like actual feelings. And, even more preposterously, that I have them for Myrtle. I mean, I'd like to think that I'd know if either one of those things was true. And try as I might, I just can't envision it.

Myrtle and I have been flirtatious, sure. But that's always just been fun and games. Playing the roles we were cast to play with each other. From the first time she came in to interview to be my assistant, I knew she was the kind of woman I'd want to have around me. Someone I could spar and parry with. That's what I liked about her. What I like about her.

It's why I was willing to do this whole thing in the first place. This peripeteia in our relationship. I'll do what it takes, because I can't lose her. I just can't. Even if things are different than they were before, just knowing she's around is enough to make me feel... comfortable.

But I'm not in love with her. That's just... that's just insensé.

I remind myself of this now so that I don't confuse the surge of excitement in my beating heart and the flow of blood making its way to my dick for anything other than what it is: The thrill of discovery and the joy of release.

Last night was the first time I can remember when I wasn't the boss. When I wasn't the one in charge. When I wasn't making the decisions and the calls and the choices. When I was just... doing as I was told.

It was thrilling.

And we only just got started. I can't wait to find out what tonight's going to bring.

I'm going to give her what she wants and then, when the weekend comes, I'm going to give her what she doesn't know she wants. Under the guise of letting her dominate me, I'm going to seize control of our dynamic once more and then everything will balance and go back to the way it was.

I never actually got around to reading the second two Fifty Shades books, but I'm pretty sure they probably ended with Anastasia Steele running a men's magazine and Christian Grey forgiving her for the fact that Ana had him publicly humiliated.

Feels like the direction the books were headed.

I hop out of my car and almost bound up the steps to the door. I ring the bell, once again expecting Kacy or whatever her name was to answer. Instead, Myrtle's voice comes over the intercom.

"Yes?"

"Uh... Myrtle?"

"Yes."

I pause, waiting for more. When no more comes, I continue. "Uh, it's Pierce. You wanna let me in?"

After another moment of silence, there's a buzz and I hear the front door unlock. I push it open, carefully, to see the inside of the main hall is aglow in candlelight. Pedestal candles in glass hurricanes fill the space. It's haunting, but elegant. It's the kind of light that radiates seduction.

Looking around, I see no one. No people. No tigers. No serval/leopard things. Nothing. Music plays everywhere. Slow, melodic, but grinding and borderline sinister. It reminds me a little of the music that a girl I went out with a few times used to favor. She owns an art gallery in the TDH. Um... Serena? Shit, I can't remember her name. But she actually kind of always reminded me of Myrtle, so this is a bit of déjà vu.

And that causes me to realize...

Huh. Every woman I've ever gone out with kind of reminds me of Myrtle. I mean no one is Myrtle. Certainly none of the women I was with ever had her wit and, um, moxie... I guess. But in the abstract, they all kind of remind me of her when I stop to consider it. I never thought of myself as having a "type," but...

"Pierce?" comes an echoing purr throughout the speaker system in the house.

"Uh... yeah?"

"Come to the dungeon."

The 'to the dungeon' part was almost a whisper. This is gonna be wild, I have a feeling. I'm doing my best not to betray my enthusiasm. "OK," I say, looking around just to make sure a lion or some shit isn't going to jump out and, I dunno, lion-fuck me or something.

I make my way through the candlelit space until I

rediscover the door to the basement. Or, I guess, dungeon. It's ajar and smoke is billowing up the stairs in thin strands. Pushing it open further, I see that the candle theme continues and extends down to where Myrtle is, I presume, waiting for me. And there's a smell. Something familiar from my youth.

Incense. It smells like the same kind the priests used to burn in the thuribles they'd swing back and forth when walking down the aisle before Mass. Holy shit… If I go down these stairs and find Myrtle dressed like a nun, I'm gonna lose my shit.

I've always had a thing for nuns.

I confessed that once and the priest just sat there for a long time, trying to decide what my penance should be. After a fair amount of silence, he finally just said, "Nuns? Really?"

I haven't been back to church in a long while.

But I have a feeling that I'm gonna be kneeling at a very different altar in a few minutes.

The music is louder here. It's dull and throbbing. It actually sounds like sex. Which is, y'know, a good mood-setter, I suppose.

"Myrtle?" I ask, as I put a foot on the first step and hear it creak under my weight. I place the other foot ahead of me as well and begin my descent.

It's dark. Just one candle at the bottom of the stairs. A very tall pillar with a high-climbing flame. I try to duck my head to see the room, but it's been blocked. Covered with—I reach out to touch the barrier—satin. Black satin.

I continue until I reach the bottom step and notice there's a hanger on a hook. On the hanger is clipped a note in red lettering. I pull it off and hold it up to the candle. It says, Take off your clothes and hang them here. ALL of your clothes.

"Take off my clothes? Now?" I announce to... well, to the black satin curtain.

Silence.

"Myrtle?" I pull the curtain aside and see nothing. I mean, nothing. Blackness. No candles, no nothing. Just blackness. "Myrtle?"

A whip cracks in the dark. "Did you not read my note?" Myrtle's voice. Or, rather, a variation on Myrtle's voice. Harsh. Throaty.

"Uh, yeah," I say. "You want me—"

"Was the note not clear?"

"I mean, it's dark, so I had to kinda squint to see it, but—"

"Stop. Talking." The whip cracks again. "You have three seconds to decide and then this is over. Either follow my commands or get out of my dungeon."

I take a deep breath and hold it. Open my mouth to say something like, Are you sure? Because this sounds like a lot of fun and I'm pretty sure we'd both be sorry tomorrow if—

"One."

Shit.

"Two."

"OK, OK. Just give me a minute."

"One minute. Starting now. When you're done, wait on the other side of the curtain for my next command."

I loosen my tie and take it off, draping it over the hanger.

The sound of tapping shoes on the floor takes my attention away from the fact that I'm pulling off my suit coat and kicking off my own shoes. Slow, methodical steps. The sound of a lighter being flicked. There's a small crack in the curtain, so I get a glimpse of shadows dancing on the other side.

I want to pull the curtain aside and see her. See what she's doing. See what she has in store. But something seems different tonight. Her mood, maybe. And I think if I pull that curtain aside she might actually send me home.

A part of me wants that. Wants to go home. And a part of me definitely does not.

I have a stroke of anxiety that what's about to go down is going to get very, very real, and I have a premonition. A premonition that I didn't previously take into account. That this could change us. Again. I changed us in a huge way this past summer and this will change us again.

But, shit, I'm not thrilled with the way things are now between us, so what the hell? May as well roll the dice and see what happens.

Because I think… I think Myrtle is done with me. I think, possibly, in her mind, she's moved on already.

It's obvious she doesn't need a job with me. Perhaps she's never needed a job with me. And every day since "the incident," it's become harder to come up with a rationale for why she sticks around.

So…

I take off my shoes, socks, and pants and start unbuttoning my shirt. When that's done, and the only other article of clothing I have left is my boxer briefs, the full realization of what I signed up for—what she's going to do to me tonight—manifests.

"Your minute is up."

"I'm—one second." I tighten my eyes, open them, take off the boxer briefs, and stand there behind the curtain. Naked. "OK, I'm ready."

"You're sure?" she purrs.

"Yes. I'm ready."

"Then pull the curtain aside, take one step into the dungeon, and stop."

I have an overwhelming urge to cover myself. Because some things you can't take back. And the moment Myrtle sees me like this—stripped bare, down to nothing—I won't be able to take that back.

I'm not embarrassed of my body. I work out. I eat right. I lay off the fromage as much as possible. So I have a very fit body. And my suits are custom-tailored. They are made not just to accommodate my physique, but to accentuate it. So it's no mystery that Pierce has, as one might say, "got it going on."

But if I do this… tomorrow at work, she'll know. She'll know what's underneath.

So I draw in a deep breath, pull the curtain aside, and take one step into the dungeon.

It's different than I remember. Which is to say, I'm not sure I really took it in at all. Last night it seemed very much like a candlelit basement in a big, weird house. Tonight, it feels like…

If the exterior of the house reminded me of my childhood home in Marseilles, this reminds me of the inside of some seventeenth-century French castle. In fact, it's almost exactly like the catacombs leading to the Palace of Versailles. If the catacombs had received a makeover and been spruced up with lace and silk and painted in hues of silver and cream.

The cages are adorned with thin strips of satin. Soft, delicate material, but strung along the bars as much for function as design. It's clear that they're there in order to bind someone to them. To hold them there. Secure them.

Off to the side is a bed. A four-poster bed with a canopy. More satiny ribbons hang from the posts. It's soft-looking and plush and elegant. But at the foot of the bed sits a chest with whips and handcuffs and bridles and some shit I've never seen before in my life.

Pillared candles are everywhere, creating a golden, amber glow that causes the metal and concrete and dark bricks in the walls to feel almost inviting. Almost. Because right in front of me is a red velvet rope. I reach to unfasten the barrier when I hear a sharp, "No!"

I look up as the billowy smoke from the candles swirls around my head and the smell of incense fills my nostrils. And then, like a wraith appearing from the shadows, Myrtle emerges.

She's not wearing a nun's outfit, as it turns out. She's got on...

Ho. Ly. Fucking hell.

I can barely process it. Myrtle. She of the dark skirts and open blouses. She of the sexy librarian glasses and the knowing looks. She who I have seen every day for the last seven years, but never, ever, in my wildest dreams, like this.

The high heels she wears are eggshell-colored. Almost white. They have petite, silk ribbons on the tops. They're sort of like Mary Janes, if Mary Jane were about to shove a stiletto into your crotch and bend you over to make you beg her to stop punishing you.

The hose she has on aren't hose per se. They're more like skin sleeves. Again, shimmery and white, they're either rubber or latex or some material that blood and liquids will just slide off clean. They come to mid-thigh, and pinch tightly enough that the strong, toned flesh of her legs is cradled inside them and then erupts into glory at the place where they meet her garters.

The garters themselves are a complicated affair, and, like the cages and the bed, have satin ribbons hanging from them that trail down the sides of her legs. And rather than being bound to a garter belt by one single strand, there are four individual straps that traverse the circumference of her thigh and attach to the waistline of her frilly white panties.

She has on a corset. A finely stitched, ornate affair with a floor-length skirt hanging from the back and lines in front detailing the shape. Vertical stripes of silver that look like boning running along the body of the well-structured piece. It fastens across the front with five metal buckles that appear as both a seduction and a challenge. Guardians of the skin within.

The same goes for the bra. White satin with beaded detail and another metallic buckle in the front to restrict entry. Long, white gloves disappear under the puffy sleeves of a silk shrug that just covers her shoulders. It fastens with a fragile-seeming brooch in the front and rises along the sides of her neck in a pseudo-military collar.

She's wearing a mask. Bedecked with rhinestones, it fans out in an arcing swoop beyond the sides of her eyes, and the way it sits across her defined cheekbones causes it to almost seem like her face is not her face, but a floating complement of cheeks and lips levitating in the air below her disguise. The hint of Myrtle is there, but this is another person entirely.

And on top of her head, she wears a tiara. Diamonds, and rubies, and sapphires. And they all appear real.

In her gloved hand she holds a shiny silver riding crop.

Simply, she looks like what I imagine Marie

Antoinette might have looked like beneath her courtly palace attire. Stripped clean of the artifice of propriety, underneath, a body perfectly built for punishment. She is a portrait in contradiction. Pleasure and pain. Hardness and softness. Abuse and mercy.

I gasp in a breath because I've completely forgotten to breathe since I laid eyes on her.

Out of instinct, I move toward her and in a flash, she has stepped to me first and raps my stomach with her riding crop.

"Ow! Fuck!"

"You may not enter until you have been given permission to enter," she says.

OK. Here we go. "Yeah, all right, fine. May I enter, please?"

"You may not."

"What? What're you talking about? Why not?"

She walks over to the chest and picks up a what looks like a studded dog collar with a chain attached. No, check that. It doesn't look like one. It is one. Yep. That's what it is all right.

"Here," she says, handing it to me as she steps back over.

"And I'm supposed to...?"

"Put it on."

"What?"

"Now that the dungeon is in its properly appointed state, a slave may only enter once they have made themselves bare and given themselves to me. Entering bare is a sign of your willingness to submit. The collar is the mark of my ownership. Now put it on."

"So... get butt-ass naked and put on a dog collar. This is what this is? I mean—"

She lowers her head. I can't expression from behind the mask, but when she lifts her head again, there is a resolve in her eyes.

"Pierce," she whispers, "if you make me count to three again I will blow out all the candles and you will be dismissed. Decide now. Because after this moment I will not tolerate insubordination. It will be an insult to my authority and a sign that you think me a joke."

I look around the space. I think of the time it took her to put all this together. I look at her. This is not an incidental thing. This isn't something she just threw together. This is who she is. This is a part of her. This is the kind of thing that we used to joke about and kid around over, but here, in this moment, I realize that this is a genuine part of what makes Myrtle Myrtle. A part of her that I always thought was kind of something to take the piss about, but that is, in fact, a mighty measure of her as a woman.

We've been kind of dipping our toes in this ocean the last few days. Feeling each other out. Playing cat and mouse, in a way. But she's right. Either we're doing this thing or we aren't. Either I'm giving over to Myrtle or I'm not.

This started out as one thing. For me this started as a way to give Myrtle what she wants. Then it became another thing. A game that we were kind of playing. Then another. A sensation—an experience I'd never had—and it kind of turned me on.

Now it's suddenly something else.

It's real.

It's real life. It's something that matters and that, if I'm going to enter into, I shouldn't do so lightly.

And so…

138

I stand, naked, and face her. It's still hard to read her, but I can see her eyes drift down to look at me. All of me. Her boss. Here. Exposed. In front of her.

I take the dog collar and clasp it around my neck. And then, because in for a penny, in for a pound, I kneel down and land on all fours on the floor just behind the rope.

I look up at her and say, "Yeah. We're doing this."

She stares at me, silently, and after a few long moments, I ask for the permission I must.

"So... may I enter, please? Mistress?"

CHAPTER FIFTEEN

Submission is all about psychology. It's a state of mind. And even though he's naked, wearing my collar, and down on all fours, this state of mind hasn't hit Pierce yet.

We're doing this. It seems like submission, but it isn't. It's a direct affront to my authority in this dungeon.

Being my slave isn't about his willingness to give in. It's about trust and respect.

And he's going to learn that lesson first.

"Did I tell you to get down on all fours?" I ask.

He looks up at me. "No, but I figured this was a good way to show you I'm serious."

I turn on my heel and take three steps. Then turn again and take three more. I stand in front of him, my legs slightly parted. He looks up at me with a smile.

I smack his ass with my crop.

"Ow, shit!"

"Did I tell you to think, slave?"

"No, but this is what you're after, right?"

I smack him again, and even in the candlelight I can see the red mark appear on his buttocks.

"Jesus, Myrtle!"

"You will call me Mistress," I say.

He sighs, hangs his head, and then looks up at me.

I smack him one more time.

"Fuck! What did I do?"

"Did I give you permission to look at me, slave?"

He clenches his jaw, bows his head, and growls, "No, Mistress."

I smile. But only because he's not looking at me. "Well done. Now stand up so I can look at you and decide if you're worthy."

He grumbles as he stands, head bowed, eyes down. And then he takes a deep, deep breath—and waits.

Well, well, well. Pierce is quite the specimen.

I know he works out. I was in charge of his calendar for seven years. He goes to the gym five, sometimes six times a week.

And it shows.

He is a tall, lean man. I don't think I realized that before this moment. His broad shoulders are perfectly muscled, his biceps well proportioned. There's a curve— a dip, if you will—as the muscle thins out and then rises again just before ending at his elbow.

I circle him slowly. Catch him watching me from the corner of his eye until I disappear and stand behind him.

If he does that tomorrow I'll punish him, but tonight I'll let it slide.

My hand falls to the red mark on his ass and I begin to rub it. "I'm sorry I had to punish you."

His back inflates as he takes a deep, deep breath.

I continue to rub the mark. "But I had to, slave. You

understand that, right?"

He stands up straighter when he realizes he has to answer me. "Um. Yes... Mistress."

I press my body up to his back, leaning in to smell his cologne because I can't help myself, and then press my lips up to his neck and whisper, "Very good."

I stay like that for a moment, letting him decide what to do next.

He stays silent.

So once again I whisper, "Very good."

I rub the short riding crop up and down the outside of his thigh. Tracing the outline of his muscle. My other hand reaches around his waist, flat against his stomach. I let it slide down. Just a little. Just enough to bump into the base of his cock.

I can tell he's already getting hard and I wish, for just a moment, that I didn't have the gloves on.

If I were really training a slave I'd punish him for that too. I'd let him know just who owns that cock of his by putting it in a cage.

But I'm not training him. This is nothing more than an entry-level session that ends on Friday and then he'll never be back. And I have plans for him tonight so that level of commitment isn't required.

"Are you ready to give yourself to me?" I ask, pulling away from him and continuing my circle. I stop right in front of him, legs wide apart, and slap my palm with my crop.

"I'm ready," he breathes. Looking down, I notice his cock is fully hard.

Hmmm. I honestly didn't expect Pierce to get turned on so fast. I must be slipping. In the old days I'd have my new slave far too frightened to even be thinking about fucking.

I slap the side of his thigh with my crop.

"Fuck! Mistress," he says, correcting himself.

I smile and turn, slowly walking across the room towards the bed. "You're a very quick learner." I turn to face him again. "Look at me."

He lifts his head up and meets my gaze.

"What do you see?"

The way he scrunches up his face in confusion makes me want to smile. He wrestles with his answer for a few seconds, then says, "A very beautiful woman?"

There's no snark in that reply. In fact, it comes out quite sincere. So sincere I have doubts. Not about his reply, but about what I'm doing.

He's showing me a vulnerability that will change my opinion of him forever.

But I'm showing him mine too.

I don't think I've ever considered that before. Not with the other men I used to take down to my dungeon, at least.

He's seeing a part of me I didn't want seen. I'm not embarrassed of it. Not at all. But I left the lifestyle behind. I thought I was done with it for good.

And now here I am.

With my boss.

I realize he's looking at me funny. I realize the silence has gone on too long. I realize... I have to make the next move.

It's suddenly hard. Being in control.

And to be sure, I'm almost never out of control, even in the old working relationship Pierce and used to have. He was always the boss, but I was boss junior. I could order him around if I needed to. I could say, "Cancel this lunch, you have an unexpected appointment." Or I could say, "Stop being a dick to your subjects, they respect benevolence."

And he'd listen. He'd skip lunch and take the appointment. Or he'd calm down and forge a new way forward with whoever was giving him problems.

But I've never been in control of him like this. He didn't have to take my advice, he just did it. And I wasn't barking orders at him, I was simply giving suggestions.

We were partners. We were a team of two.

And we don't feel like partners anymore.

I turn away and stare at the wall.

"Myrtle?" he asks. "You... OK?"

I don't think I can do this.

I don't think I should do this.

"Mistress?" he says.

It's not that I feel rusty or somehow incapable. I'm quite capable of making him submit. It's just... I don't think it's going to make me feel better. I don't think, that when this is all over, I'm going to feel better about things.

I think I'm going to feel worse.

I spin on my heel and open my mouth to tell him to get dressed and leave, but he's looking at me. Nodding his head. Just a little nod. Very slight. But it's definitely a nod.

Is he reassuring me?

I spy the bottle of wine I was drinking earlier. I thought it would be enough, but it wasn't. It's forbidden to get drunk in a dungeon. It's just... not done. But I had a long afternoon. I spent hours getting everything ready. I needed a little extra courage and now I know why.

I shouldn't be doing this... but I am.

I walk over to the bottle, pour myself half glass, and drink it down. The warmth fills my stomach and radiates outward. I pour another half a glass and do it again.

What could he possibly be thinking right now?

And then I know what he's thinking. He's thinking, She's gonna give up. She's gonna give in. She's gonna let me out of this stupid game and—

"Lie down on the bed," I say, turning to face him again.

He steps forward, hesitantly, at first. But then I grab the chain attached to the collar he has on and tug at it. He walks over to the bed. I circle around him, still holding his leash, and allow him to slide onto the bed and lie back.

I stare at him. At his cock, lying across his stomach. Fully hard.

He's turned on. He's waiting for me to do something. He wants this.

"Now turn over and spreadeagle."

He hesitates. I yank on his leash. And then he turns over, lifts his arms up, hands stretching outward toward the bedposts, and then spreads his legs.

The wine is hitting me. I feel loose now. Ready to begin.

So I drop the leash, walk over to the bed, and begin restraining him. I tie the long silver satin ribbons around his ankles like I'm securing a ballet shoe. Making sure they lie flat, that there are no wrinkles, and that they're tight enough to let him know he can't move, but not tight enough to cut off his circulation.

I do the same to his wrists. I don't look at him, even when I'm on the side of the bed he's facing. I just concentrate on my job.

When I'm sure he's tied down properly, I walk over to one of the candelabras, pluck out a candle out, and walk back over to the bed.

"I'm going to show you how pain is pleasure."

He sucks in a long breath of air, eyes on my candle.

Then I climb onto the bed, position myself between his legs, and watch his face carefully as I tilt the candle until the hot wax drips down the inside of his thigh.

He hisses. But my hand is there, peeling the already hardening wax off his skin. Gently caressing away the pain.

He closes his eyes. Relaxes.

But this time I drip it onto the underside of his hard, round balls and his eyes fly open as his chest comes up off the bed. "Jesus Christ!"

"Shhh," I say, peeling the wax off. Letting my palm ease around his balls so I can take away his pain.

He closes his eyes again, clenching his jaw, waiting for the next drip.

I tilt the candle over his lower back this time. Hold it like that, letting drop, after drop, after drop spill down and make a line across the dip where his back meets his ass.

I don't peel it off this time. I let the wax harden, trapping the heat.

This feels good. I know it does. I've had this done to me before. It was a reward. And I know he likes it, so he's very relaxed when I drip it onto his balls again.

"Fuck," he hisses. His chest rises and falls. Just a little faster than normal.

I don't reward him for that. I drip onto his inner thigh, letting the wax run down his leg, then the edge of his buttocks, so that it comes perilously close to dripping into his ass, but doesn't. It lands on his balls again.

"Goddamn it!"

I take his mind off the pain by peeling the hard wax off his back.

Or not. Because it pulls on his skin, leaving a bright

red mark, and he wriggles frantically, looking over his shoulder at me with a glare.

I smile and shrug. Then I drip wax across that same line, only this time I peel it off before it's fully hardened, and softly caress him. Making him forgive me.

OK. I can do this, I decide. I'm feeling better now. Maybe it's the wine or maybe I just needed to get over that point of no return. I'm not sure. I just know... I'm having fun. And I think he might be too.

So I lean across his body, letting the satin covering my breasts slide along his back as I place my candle into the waiting candlestick. Then I get back in position, take off my long gloves, and reach forward, palms sliding all the way up his back. I drag my fingernails down his taut muscles, not hard, but not softly either, and caress his ass cheeks.

"That was very good, slave," I purr. "You did very well."

He smiles a little. Pretty proud of himself. He probably thinks we're going to fuck now. He probably thinks I'm as turned on as he is and hey, this isn't so bad. Submission is pretty damn cool.

But then I say, "Now it's time for the paddle. Because you've been a bad, bad boy."

CHAPTER SIXTEEN

The collar hurts. The ties around my wrists are tight and tugging at the skin there. The wax on my back, ass, and balls fucking stings. My cock throbbing and pulsing into the sheets as it fills with blood is uncomfortable and I can feel it in my lower abs.

I love it.

Which brings me to an actual problem. Do I let her know that I love it? Do I show her how much joy this new experience in my life is bringing me? Do I stop thinking about it right now and give over to the moment?

Or. Does that undermine the very point of this exercise? The intention of this entire agreement was that by letting Myrtle have a certain amount of ascendancy over me, she would feel vindicated and we could start figuring out how our relationship might look anew.

Jesus, that's fucking weak.

What a load of shit. There's no version of any of this where that story holds water. Our dynamic was fractured by me and nothing can put Humpty Dumpty back together again. But all I guess I really wanted was for a new relationship between us to not be shitty. Because, God knows, this is definitely a new relationship already, and there'll be no repairing what comes of it.

The only thing I can hope for is that it goes ahead and just breaks us into a million tiny shards, and then perhaps we'll be able to pick up the ones that won't cause us to hurt too much and build from there.

Speaking of hurt.

"Oh, fuck!" is the muffled sound that escapes my lips as I bite into a pillow and shake my head back and forth. My fists tighten and my forearms pull against the satin ropes. The smack of the paddle hitting my ass rings in my ears as I half-cry, half-laugh silent puffs of air out of my lungs.

Hazarding a glance over my shoulder once again, I see the paddle in all its glory. It's formidable-looking. A foot long, black, with the word BITCH in red lettering etched into the part that I presume just made contact with my suddenly tingling ass.

She puts her finger to her lips and whispers, "Shhhh."

A couple of small moans escape my throat as I nod to show her that I'll behave. This seems to satisfy her because a tiny grin lands on her lips and she moves toward me. She places her hand on my ass and begins to rub the sting away. Her thumb slips down into the inside of my thigh and rubs against my semi-wax-covered balls. I moan longer now, burying my face in the satiny pillowcase.

I'm working hard not to step outside my body and see this from above. Not to get a picture of what's happening and how it looks. Not to judge myself. Or Myrtle, for that matter.

Because as much as this is about me and her, it's also simply about me. Period. Full stop. In the limited contact I had with my father as I was growing up, one thing he emphasized with unflagging commitment was that it was incumbent on me never to give up my power. He has, to this day, an extremely rigid perception of what it means to be in control.

Ha. I wish he could see me now.

I must actually laugh aloud, without intending to, because suddenly another smack! welts my ass and I bite into the pillow again.

"Did I tell you you could laugh?" she asks. When I don't answer quickly enough to satisfy her, she asks again, "Did I?" This time she grabs the leash attached to my collar and gives it a nice, healthy tug. It strains against my Adam's apple and I cough.

This seems to freak her out for a second, because she drops the tension on the chain and the next thing I feel is her hands on my neck. Not in a strangulating way, which for about half a second is what I expect, but in an attempt to remove the collar from around my throat.

She unfastens it, slides it away, and then her hands are acting as the collar. A soft, sensual massage that loosens my spine, which has been, unacknowledged by me, tightening as we've gone along. I allow myself, for a moment, to relax into her touch.

I wonder if she knows that she's giving me as much as I'm supposedly giving her. That she's offering me an excuse to let go. To release my grip on myself and be handled. Be manipulated. Be owned by someone.

I haven't had a romantic relationship in ten years. I've had encounters. Interludes. Distractions. But nothing close to approaching a relationship. The only enduring relationship I've had with a woman at all has been my time with Myrtle. That's what's causing this to feel so unusually intense, I suppose. This is the kind of thing you do with a lover or a partner. Not an employee.

But Anastasia and Christian didn't really have anything between them before he started working her over either. Their relationship was forged in the crucible of a red room. I wonder if the basement of this big cat sanctuary is the tipping point for me and Myrtle.

Wow. There's a sentence you really don't think you'll ever say.

Maybe Eden was onto something. Not about me. I continue to want to think that I know myself well enough to know whether or not I'm in love with someone. But perhaps she was right about Myrtle's feelings for me. The way she's taking care not to hurt me too much. The way she's caring for me even under the framework of making me feel shame. Maybe there's something there after all.

Oh, fuck. This could go sideways real fast.

And speaking of sideways…

She leans close to my ear and whisper, "I'm going to untie you so that you can roll over. Do not attempt to get off the bed. Do not attempt to touch me. Do not do anything I don't tell you to do. Do you understand? You may speak."

"Yes. I understand."

"Good."

She straddles my back. The feeling of the latex from her boots, her powdered and scented flesh touching my ribs, and the warmth of her pussy through the shimmery panties touching my back is causing me to forget who I am. Who she is. Why we're here.

It may just be my imagination or the touch of the fabric on my startled and traumatized body, but I could swear she's wet. She feels wet. She feels like she's getting off on this as much as I am. I'm pretending that it's not turning me on so that I can keep up pretenses. What's to say that she's not doing the same?

She finishes untying both my wrists and I let my arms slide down in front of me. I'm splayed out on the bed, completely prostrate, totally vulnerable. I have no idea what happens now.

She slides her crotch down my back, across my ass, and down my legs as she reverses off me and stands. She hits my ass with the paddle again. Delicately this time. Just a kind of reminder. Just enough to let me know she's still there.

"Roll over," she says.

"Does it matter which direction?"

"On your back."

"Yeah, but left or right, or… I don't wanna presume."

An almost impossible to detect smile is present in her answer. Almost impossible, but not totally. Not for me. I know her too well. "It doesn't matter," she says. "Just face me."

I choose to roll to my left. Seems like the correct choice. Once I'm completely onto my back, I catch her eyes behind the mask. Which is to say, I catch her staring at my rock-hard cock. I don't know if she's bothering to notice my eyes at all.

I want to ask, What now? It's almost compulsive, my need to have control. To know what's happening. What's about to happen. To have answers. I fight with my mouth to keep it from opening uninvited. I bite my lip.

She stares at my cock. The droning, orchestral, bass-heavy music thuds on. I think my dick might be bouncing a bit, in time with the rhythm.

Myrtle approaches the foot of the bed again. She lifts her paddle and presses it into my cock, forcing it to lie flat against my stomach once more. She shifts her head to the left and then to the right, studying it. Studying me. I still have my arms above my head. I grab at the headboard.

"You have a nice cock," she says. I don't say anything. Because I haven't been told to, and also because there's a foot-long piece of wood that reads BITCH pressed against my junk and if I do something I'm not supposed to, I worry about what might happen.

She lifts the paddle and my dick springs back to vertical. And now...

Oh, Jesus. She's climbing on top of me. She's sliding up my body. Her panties are pressing into my bare dick. I'm less than a centimeter away from being inside her right now. What the hell is happening?

"Do you want to fuck me?" she asks.

I swallow, hard. I'm not sure if it's a trick question.

"I... don't know," I finally manage out.

She closes her eyes inside her mask and nods, slowly. Then she reaches down beside her hip and unties one of the pieces of ribbon that was attached to a garter. She draws it out with both hands and stretches it taut. Then she leans over so that her mask is an inch from my face, and after that... I no longer see anything.

She has me blindfolded.

I am in the dark.

I am in the dark.

I am. In the dark.

CHAPTER SEVENTEEN

He thinks he's so cute.

So in control. So excited about what we're doing. So expecting something good to come out of this.

"It's not gonna happen, Pierce."

I bet he's furrowing his brow. But I can't tell because of the blindfold. I only see his mouth. Slightly parted, breathing air in and out.

I get why a man would be hard at this point. I am a goddamn sex goddess. I have manipulated him perfectly. Started out with just the right amount of tension, and fear, and pain. And in between each of those things I've allowed him to let his guard down. Let him think this has been what he's been looking for his whole life.

That's how it started. But it's not going to end that way.

He wants to fuck me. Actually, he wants me to fuck him. And I'd be lying if I said I wasn't interested. I am. But if all I'd wanted out of this last hurrah with my boss was an orgasm I'd have handled that at work. I'd have let him bend me over his desk or ambushed him in the parking garage. Waited until he got in his car and then climbed in his lap and fucked him with my back pressed into the steering wheel.

He gave me his body tonight. He submitted that and did quite well. He still has his dignity. He's breathing hard, but not too hard. He's excited.

But he never surrendered his mind. Not one bit. And this is all about mind games.

"Why are you hard?" I ask him. "You may speak."

"Ahhhh… well, Myrtle"—he pauses to grin here—"you're turning me on."

I wriggle against him, his cock so stiff and ready beneath my panties. "And do you think that was my purpose tonight, Pierce?" I accentuate each syllable, making sure my t's and p's are precise. "Do you think," I say, "that was my goal?"

I swear, I can see his eyeballs moving back and forth under the satin ribbon. Confusion.

"You may speak," I add, even though he's not hesitating because he was waiting for my order.

"I… feel like this is a trick question."

"It's not. Now answer me."

"I want to say yes. But I have a feeling that's wrong."

I lean down, pressing my lips up to the soft skin of his earlobe, and whisper, "So. Wrong."

He swallows. But his cock is still pressing up against my pussy. So hard. So confident that it will get what it came for.

"I'm afraid you have missed the point of tonight's lesson. So I'm sorry I have to do this." Which isn't true. Not even a little bit. "But you may not leave until the lesson has been learned."

"What lesson?" he asks.

I pinch his nipple.

"Ow! Jesus!" His hand snaps forward and grabs my wrist.

I just stare at his touch. And it's like he can feel the heat of that stare, because he withdraws his grip and places his hand above his head once more.

I pinch his nipple again.

"Myrtle!"

"Did I give you permission to speak or cry out in pain?" And then I rub my pussy against his cock. Sliding back and forth along his hard shaft.

He shakes his head and bites his lip.

"You didn't learn my lesson. Do you know what my lesson is?"

He shakes his head again.

"Well, I had three. One, that you learn to trust me. You did a fair job at that. For a first-timer. Two, that you submit. And you did that almost as well. You gave me your body. But it's still a joke to you. A game. A—"

"No, it's not. I'm here. I told you that."

I should punish him for speaking out of turn. Another nipple pinch or get my paddle ready. But I have something else in mind and besides, these little corrections are getting boring.

"That's not true, Pierce. But it's my fault. For not explaining things to you immediately. You see"—I scoot backwards so I'm kneeling between his legs. I take his rock-hard cock in both hands and begin to massage him— "when you're in my dungeon, this cock belongs to me. And I never gave you permission to get hard."

"Wha—what? What are you saying? I don't know

that—I can't—How—?"

I smile now. A genuine, really big smile. Because the confusion on his face, apparent even from behind the blindfold, is so very, very satisfying.

"I think you heard me just fine. But I'll repeat it. I did not. Give you permission. To get hard."

I pause to let that sink in and give his cock a few more pumps with my hand.

"And even though it's my fault for not explaining the rules, I'm going to have to punish you for that."

Right now he's imagining all the ways that can happen, but I'm pretty sure he's imagining all the wrong ways.

"Do you want to know what your punishment is? You may speak."

"Yes, Mistress. I would very much like to know."

I get up, off the bed, and walk around to the chest set up with my toys at the foot of the bed. I pick up my punishment of choice, which is quite scary-looking, if I do say so myself, and slowly walk back to Pierce. I lift the blindfold over his head and let it fall back on the pillow.

He stares up at me, eyes wide.

But still, there is a little hint of a smirk.

I hold up my punishment. His eyes track to the stainless-steel device and then he squints, like he's not sure what he's seeing.

I showed it to him last night, but I don't know how much of what I said actually... processed.

"This is a cock cage," I say. "It helps you understand that last rule, Pierce."

"Helps me... you're going to put that on me? Now?" He looks down the length of his body to his rock-hard cock. "That little... thing?" And then he laughs. "I'm sorry, but my cock won't fit into that cage."

"Oh, yes, it will." I turn the small key in the lock and open the cock cage. "Because I'm going to make it."

"Myrtle," Pierce says.

"Hmmm?" I ask, fingers fondling the stainless steel.

"I have to wear that?"

"Yes. It forces you to obey the rule."

I bend down and take his cock in my hand.

He sits straight up, his hand on my wrist. I glare at him and he immediately withdraws his grip. "I don't think I'm ready for this."

I look down at his still semi-hard cock. It's a lot smaller than it was ten seconds ago, for sure. But… not quite soft. I can almost hear the 'sacapuntas' building in his throat. I push, just a little, to test. "You're almost ready."

"Myrtle, wait. I get it, I understand. I swear. Mistress!" he says, loudly. "Mistress! I understand the rule. I'm begging your forgiveness. I will never disobey again, I promise!"

And with that, all his excitement vanishes. "Oh, look," I say, fondling his now soft dick. "You're ready. That's perfect."

"Mistress," he starts again. "I am deeply, deeply sorry that I have offended you. I did not understand the… depth? Of your rule. And I regret that." I place the cock cage near the top of his dick, getting ready to squish it inside. "And wait!" he says, voice an octave higher, slightly desperate. "Wait, wait, wait! I'm going to worship you now, Mistress. Show you the proper amount of… worshipness. I'm going to make it up to you. How can I make it up to you?"

He didn't use the safe word. He didn't pull the plug

on me. On this, I mean.

I let go of his cock and stand back up. "Hmmm. Well… I suppose this is all my fault for not fully explaining the rules to you."

"No," Pierce says. "No, it's my fault for not thinking ahead, Mistress. All. My. Fault."

Oh, he's such a quick learner. "You're right. It is your fault."

"It is! Yes! My fault. But—" He swings his legs out of bed and drops to his knees. Pressing his face down to my shoe. Kissing it. Right on the toe. He looks up at me, eyes bright and pleading. "I understand now, Mistress. And I will never, ever disobey you again."

"Never?" I ask.

"Ever," he assures me.

"Even at work tomorrow?"

"What?"

"Come up here, slave," I coo, doing one of those little come-here motions with my pointer finger. "Come close to me."

He makes a face that might be a grimace. But he stands up and leans into me. I caress his broad shoulders, liking how his muscles feel under my fingertips. I lean into him now too. Right into his neck. Pressing my lips to the skin right under his ear. One hand goes to his cock and begins to fondle him.

He sucks in a breath and starts muttering something. Some mantra to take his mind off what I'm trying to do.

I admit that little coping mechanism makes me proud. I have a proud mistress moment.

"Well," I whisper into his ear. "That was very good, slave. Very good. So I'll tell you what."

"Please… tell me something good, Mistress."

"I'll give you another chance to show me you understand the rule."

"I will not disappoint you, Mistress. I promise."

"I believe you," I say, stepping away from him, walking back over to the chest and putting the cock cage down. "I do. But tomorrow at work I'm going to test you. And if you do well, there will be a reward for you tomorrow night."

"A r-r-reward?" he stammers.

"Mmmm-hmmm," I say, panning my hand over the top of my devices all laid out pretty on the top of the chest. "A very nice reward for you."

He swallows hard and then nods his head. "I'm looking forward to pleasing you and getting my reward, Mistress."

I stare at him. Just long enough that he begins to shuffle his feet. "Very well. You may get dressed and leave, slave. I'll see you tomorrow."

CHAPTER EIGHTEEN

"Andrew. Psst. Andrew. Over here."

"Pierce? Where the hell—?"

I poke my head out from around the side of the concrete column in the parking garage. I lower my sunglasses. I wave Andrew toward me. "C'mere…"

"What the fuck?" he mutters as he makes his way over. "Dude? What are you—?"

"Shhh." I pat him up and down, grab for the phone in his back pocket.

He swats at my hand. "Stop grabbing my ass! What're you—?"

"Shhh!" I hiss again. "I don't trust that you aren't bugged."

"Bugged?"

"That Declan isn't listening in on us."

"Dev?"

"Sure. Gimme your phone."

"Dude…"

"Gimme me your phone, bro!" I whisper-yell.

A security guard comes wandering over. Great.

"Gentleman, can I—? Oh, Mr. Chevalier. Mr. Hawthorne. Sorry, I didn't realize it was... Are you all right, sirs?"

"Yeah, Kenny, we're fine. Just talking a little TDH business," Andrew says. "Thanks."

"Oh..." says the security guard, whose name Andrew seems to know for some reason. "OK. As long as everything's—"

"All good, Kenny," I say. "Thanks, Kenny. Appreciate the attention to detail, Kenny. Kenny. My man." I point finger guns at him. He seems like the kind of guy who'd dig finger guns.

"O... K," he says, dubiously, for some reason. Odd guy. But then he's gone.

"I'm actually not sure his name is Kenny," Andrew says. "Anyway... what the fuck is happening? Why did you bring me down here? Why are you Deep Throating me?"

"What? "

"What what?"

"You think I brought you down here for some weird sex thing?"

"What? No! Deep Throat! Like from Watergate?"

"Oh. Right. That guy."

"Jesus."

"Sorry. My head's a little... Come with me."

"Where?"

I look around to make sure no one else is going to roll up on us, and then take my friend by the arm and drag him over to my McLaren. I open the passenger door and usher him inside. But first...

"Your phone."

"My phone?"

"Gimme your phone, man. I'm putting it in the trunk. This car is going to be our SCIF."

"Our SCIF? Why do we need a SCIF?"

"Because the last time I tried to talk with you in confidence, your lady burst in and fucked my head all up. And also because you work for the NS fucking A!"

He pokes his bottom lip out. "Fair enough." He hands me his phone and I toss it in the trunk along with my own as I swing around the back of the car on my way to the driver's side. I open the door, slide into the seat, and take off my sunglasses.

"OK," he says. "So what's…?"

I put my finger to my lips to silence him. I'm still not sure we're in the clear. And what I have to tell him today, no one else can hear. No one. I can't even risk it. For so many reasons.

I turn the stereo on and the speakers start blaring the dubstep playlist that I last had on.

"Ahhh! What the hell is that?" Andrew shouts over the music.

"Knife Party, I think! They're Australian!"

"It sounds like a grizzly bear with chainsaws for paws trying to hack a tunnel into my brain!"

I turn it down slightly so that the squealing electronic musical effects still cover our voices, but that it's not loud enough to hurt Andrew's delicate baby ears. Christ.

"What in the name of jumpin' Josephat is going on, man?" he asks.

"Um, well, couple things. Remember how excited I was about what happened with me and Myrtle?"

"You mean do I remember what you told me yesterday? Uh. Yeah."

165

"Yeah, well, less excited today."

"What? Why? What happened?"

"I dunno, man. I mean… dude…" I don't even know how to go about expressing the things I need to tell him. So I start with the facts. "She made me get naked."

He nods. "Right. Yeah. Well. I mean, you're doing some weird BDSM shit with your old secretary—"

"Executive assistant, man! Jesus, join us in the twenty-first century. Hey, did you hear women can drive and vote and shit now, too? Fuck, bro." Honestly, Andrew is a great guy, but there's a lot of that old South rearing that must've gotten stuck in there. I mean, get woke, friend. Sheesh.

He shakes his head. "Fine, man. OK. So, you're doing some weird BDSM shit with your former executive assistant, and yet you didn't think getting naked would, at some point, be part of the drill?"

"No. No, I did. I just didn't…"

"Just didn't what?"

"I dunno. It was very… it was… I got hard, man."

There's a pause before he says, "Well. Yeah."

"No, I don't think you get it. I mean, like, hard. Like…" I raise my forearm and make a fist. I tense it and shake it in his face to emphasize my point.

He puts his hand around my fist and pushes my arm down. "Yeah, yeah, no, I get it. OK. And…?"

"And… I dunno. It just… it didn't feel like an agreement or a contract or whatever it's supposed to be."

"What does that mean?"

"It means… it started to not feel like this is just something I'm doing to make Myrtle happy, or something I'm doing to avoid a lawsuit, or—"

"If you were doing BDSM to avoid a lawsuit, I've got some sobering news for ya."

"Will you just shut up and let me get this out?"

Knife Party screeches a staccato siren into the air. Andrew nods and does the 'lock my lips with a key and throw it away' thing people do when they're being annoying.

"I'm saying, I felt something. Like felt something. I'm trying to say that I wanted her."

I let that land as the sound of something resembling machine-gun fire plays in the background.

"You get me?" I go on. "I wanted her. The way you want someone when you're... you know..."

Andrew cocks his head and raises his eyebrows. "Falling in love?" he asks.

"No! No. That's... no. That's not what I'm saying. I don't... I mean... I don't..." I pause, trying to find the right words. The closest I can come up with is, "I don't think so."

"Pierce? "

"Yeah?"

"Have you never been in love before?"

"Not sure. If I had, would know for certain?"

He lets his head fall back into the head rest and says, "Holy shit."

"What? Holy shit what?"

"I'm... honestly, I feel kind of embarrassed. I've known you all these years and I never once bothered to notice that you've never actually been in love."

"That's not... that can't be true, though, can it? I mean, that girl in college. That first one you dated who was terrible to you—"

"Jilissa?"

"I couldn't remember Eden, you expect me to remember fucking Jilissa?"

"That's fair."

"But, yeah, I guess. The one I wanted to be with but that you dated first. I think I was kind of in love with her."

"No, you weren't. You just wanted to, whatever. Win. She was hot and mean. Which is your shit. You just wanted the challenge. No offense."

"None taken. But, yeah, OK. So, but that's what this is with Myrtle. Right? My whole plan in taking her to Vail this weekend is to let her think she's won, but then to, y'know, PIERCE her—"

"Nice. You just make that up?"

"Eh, I've used it once or twice before."

"Clever."

"Thanks. But, yeah, it's to let her think she's won, but then actually win myself and then we both get to feel like we've won and save face and then move on with business as usual. It's a classic political strategy move. I think. I may have made it up, but it makes sense to me."

He stares at me. I stare at him, waiting for a response of some kind. In the background, Knife Party... knife-parties.

And then something I'm not expecting happens.

He takes my face in his hands.

"What's happening? Why are you doing that? You're touching me. Why are you touching me? Stop that."

He doesn't. He just grips me tighter and looks at me in the eyes. "Listen to me..." He takes a breath and says, "I love you. Do you know that?" I nod inside his grip. My cheeks feel squishy. "And you love me. I know you do."

"I do," I mutter out through my squished fish lips.

"I'd do anything for you. Anything. Do you know that?"

"Uh-huh."

"And you'd do anything for me. True?"

I nod.

"Would you do anything for Myrtle?" he asks.

"Whattayou mean?"

"I mean would you, I dunno, go to incredible lengths to publicly shame her when you thought she had betrayed you? Because somewhere inside you, it cut you so deep and you felt so hurt that you didn't know what to do with that pain?"

"I—"

He tightens up his hold on my face and shakes it a little. "No! And"—he pauses, to make sure I'm listening, I guess—"and... when you realized you had done something terrible, would you do anything... anything... to make it up to her? Would you submit to whatever wild abuse she wanted to put you through just to prove to her that you're sorry? And that you care about her? And that you love her?"

I roll my eyes up, thinking. "I mean—"

"Because if all that's true, and if you can't help getting hard when you're with her, and if you're still willing to put yourself through it, and if you're taking her to fucking Vail this weekend, then, I mean, I'm no shrink, but I dunno, dude. You may—may—really like this woman. A lot."

I blow air into the inside of my cheeks, which pushes Andrew's hands outward, and finally he takes them away and lets them drop in his lap. He says, "But hey, I'm just spitballing."

I can feel my jaw slacken and I kind of stare at the steering wheel. In fairness to Andrew's point, the music is pretty distracting. I reach out and turn the stereo off. I stare at the steering wheel some more. Out of my periphery I can see Andrew looking at me. When I look over, the expression he wears is something like a cross between pity and affection.

"What?" I ask.

He shrugs. "I just like seeing you happy."

"Happy? I feel like I'm going fucking crazy."

"I know. That's when you're happiest."

Yeah. He's right.

"What're you gonna do?" he asks.

"About...?"

"Whatever."

I breathe in long and hard, let it out through my nose. Contort my mouth. "Dunno. Go upstairs and find out what happens next, I guess."

"What do you mean?"

"She told me when I see her at work today she's going to test me, and if I pass, I get a reward tonight."

"Really? What test? What reward?"

"Gee, And, I don't fuckin' know. Maybe that's part of what's got me all twisted up."

"OK. OK. Sorry. And you haven't seen her yet?"

"No. Not yet."

"It's three o'clock. How've you avoided her all day?"

"I've been down here, trying to go up for six hours."

"Here, in the parking garage? All day?"

"I wandered over and talked to that woman at the dry cleaners for a while."

"Svetlana?"

"Dude, I don't know. I asked her how to get candle wax residue out of the lining of suit pants."

"Why did you have..." I shoot him a look. "Ooooooooohhhhhhhh."

I shake my head. "OK. I gotta... I gotta go figure out whatever." I open the door and step out. Andrew does the same. We meet at the trunk. I open it and hand him his phone back.

"Thanks, man," I say, giving him a hug.

"I got you, man," he says into my shoulder. "I mean, I wish I could be more helpful, but this is maybe just one of those things that…"

"No, I know. It's cool. I appreciate you letting me Deep Throat you, anyway."

And no sooner is that out of my mouth than Andrew's cell rings. He answers it on speaker.

"Yeah, Dev?"

"Uh… boss…? We've got that call with… I'm sorry to… I mean if you're busy doing stuff… then…"

"Aha! I knew it!" I shout.

Fuckin' Declan.

CHAPTER NINETEEN

I won.

End of story. We turned the last page and it's time to close the book.

I just… won.

So I'm humming as I pretend to work. Been doing it all day. I cannot even remember the last time I felt this happy.

Well, no. Maybe that's not true. That morning Pierce accused me of being the Sexpert I was pretty happy. I got a little rush as I took my seat with Eden and stared up at the stage where Pierce was standing. He of Chevalier royalty. Tapping the microphone with his finger, asking for our attention.

I was fixated on him. Ready for whatever words came out of his mouth. I wanted to stand up, clap my hands three times and say, "Your leader is speaking, subjects! Hush up!"

But it wasn't necessary. He had everyone's attention that morning. I was a little breathless with anticipation because I didn't know what he was gonna say. I had no idea what this impromptu meeting was about. It was one of his classic Pierce reactions to things. Which I admit I find exhilarating.

So yes. I guess that was the last happy day I had at work. Looking up at him on stage.

But today my happiness comes from his absence.

Do I find that weird? Yes. And normally when Pierce is out of town or away from work and I'm here at Le Man alone, I feel a little sad. Like I'm missing something. And I have to rally myself because eventually a shitstorm lands on my desk and Pierce isn't there to hand it off to, so I take care of things. Not because I want glory. That's not why I rally when he's gone. It's just... I want people to see him in the best light. I want them to see him the way I do. Because Pierce is probably the only person I've ever met who... understands me.

Or I thought he did.

Turns out I was wrong about that.

What was the point of my pointless musings again?

Oh, yes. Humming. I'm humming.

"What are you doing?"

I look up from my computer to find Eden standing in my doorway. "Oh, just looking at these design ideas Maggie sent over for the party."

"No, that noise. What was that noise? Were you... growling?"

Eden. She's so adorable. "I was humming. I'm happy today. Pierce and I had quite the night last night and today he's missing."

"Missing? Did you leave his body somewhere?"

I close my email, fold my hands in my lap, and look at her. Maggie can wait. "Not his body. His body is juuuust fine. His spirit, well, I might've broken him."

"Broken him how?" She closes my door, walks over to one of the chairs in front of my desk, and plops down. "What did you do, Myrtle?"

I take a deep breath and all the words spill out on the exhale. The whole story, starting with 'velvet rope' and ending with 'cock cage,' fills the room. Eden is quiet as she listens and when I finally finish by saying, "And then he didn't show up for work today." She blinks her eyes at me. "He's avoiding my test."

I have to admit, I'm sorry this game ended so soon. I'd have liked to see him try to pass that test. Of course, there's no way he could. I'm just that good.

"Are you crazy?" Eden says. "You did that to Pierce? You do realize he's your freaking boss, right?"

"He wasn't my boss last night." I cackle. And then I begin to hum again. I can't help it. I'm so happy.

"Stop that growling. It's... disturbing."

"I won, don't you see? I won. He came over, I humiliated him, and now he's so embarrassed, he can't even show up for work today. He can't face me. It's just like... no," I say, stopping to collect my thoughts. "It's exactly the way I felt after that whole Sexpert debacle." And then I sigh. "I think I'm done here. I can now walk out on my own terms."

I lean back in my chair, clasp my hands behind my neck, and luxuriate in my own self-satisfaction.

A knock at my door makes me lean forward again. Eden spins in the chair, and we both stare at the door.

Pierce is peeking through the tall, skinny side window, smiling at me.

Eden turns to me and says, "Well, would you look at that," just as Pierce opens the door and pops his head in.

"Eden," he says.

"Hey, Pierce. Um..." She glances at me, then back at him. "Everything OK today?"

"Just fine," he says, eyes meeting mine, then darting to Eden's, then back to mine. "Just wanted to check in with you, Myrtle. Make sure everything's running smoothly, since I had to take care of business today."

"I'm sure Valerie has it all under control," I snap.

"Yup," he says. Smiling. "Yup. I'm sure she probably does. So..." he says, leaning into the word, still smiling. "Yup. Great. Good talk. Catch you later, Myrtle."

And then he closes the door and disappears.

Eden turns to face me again. Then she stands, straightens her shirt, and says, "Better reconsider your exit strategy. Because he didn't look like a man humiliated."

"No," I growl. "He didn't. What do you think he's been doing all day?"

Eden laughs. "Probably reliving last night on repeat with his hands down his pants."

"Eden!"

"What? You tied him up, smacked him with a paddle, dripped wax over his balls, and then threatened him with a cock cage! And he just hinted that he's looking forward to more. So... I mean, what did you expect, Myrtle? He liked it! I don't care who you are or how vanilla your sex life is, if Mistress Myrtle gives you the full treatment, you get off! How do you not understand this?"

I just look at her. Is it true? Did he like it that much? Is he making fun of me and my attempts to scare him into humiliation? "I didn't give him the full treatment," I say.

"Oh, my God. You're gonna do it again tonight, aren't you? That's stupid! Because if I was making a Twitter campaign about this moment I'd call it #Fail."

I glare at her, but Eden isn't afraid of me. She might've been, once upon a time. And I used to make her uncomfortable in lots of ways, but not lately. It's like she's immune now.

Shit, is Pierce immune too?

Is everyone immune? Am I really just that weird woman who makes more than Josh Washburn now?

"You don't double down when your plan doesn't work, Myrtle. You reconsider. And I think that's what you should do now. Reconsider. Everything. The leaving, the sex games, all of it. Because this is going to end badly. You're not getting what you want and he is. How is that winning?"

Is he getting what he wants?

"Just tell him you miss your old job and you want it back. And then tell him you love him and can't live without him—"

I laugh.

"—because both of those things are true and one day, you're gonna realize that. Stop denying your feelings!"

"I don't have feelings," I snap.

"Everyone has feelings, Myrtle. You just bury yours deep for some reason."

"Don't psychoanalyze me. I know what I want and how to get it. And this is working. I just need to push on. Besides," I say, standing up and straightening my jacket. "I promised him a test today at work and when I make a promise, I deliver. There is no way he'll pass my test. And when he fails, and he will, I'm going to humiliate him in front of everyone and then… then I'll have my satisfaction. Stick around, Eden. You're about to see the mistress at work."

She grabs my arm as I try to walk past her. "What are

177

you going to do?"

I shrug her off. "I'm going to dirty-talk him until he's rock hard and then I'm going to parade him in front of every one of his fiftieth-floor executives. Hell, I might take him downstairs and walk him past the underlings too."

"Myrtle," she hisses.

I reach into my pocket and pull out the cock cage to hold up as proof. "And then I'm going to take him into his office, strip him naked, force my chastity device over his dick, lock it up, put the key in an envelope addressed to him, and dismiss him for good. I'm going to tell him it's over. All of it. I'm going to end this little game the winner and give him my notice. Then, after the Halloween party, I'm going to drop that key into a mailbox and forget about him. Forever."

"Myrtle!" she hisses again. "That's crazy! Just wait!"

But I'm already past her, pulling my office door open.

I'd like to see him try to have a romantic weekend with me when I've got his cock all bunched up inside a cage.

This is gonna be so much fun.

"Pierce," I coo. "Oh, Pierce! Where are you?"

CHAPTER TWENTY

I sit in the throne in my office and try to look casual. Problem with thrones is that one can only appear so relaxed. I could throw my leg over the side, but then it'd just look like I was trying too hard. Also, it'd look like I'm trying to show my dick off. I don't wanna show my dick off. Feels like that sends the wrong message.

The sofa. I could lounge on the sofa. I run to the sofa and assume a position of repose. No, this is no good. Now I just look like a cheesy velvet poster of a seventies porn star. Shit.

Why is looking relaxed so damn stressful?

In about two seconds Myrtle is going to walk in here and 'test' me. I can feel it. Unless she isn't. Maybe that's the test! Oh, Myrtle, you sneaky minx. The test was to see if I'd feel tested and react as though she's going to give me a test when that's the test itself! Crafty vixen.

Oh. No. Guess not. Because here she comes. Oh, hell.

I see her approaching from down the hall through the glass wall. Shit. There is a test after all. Oh, Christ. I can't show her that I feel stressed about the test. Stress test. That's what this is. Aha! OK. Stand. Maintain composure. Look casual. Read something. Grab a magazine.

I have no magazines in here to grab. Are you kidding? This is a magazine and there are no magazines in here? Well, that's ironic. Maybe—

"Pierce?" she says, entering the office. Which is wildly unnecessary. A) It's my office. And B) she knows I'm in here because she can see me through the wall. Maybe I shouldn't answer. She hasn't given me permission yet.

Wait. What? What the fuck am I saying? It's my office, not a dungeon. Oh, Jesus, she's in my head. I can't let her know that she's—

"Oh. Hey, Myr. 'Sup?" I stand and lean on the arm of the sofa, super chill.

She blinks at me. "Did you just call me Myr?"

"Uh… I think I may have, yes."

"Don't do that."

"Copy. I shall do it no myr." I smile. "Get it? No myr? It's a play on—"

"Yeah, no, I got it."

I give her an o-kay sign with my hand and I wink. She takes in a breath and starts walking toward me. She's wearing typical Myrtle-at-work wear, but as she moves in my direction, all I can see is what she had on last night. The dirty, Parisian dominatrix motif. I imagine that when she looks at me all she sees right now is a dog collar and a hard dick.

And… I kind of hate that. Not the second part. The dick thing doesn't bother me all that much, but the first part…

"What's up, Ms. Rothschild? How can I help?"

She gets close. Not so close as to cause anyone (aka Valerie) to notice, particularly, but close enough that I can smell her perfume.

"Well, I was worried that I wouldn't see you today. I thought maybe you were avoiding me."

"Pffft," I scoff. "Why—Why—Why would I be avoiding you?" Not sure the stammering gives me the strongest position of authority, but—

"I thought maybe you were trying to get out of your test."

"Test? Oooooh, right. The test. Y'know, I forgot all about that."

"Did you?"

"Sure did."

I've never been in a Mexican standoff, as they are called, but this feels like maybe what one is. Everybody with their gun drawn, waiting to see who shoots first.

"Well," she goes on. "I didn't forget." She steps closer still. Man, she smells nice. "Because, remember, if you pass the test, there will be a reward waiting for you when you come over tonight. You are still planning to show up tonight?"

"You betcha. Deal's a deal."

"Oh, good. Because I was afraid that after last night—"

"Deal's a deal, Myrtle."

It feels like the temperature in the room just dropped about ten degrees. That last bit came out of my mouth unexpectedly cold and a more than a little harsh.

It surprises me. I can tell it surprises her because it stops her move toward me.

I'm not sure why I just got so stern.

Garbage. Yeah, I am.

It's because… this isn't me.

This submissive bullshit. And, y'know, it's fine to do it in her basement or whatever in order to honor the agreement I made with her. Because I always honor my agreements. But now she's bringing this shit to where I work. My place of business. The company I built. And it suddenly occurs to me that hiding in a goddamn parking garage to avoid seeing someone who works for me is pretty fucked up.

And also, what Andrew said about the lengths that I'm willing to go to for the people I love…

I don't love Myrtle. I'm not in love with Myrtle. I like her. She was a great assistant and I appreciate everything she's done for me over the years, but I'm not in love with her.

I'm not.

I'm definitely not.

This is just a game.

A weird, fucked-up, totally absurd game that I'm willing to play right now because I have nothing better to do. But it's starting to intrude too much into my real life. My everyday life.

And out of the blue, I hear my father's voice, in his thick, French-accented English, reminding me to never give up my power. I've worked incredibly hard to be who I am. To shake off all the anxiety that I had as a child, when I felt abandoned and unwanted. I've worked incredibly hard to earn the respect I garner. To be the man I am. To be seen the way people see me.

I know that most of the time people see me as this bigger-than-life personality who kind of fancies himself as a twenty-first century monarch. That's OK. That's the role

I've assumed in life and I'm happy to play it. It's fun. It's easy. And most of the time it allows me to get everything I want. I have no problem being seen that way.

But I am not a joke. I am not a fool. And I am not someone who loses.

I know who I am.

And like an unexpected bolt of lightning on a clear blue day, I am now shocked into remembering that.

I look around at the throne, the glass wall that allows me full view of my kingdom, the mountains outside my windows, and I feel pissed. You can make me simper. You can make me crawl. You can burn me and shove my dick in a tiny box (again, weird), but you do not get to walk into the sanctity of my sovereignty and push me around.

"So," I say. "What's the test?"

She looks a bit distracted now. "What?"

"The test? You got a test? What's the test? You said you had a test for me and that if I passed I'd get a reward tonight. Give me the test. I want to earn a reward."

I'm walking toward her now and she's backing up. The heel of one of her shoes buckles a tiny bit and she almost, but not quite, stumbles. I've never seen her do that before.

"Um," she says.

"Let's go. Test me. C'mon. Let's do it."

She reaches into her pocket and grabs at something. I can't see what it is. She doesn't draw it out.

"What's that? Whatcha got there? Is that it? Is that part of the test?"

She doesn't say anything. She looks a little... Jesus. She looks a little scared. And I hate it. I really do. But I can't stop.

"Myrtle? What are we doing? Are we doing this thing

or not?"

"I, uh… I don't…"

"Because honestly, I've lost some of my day and I've got work to do and a company to run and things that actually, y'know, matter to take care of. So, if we're gonna get into it, let's get into it so that I can get on with the business of my business and then get my reward tonight. Let's make moves, ma chérie. Chop chop." I snap my fingers.

She steps back again, her brow furrowed, her chin drawn in toward her chest. She pushes her librarian glasses up the bridge of her nose. Out of the corner of my eye, I can see a couple of my VPs chatting with Valerie. All three of them are trying to pretend that they aren't looking over this way and don't see Myrtle's back almost pressed against the glass.

Fuck it.

I take another step toward her and finally stop.

"So… Myrtle?" I say. "What are we doing?"

She looks down at the ground and it's almost like she's another person. That's fine. I imagine that's how I look to her too.

"Myrtle?" I ask again.

She glances up at me. Stares in my eyes. "What are we doing?" she repeats.

"Yeah. What are we doing?"

She's breathing heavily. I watch her breasts rise and fall under the blouse that's always open one button more than everyone else's. I meet her eyes. The way the afternoon sunlight is hitting them causes her to almost look like she's tearing up. If I didn't know better, I might actually believe that was the case.

But I do know better. And I choose to believe it is

not.

Finally, after several long seconds, she says, "We're not doing anything."

I squint. Draw back. "No?"

"No," she says. "See you tonight."

She reaches for the door and swings it open. She steps into the doorway and starts to exit.

"No test?" I ask.

She stops, turns her head to the side so that I can just see her profile, and lets out a long, jagged breath...

"You passed. See you tonight."

CHAPTER TWENTY-ONE

The rest of the day was a blur. A disturbing, nightmarish blur. I went back into my office and closed the door, shutting out Eden, and Valerie, and the whole damn office who all witnessed me cowering before Pierce with my back against the window.

What the fuck happened back there?

It's like I... it's like I went back in time. Became old, old Myrtle. That girl who entered her first dungeon a scared, timid wallflower.

I just packed up my bag and left after that. Didn't even say goodbye to anyone. Just left.

And now I'm home, it's dark, Pierce will be here any minute, and even though I'm dressed in an outfit I've always called the Queen—thick, light blue silk-jacquard corset binding me tightly with cream-colored satin ribbons and full rear-shirt made of chiffon; my breasts lifted so high they practically touch my chin; the stockings thin and silky, same color as the ribbons; hair piled on top of my

187

head so that my silver tiara is fastened securely, and long, wispy tendrils flowing down to my shoulders like spirals; quite simply the most beautiful dungeon apparel I own— I don't feel much like a queen.

I look at myself in the wardrobe mirror and feel a lot more kinship with the peasant-girl outfit that got tossed with the submissive collar the minute I did the switch from bottom to top than the queen I am now.

How did he do that?

I don't understand it.

And all he did was speak. It's not like he was holding anything over me. Not like he was threatening me with punishment. And the whole office seemed to be watching, so there was no chance of him dominating me.

But he did. He dominated me.

And I reacted.

I have several justifications for this.

One. We were at work. His kingdom. And while at work, I am his subject, just like everyone else.

Two. He's not a submissive. In any way. So it was bound to come out, and that's the moment it emerged.

Three. My power isn't what it used to be.

And the thing is, it's all three of these possibilities. I was in his dungeon, he's not a submissive, and I am not the woman I used to be.

And there's nothing wrong with any of those things.

I close the wardrobe to make my reflection go away just as my phone dings a text. I glance down at the screen.

Anastasia is here! That's the message from Samantha at the gate.

"Great," I mutter. "Figures he'd be punctual." I was hoping for a little time to figure out all my… feelings… which I'm also trying to deny I have, but that's a luxury for another time.

I was going to wait for him down here in the dungeon, but I've changed my mind. I go upstairs, get to the living room just as the lights on his McLaren switch off, and then open the door.

Pierce is absently adjusting his coat collar with leather-gloved fingertips, looking around at the house as he travels up the long, curved walkway, looking like he hasn't got a care in the world.

Eden was right. #Fail.

I have failed. And to be fair, it was doomed from the start. I made a mistake with Pierce. Well, not true. Many mistakes.

That's when he notices me standing in the doorway. He's about fifteen feet away when he stops and says, "Myrtle?" with equal parts confusion and… what is that? Worry? "What are you doing? Go inside, it's freezing out here tonight."

I sigh. Massive. #Fail.

"I wanted to stop you," I say.

"Stop me from what?" he says, smiling. Walking forward again.

"From coming inside," I say. "The deal's off, Pierce. We're done."

"What? No, no, no. I passed your test. I get a reward." He does that cute eyebrow lift thing I've come to love over the years. It's a playful expression, one that says he's in a good mood. And why shouldn't he be? He won. Again.

"I'm afraid I owe you an apology, you see—"

"Can we go inside?" he says, looking down at my legs. Bare, except for the silk stockings. "It's like twenty-two degrees out here."

"No," I say, shaking my head. "We're not going—"

189

But he grabs my hand as he pushes past, taking me with him. "Whatever's going on, we're not doing this outside. Come on."

I follow him, stopping in the large foyer, just underneath the massive chandelier, and he closes the door, once again reminding me that I'm not the one with the power in this relationship, he is.

And the thing is—the most important thing is—he's not doing it to make a point. He's not trying to be a dick, or throw his authority in my face, or ask me to submit to him. Not at all.

He's acting this way because this is just who he is. This is just him, being him.

"OK, now… what's going on?" he asks. "What's the problem?"

It's a thing I loved about him. The very first thing I noticed when I came in for the interview as his assistant at Le Man. He was the fresh-faced rich boy. Eager to show his father what he was made of. And I was…

"Myrtle?"

I was coming out of something. Something I thought I left behind a long time ago but now find myself fully immersed in once again. I wanted something normal. Something that would ground me to the real world and take me out of the fantasy life I'd been living in since I left my mother's school and went to college.

I wanted to reinvent myself, but not the way I did when I entered the lifestyle. Because the girl I was at the Quaker school was something I was happy to discard. The woman I became in the lifestyle was something… else.

"Myrtle? What's going on?"

I wanted to keep parts of her. Wanted to dress like her at work. Tight pencil skirts. Crisp, white button-down

190

shirts with one too many buttons unbuttoned. Red lipstick on my full, pouty lips. Dark hair done up tight and severe, but in a way that had every man who looked at me wondering what it would look like down. And real silk stockings held up with a garter belt and ending in four-inch heels.

"Talk to me. What's happening here?"

I realize he's still holding my hand. He squeezes it.

"Is this about today? I'm sorry, OK? I don't know what came over me. If I scared you, then I'm sorry."

"You didn't scare me," I say, my words very low and soft. "Not the way you think."

"What? Then... how? What's happening?"

"I want to apologize," I start again. "For talking you into this when I knew this isn't who you are. And I know better, Pierce. I shouldn't have asked you to sign that contract, and I shouldn't have been drinking down in the dungeon yesterday, and I should not have let my emotions cloud what should've been a serious, serious decision."

"Hey," he says, taking my other hand now too. "We're having fun, right? I am. I mean, yeah"—he laughs—"it was... a little bit intimidating yesterday, but I'm prepared now. I'm up for anything, Myrtle. Let's do it."

"No," I say, pulling my hands from his and folding my arms across my chest. It is cold out tonight and that cold came in with him. It's lingering in the foyer. "No," I say again. "You don't understand what you're doing."

"Sure I do," he quips. "You get to boss me around. I've made my peace with it. I'm fine, I promise. If this is all you need to stay at Le Man, well, I'm getting off easy. I want you there. I do. And I am sorry for this summer. I made a mistake and I'm willing to do my penance."

191

"This isn't penance!" I say, too loudly. "It's not a punishment! I'm doing this all wrong! I'm using you, Pierce. Can't you see that?"

"Hey," he says, taking a step towards me. "It's OK."

"No. Nothing about what we're doing is OK. None of it. I'm doing this out of revenge. I've turned you into my submissive and that's not how it's done! Don't you get it? I can't make you be a sub, Pierce. No one can just become submissive. Either she is one, or she isn't!"

"She?" he says.

"He. You," I say, wanting to stab myself in the eye for that little slip-up.

"Uh... what are we talking about?"

"You," I say. "Me." And then it's out. And I regret that immediately. So I turn away and say, "You need to leave. Now. This is over."

"No," he says. "This isn't over. And I'm not leaving until I understand what just happened."

"I just told you. I'm doing this for all the wrong reasons. This... lifestyle. It's not a joke, Pierce."

"I didn't mean to treat it that way, Myrtle. I swear. I'm just... I was just trying to make you happy."

"It's not you, don't you see? It's me."

"It's not you, it's me?" He chuckles. "Uh, well, I've heard that plenty of times in my life but it's never rung true before and it's not ringing true now either. So just what the hell is going on?"

I shake my head and turn away from him. "Just go. Please."

I don't know what he does then. He doesn't leave. Just stands behind me, quiet. Seconds tick off in silence and then he brushes past me and walks over to a picture hanging in the hallway. "Who's this? Your father?"

I stare at the picture. It's old. Very old. The years have changed the black and white to a dull sepia color. "No, my grandfather."

"Rangy Ron, Wild Beast Whisperer," Pierce says, chuckling as he reads the sign over my grandfather in the picture. He's a tall, thin man surrounded by lions, wearing the classic lion-tamer circus costume, whip in one hand, outstretched chair in the other. "Nice. He looks... formidable."

"He was," I say, some of the tension I've built up in this room leveling off.

"And this one?" Pierce asks, pointing to the next picture on the wall. "This is your dad?"

I smile as I step closer to look at the photo. Because I walk past it every day on my way out of the house but I can't remember the last time I actually stopped to look at it. "Yeah," I say. "He was about seven, I guess. That's when he started working with the cats."

"How old were you?"

"Me? No. I don't work with them. I just..." I shrug. "Hang out with them, I guess. When I was growing up it made me sad to see them working. I didn't like it. My father would take me on set when he was training them for movies and I'd watch him. Whole summers, sometimes. But I never wanted to make them do things."

Our eyes meet. I look away first.

"I mean, I never wanted to train them. I just wanted to know them. They were like friends to me when I was a kid." I chance a look up at Pierce and he's nodding.

"OK," he says.

"I didn't have a lot of friends as a child."

He squints his eyes at me. "Honestly, I can't even picture that. You're so... intriguing."

193

"Not back then I wasn't."

"No? What were you like?"

I suck in a deep breath, so uncomfortable talking about this stuff.

"Were you... quiet?" he asks.

I nod. "Very."

"And shy?"

"Right again."

"Did you read a lot?" When I look up at him this time, he's smiling. So I look away and don't answer. "I did," he says. "I mean, probably not a lot. But enough. I was a little quiet at times too."

I chuckle, can't help it. "You? Quiet? Ha. Nice try, but I'm not falling for the old we're-the-same routine. I picture you in your royal sailor suit"—he guffaws—"running around expansive green lawns trimmed so well you could bowl on them, smacking things with a croquet mallet."

"Close." He laughs. "But I was... an outsider, I guess. Too much of everything. Too loud one minute. Too quiet the next. Too tall, too skinny, too smart, too hungry, too satisfied. All the toos. That was me." He moves to the next picture and I inch along with him. It's of me. Sitting on the back of a lion holding a balloon. "I was all the toos. This is you, right?" I nod. "How old?"

"Mmmm... four, I guess."

"Were you ever afraid of them?"

"I was too small and too innocent to be afraid."

"So we have something in common then."

"What?"

"You were all the toos too." He smiles at me. And then his smile falters and he's frowning. "I'm here because I wanted to come. And you did promise me a reward."

"We're not going back down there and that's the end of it."

He inches closer to me. I glance down as he places his hand on my hips, fingertips spread out across the light blue silk jacquard pattern. His chest presses up to my back and his head dips down until his mouth is on my neck. "We could just... stay right here, if you want."

My eyes dart to the little girl in the photo in front of me. And I wonder, not for the first time in my life, just what the hell I'm doing.

CHAPTER TWENTY-TWO

"What are you doing?" she asks.

"I dunno," I reply. I feel a twinge of guilt, lying to her. But it doesn't matter. Because we both know what I'm doing. It is of no consequence whether I admit it or not.

"Why?" she asks.

I maneuver her around to face me. Corseted and tall and lithe, as she turns she calls to mind one of those music boxes with the ballerinas that spin in a perfect pirouette. Ceramic or porcelain or whatever they are. Beautiful and ever there when you summon them to dance.

"Why what?" I ask once her eyes are in front of mine.

"Why me?"

I have to cock my head because my neck kind of gives way. I was not expecting that to be her response. The Myrtle I know has never questioned herself. Never once. At least not as far as I know. But hell. What do I know anyway?

"Why you?" She nods. I blow out a breath. "Well, I

mean, look. I think, after Andrew, you represent my most enduring adult relationship. Also, you're the most reliable and trustworthy person I've ever met."

She starts to make a point. I anticipate it even before the words are out of her mouth.

"I know! I know! I accused you of something that belies what I just said. Listen. Listen to me." I take her by the shoulders. "Are you listening to me?"

She nods. "Do you think holding my shoulders will make me listen harder?"

"No."

"It won't. "

"I know."

"I listen with my ears, not my shoulders, so—"

"Will you shut the fuck up and stop deflecting for a second?"

She pulls her chin into her chest.

I start again. "Listen to me. I—"

"You don't have to yell."

"Jesus Christ!" I let go of her and turn around in a circle for no reason. "I fucked up! OK? I fucked up. I was in a very, very bad place. The magazine was hemorrhaging money and I was kind of scapegoating and I might have gone a little crazy and—"

"Might?"

"Whatever. Listen, honestly, I've apologized in every way I know how. I feel like I've kind of gone well beyond what most would consider the normal scope of a reasonable apology. And I've, I think, really illustrated my commitment to make things right between us. Myrtle Astrid Rothschild… you are one of the best people I know, you are one of the finest people I've ever met, you are one of my favorite humans of any persuasion, and at this point, I don't know what more I could do to show you that other than chop my own dick off. Which I really, really don't want to do. But I will if... No. Sorry. That's a lie. I won't chop my dick off. That's where I draw the line. So, if you need that... Fuck you. But my point is, I'm sorry. And you look amazing tonight. And I feel like I did earn a reward. And whether you believe it or not, I think you deserve one too, and also whether you believe it or not, I feel like what I want to do to you right now could serve as one, and even though I'm not entirely sure what I'm saying makes sense because this whole thing has me super fucked up, I think you get the point I'm making because I kind of feel like you also understand me better than anyone. So..."

Had I known I was going to be making word salad, I would've brought dressing.

Jesus. That was... I have no idea what she'll make of that, so I decide to just shut up and wait to find out.

Her highly bodiced bosom is heaving. She swallows. Her eyes are rimmed with wet. She tightens her jaw. Her chin shakes.

I watch. My eyes dart to the photos on the walls. A strange imagining of her over the course of her life whizzes through my mind. I don't know if it's accurate, but it's vivid. "What?" I ask, with the caution one would use when attempting to tame a wild lion.

"You..." She stops herself. Swallows again.

"Yeah...?"

"You..."

"Me... What? Her head shakes back and forth slowly. "You... you actually remembered my middle name?"

Huh. That was not where I thought that was going. "Uh. Yeah. I guess I did."

And before I can say more, she's on top of me.

She jumps right into my arms and I grab her under her ass to hold her there. I keep her lifted with one arm and with the other, I grab the nest of black hair she has pinned to the top of her head. I force her mouth onto mine and my tongue gallops inside.

She allows me to lick her up. Our lips wrestle and our tongues joust. I open one eye long enough to spy the Persian rug in the adjoining room, next to the entry hall, and begin walking us in that direction. Her hands paw along my top coat. Paw seems like the appropriate word.

Once we're onto the rug, I loosen my hands and allow her long legs to land on the floor. I don't let go of her with my mouth as I strip both my overcoat and my suitcoat off, and she helps me push them off my shoulders and down my arms. It's dark in here, but the candlelight from the hurricanes she has lit in the foyer cast us in a half-glow, and the shadows dancing across her face make her appear as some sort of half-cherub, half-devil. In other words, the perfect creature for someone like me.

She reaches for the buttons on my vest and I go for the satin ties on her corset at the same time. We are fumbling and clumsy, our eagerness making us frantic. I jerk at the knots in the ribbons that I think will cause her body to fall free of its captivity, but it must be some kind of... It's not a slip knot, because it doesn't slip. So it... I can't... It seems to just be... I think it's getting tighter, so... maybe if I just...

She gasps in an, "Oh, shit," as the tight satin cinches her harder, causing her to have to suck in her ribs.

"Fuck. What? What did I do?" I go to try to rectify whatever I just caused to go wrong, but she waves me off.

"No, no," she chokes out. "It's not... hold on."

She fiddles with the knot that I drew in, trying to get

it unwound. She kind of slaps at her stomach as if she can maybe knock it off.

"Seriously, let me help," I say, coming toward her.

She waves me off again and turns to head to a writing desk. There's an antique letter opener. She snatches it up, slices at the ribbons, and cuts them loose. She gulps in a breath and releases it on an exhale as the satin binders fall loose and limp and hang unceremoniously from her torso.

"They're just... they're ornamental," she says. And then, to illustrate the point, she pops a snap in the front which opens the top a fraction, allowing the smooth flesh of her breasts to spill forward a bit. Which is distractingly pleasant.

"Shit. I'm sorry," I say.

"It's OK."

"I hope that wasn't like, your favorite outfit or anything."

"I mean... it was."

"Oh."

"And it was designed by maybe the most famous dungeonwear designer in the world."

"Oh."

"But, y'know... no big."

Fuck me. "Fuck me. I'm sorry. Tell me her name, I'll have her make you ten more."

"His name."

"His?"

"Yeah. He was a he."

"Was?"

"He died last year."

For fuck's sake. "For fuck's sake. I'm sorry... um... how'd he die?"

"Auto-erotic asphyxiation. Which is probably an

JA HUSS and JOHNATHAN McCLAIN

occupational hazard."

I don't know if she knows she's making a joke, and I know I shouldn't, but I can't help it. I start laughing. Hard.

"Stop!" she says. But then she starts laughing too. "Stop! I'm serious!" She's not serious. "Stop! It's not funny!" It is funny.

"OK, OK," I say, slowing my laugh down. "OK. But I am sorry. Shit. That was ridiculous."

"Yeah."

"It feels kind of like... Know what it's like?"

"What?"

Andrew told me a story about when he and Eden first—"

"Eh, eh, eh. No thanks. I don't need to hear about what your friend and my friend do when they're... whatever."

I nod. Put my hands up. Bow my head. "So. Uh. What now?"

"What now?"

"Yeah."

She nibbles at her bottom lip and says, "Well... you did earn a reward."

I smile. "Yeah, I guess I did, right?"

"So..." She walks over to me and starts backing me up.

"What're you...?" She pushes me in reverse until my knees hit a tufted leather accent chair and I fall into the seat. "What're you doing?"

"I don't know. Slowing this down."

"Why?" I say, starting to stand.

"Because," she says, pushing me back down. "Because I know what I'll be getting, but you don't yet."

I squint. "Whaaaaaat does that mean?"

She shrugs. "Just means I've seen what you're working with. You haven't had the same insight. You should make sure this"—she gestures down her body—"is something you really want."

"Why wouldn't it be? Myrtle?" Suddenly, I have a horrible feeling that she might be trying to tell me… "I hope you don't… I don't wanna offend, but—"

"I'm not a hermaphrodite."

"Oh, good. OK. Great! I mean, I didn't think so, but—"

"Shut up, Pierce."

"You got it."

I do. I shut up and I let her have control. In a very different way though. A very different way than I have been these last days.

Now, I simply give over to the fact that she wants to bare herself to me. That she wants me to sit here in my shirt and tie while she strips down in front of me. That's what she's asking for. She's telling me to let her expose herself to me and in so doing reassert her dominance.

Not over me.

But over herself.

Or maybe she just knows she's got a rockin' bod and wants to show it off.

Either way, we both get something we want right now, so I'm good.

She picks up where she left off, unbuttoning the rest of her gorgeous and violated corset. Each snap that she pops open drops loose the strands of creamy satin and replaces it with more and more and more and more of her creamy, creamy skin, until…

The corset falls to the floor.

Heels. Thin, silky, cream-colored stockings. Creamy,

white panties. Silver garters snapped onto a matching garter belt. And above that...

Her.

Her naked, lean torso. The breasts that I have seen for the last seven years, always on display underneath blouses and dresses, occasionally peeking out from behind their shroud, occasionally not, now on full display. Oh, mon Dieu, she is... she is a sight to behold.

The tiara is still squarely planted on top of her head and the black tendrils falling around her cheeks frame her face as though it were a Renaissance painting.

Candlelight flickers around us still.

My cock stiffens in my suit pants. I rest my elbow on the arm of the tall leather chair and rub my palm down my face. When it falls away and I open my eyes, she is still there.

She says nothing. Just stares at me intensely with unblinking eyes as she unfastens the garters from her stockings and they snap against her legs.

She slides her heels off and, in stockinged feet, she saunters toward me. I squirm in the chair. My dick is kind of stuck in between my thighs. I just need to pop it loose... To shift... So... OK. Good. There it goes.

She lands in front of me and straddles my knees. I look up at her, awaiting instructions on what she would like. This isn't a game, and there are no rules now, but I am happy to submit to whatever she asks in this moment.

Unless she wants my cock in a tiny box. Then I draw a line. But that doesn't feel like what this is. So...

She reaches out and takes my hands. She places them on the outside of her thighs, right along the waistband of her underwear. I continue to stare into her face. She nods, subtly, and I oblige by sliding my hands down, dragging the delicate fabric with me as I do.

My breath is heavy. My heart is beating faster than I'm used to. I pause and look back up at her one last time. Her expression doesn't change.

And then I draw the covering down to her ankles, she steps out, and I find myself facing...

I look up at her one more time and she smiles a mischievous smile.

When I told Andrew that I was going to Pierce her, it was a play on words. A joke.

I had no idea that it would be literal and that someone had already beaten me to it.

I swallow. "Wow," I say.

She shrugs. I stand, keeping my hands on her hips.

"Does, uh," I start. "Does that stay in when...?"

"It can," she says.

"And does it make it feel...?"

"Like nothing you've ever experienced."

I gulp. I suck at my teeth. I nod. "Well. That is, uh... that's pretty cool."

I lift one hand up to her neck to draw her in for a kiss as my other hand stays down by her crotch, presumably trying to decide if it's brave enough to attempt to touch the impressive-looking silver ring that's down there.

And just as I'm about to lay my lips on her mouth and allow my hand to find its courage...

"Holy fucking shit!" That's me. Or, actually, that's me reacting to a galloping, mewing caterwaul that stampedes into the room and crashes into my legs.

"Betty! Dave! Stop that!" Myrtle shouts at the uninvited servals who chose this fucking moment to remind me that they live here.

Watching Myrtle chase two rambunctious servals

205

around a candlelit big cat sanctuary while wearing nothing but stockings and unfastened garters is probably going to be the image that visits my memory on my deathbed. I can't imagine it'll be bested.

"Shoo! Shoo! Go on!" she says, waving them out of the room.

Once they're good and gone, she turns to me, lowers her head, shakes it, and says, "We should have just gone down to the dungeon."

I laugh.

"Shit," she says, "I'm sorry. Fuck."

"What?" I go to her. "Hey, no, no, what's wrong? Hey don't do that."

"This is just... this whole year has not gone the way I expected."

"No?" I ask, pushing a tendril of hair aside. "Why? What did you expect?"

"I don't know. My resolution had been to just be... normal. Y'know? Like, more active in the community. Just teach a class at the community center, or... oh, shit."

"What?"

"That woman Pearl is still expecting me to teach a Subs for Hubs class." She groans. "Nooooooo. Jesus. I forgot about that. Christ. OK. That's it. I have to move."

"Move? Whoa. Slow down. What are you talking about? Move where?"

"I dunno. Away."

"Why?"

"I think I need another reset."

My palms start sweating very unexpectedly.

"No, no, no. Hey, look at me. Look at me." I take her by the shoulders. She looks back and forth at my hands.

"Why do you keep doing that? I can look and listen

without being handled."

"Hey," I say. "Don't get weird."

"Don't get weird? Oh, OK. Yeah, I won't get weird."

"Stop it. Just... we're going to Vail this weekend, and—"

"What? You still wanna go to Vail?"

"Of course. We had a deal. Why wouldn't I wanna go?"

"Um, well, the deal has pretty much fallen apart, don't you think?"

She gestures at her naked body and I try not to think about it too much because I have a point to make.

"Whatever. Vail was still part of the deal. And beyond that... I just want to take you to Vail. So, let me take you to Vail. OK? Can we go to Vail tomorrow? Vail?"

"Stop saying Vail."

"Will you come with me?"

She takes a long moment, sighs, but finally... nods her head.

"OK. Great. Cool," I say.

"What about tonight?" she asks.

"What about it?"

"Your reward. You don't still want your reward?"

I look at her. Smile. Breathe out. Stroke her cheek and tell her, "I got it."

CHAPTER TWENTY-THREE

So... that was one of the weirdest nights of my life. Which is saying a lot, I realize. Because my life was weird from the first breath of air I breathed. Librarian mother meets lion-tamer father. I mean, that right there is the stuff ridiculous sit-coms are made of.

Only it wasn't a sit-com. My parents are serious to the nth degree and I guess with that kind of atmosphere permeating my formative years, there was no chance of me turning into a something other than what I am.

The way I look at it, I had two choices. One, be a mousy academic who hides her true self away in shelves of books. Or two, fall into the trap of adrenaline-induced exhilaration and spend the rest of my days wondering when my lifestyle was going to kill me.

To be fair to them both, they came out of it just fine.

My father has navigated his dangerous lifestyle very well. He's still alive, so that's saying something. And he's happy, as far as I can tell. Maybe even extremely happy. Not many people get to live the dream like he has.

And my mother has settled down with a sensible man who accepts her for who she is and won't be eaten by carnivorous animals one day at work.

Both of them just live their lives in a way that makes sense, but I never quite got the hang of that.

I fell into both those worlds at one point. If you looked at me at age fifteen you'd have said with one-hundred-percent certainty that I'd grow up to be just like my mother. And if you had seen me at age twenty-three, you'd have said my lifestyle was going to kill me just like it did the designer who made my dungeon queen outfit.

There was, at no point before I came to Le Man Magazine, any kind of... intermediate middle. I was one or the other and it took a long, long time for me to realize I didn't have to be one or the other. That I could just be myself.

And for the past several years that's who I truly thought I was. Myrtle Astrid Rothschild, executive assistant to Pierce Chevalier at Le Man Magazine.

Myself.

But it's not true and it took Pierce promoting me to VP to realize it. I took my job as his assistant too seriously. I realize that now. I based my whole new identity on that role and so it was inevitable, that when it was taken away from me, I'd be lost.

That's how I feel now. That's where I'm at.

Lost in an identity crisis.

It was nice. I do admit that. Being with Pierce as a woman who might be starting to understand who she is, was nice. We didn't have sex. In fact, after he basically said he was satisfied just looking at me in this new way, he and I made our plans for this afternoon and he left. I accompanied him to the door, opened it up still mostly naked as the cold night wind wrapped around my body, and watched him walk away.

He was already at work when I got here this morning. He looked up from whatever he was discussing with Valerie when I paused at my office door and smiled at me. And for a moment I debated if I should say something. But then he took his attention back to work and I didn't.

I didn't know what to say.

Thank you felt appropriate, but I'm just not sure what I'd be thanking him for.

Relieving me of my corset? Unbinding me? Allowing my true self the opportunity to spill out?

I'm just not sure.

I live with danger every day. Down the hill from my house live thirteen lions, eight tigers, six mountain lions, two jaguars, and a snow leopard. They are all tame in their own way, but still, deep down inside they know who they are. They know what they are. And at any moment one of them could just decide... you know what? This is not who I am and I've had enough. I need a reset.

They could have an identity crisis too.

I understand this. Have lived with it my whole life. That's why there's what constitutes a cage surrounding my home. That's why there's a guard at the gate with a small arsenal of firearms locked in a safe behind her. That's why we keep tranquilizers in the fridge and hundreds of pounds of fresh meat in the freezers.

I was taught at a very early age that the proper precautions can save your life and maybe I took that too seriously too? Maybe I applied it with too much rigor? Maybe I, like Pierce, really am all the toos?

Maybe the corset is my cage? Maybe the whip is what keeps them tame? Maybe the blindfold is my hope that one of them won't wake up one day and have an identity crisis?

Of course, I'm not talking about the cats. I'm talking about the men in my life.

Or lack thereof these days, because Pierce is the only man in my life. Has been the only man in my life for a couple years now. I used to date when I first came to work at Le Man, but I stopped. I don't even know when that happened, exactly. I just know it's been a while now.

And up until that morning when he pointed his finger at me and told the whole world I was the Sexpert, I was happy. I really and truly was.

And since that day I've been sad. Because it was a wake-up call. It was a sharp slap in the face that nothing I thought was real, is real.

I'm sitting at my desk running all this through my head when my phone buzzes.

I press the speakerphone button and say, "Yes?"

"Hey," Pierce says.

"Hey," I say back.

"Did you bring your weekend bag with you this morning?"

"Yes."

"Then... you wanna get out of here early and beat the traffic?"

I get a strange tingling feeling in my body as I say, "Yes. I'd like that a lot."

I can feel him smile through the walls that separate us. "Let's go."

There's nothing to clear off my desk for the weekend because I truly do not have a purpose here, so I just log off the computer, grab my purse, and exit my office.

Pierce is waiting just outside. He smiles at me, which for reasons that remain elusive, gives me that tingling feeling again, then places his hand on the small of my back, urging me forward with him, and looks over his shoulder at Valerie to say, "Have a nice weekend."

I am lost in the feeling of his guiding hand on the small of my back, so I don't even hear if Valerie responds. I just know we leave together. And that it is very apparent we are leaving together because by the time we enter the elevator with a half a dozen other people, he's holding my hand.

I stare straight ahead at the elevator doors. Afraid to move. Afraid to speak. Afraid to do anything.

When they open to the garage, we spill out like a herd, which dissipates quickly, and then Pierce is asking me, "Is your bag in the back seat? Or the trunk?" Because he has successfully guided me to my parking space, where my Tesla sits right next to his Escalade. This makes me let out a small laugh.

"What?" he asks.

"I must've been lost in thought when I pulled in this morning and didn't notice the Escalade, because for some reason I pictured us driving up the mountain in your McLaren."

"I would never drive you up a snowy mountain in a McLaren." And then he smiles at me. "That would be irresponsible."

Yes, it would, I think to myself. And that's not who he is. Not with me, anyway. Not anymore. "Trunk," I say, thumbing my key fob to release the lock.

He lets go of my hand and approaches the rear of the car, then plants his hands on his hips, looking down into the abyss of my trunk, and shakes his head.

"What?"

"We're not going to Paris. It's just a weekend."

"I like to be prepared," I say, hiding a smile as he takes out the matching three-piece set of Tiffany luggage. "And believe me, I'd bring all six pieces for a Paris trip."

"Here," he says, leaving the luggage as he clicks his key fob and motions me over to his car. "Get in while I load." We walk over to the passenger side and he opens my door, waits until I'm comfortable, and then closes me in.

I admit, I like being on the receiving end of his good manners. I have always known he was a cultured man, but this is the first time I've ever experienced it as his… date.

It's nice.

I check my watch. Almost one-thirty. Then fidget as I decide how to appear… casual. Do I cross my legs? I cross them. But today's pencil skirt lands above the knee, which means it's now mid-thigh, so I uncross them. Press my knees together. Decide that's a position my mother would choose and stop doing that. I cross my ankles like a lady, decide I'm not really the ankle-crossing kind of lady, and cross them the regular way again, angling my body a little so I'm facing Pierce, just as he opens his door and slides into the seat.

The Escalade is roomy but his long legs take up all the space under the steering wheel.

"Have we ever been in a car together?" I ask.

"No," he says, hiding a smirk.

"You're sure?" I ask.

"Positive." His eyes meet mine for a moment as he backs out of his parking space, then refocus on his task.

But wow. That was some look he just gave me.

We're silent as we make our way out of the TDH and get in the freeway, and that silence is deafening. I want to say something to break it. Anything. But nothing comes to mind. I am literally speechless.

It's several more painful minutes, when we've settled into the ride, when he finally speaks. "I think I need to give you a safe word."

"What?"

"You know, a safe word. Like you gave me for the dungeon stuff."

"Did you pack whips and handcuffs?" I laugh. "Why in the world would I need a safe word?"

"Because you seem... guarded. And you're entitled to your privacy, but I think..." He sighs. "I think I need to know more. About you, I mean. So, I'm going to ask a lot of questions. And I don't want you to feel obligated to answer. I'll accept whatever, but at the same time, I don't want to feel like some things are off limits." He glances over at me. "You can have all the decision-making power. I'm fine with that. But I want to lead."

I have to run these words over and over in my head for almost a minute. "You want to lead," I say, finally able to reply.

He nods. "Yup. I'm just... that kind of guy. I like to lead. But you know that."

More silence from me. Because I don't know how to respond. When I agreed to this weekend I figured we'd look at the aspens from the safety of the car. I pictured us eating at nice restaurants. Maybe strolling through Vail Village looking into shops. Possibly there's snow up there and the runs are open, so there might be some skiing. And... probably some sex. I mean, he didn't hide the fact that he was turned on this week. And I'm not averse to sex with him if that's where it goes. Pierce is what I'd like to call "the total package" as far as I'm concerned.

It that weird? Plenty of people are sexually attracted to their boss, right?

Yes, but most of them do not take him to their sex dungeon to get him hard.

Actually, getting him hard wasn't my plan. My plan was... well, derailed comes to mind.

Which reminds me of what's happening in the present moment.

I did not figure intimate conversation was going to be part of this.

Which is stupid of me. Just another example of how far away I am from that domineering, powerful woman I used to be. Because she would've thought of that. She would've had rules in place from the start. She would not have been blindsided by the threat I might need a safe word to communicate with him this weekend.

"So what is it?'

"Huh?" I say, absently looking at him.

"Your safe word. Because I'm dying here. I'm dying to know more about you and I'd like to get started right now."

"Wallflower," comes out of my mouth unexpectedly. And I really do want to stab myself in the eye for that. But it was automatic. It's the only safe word I've ever had so it just... came out.

"Wallflower?" he laughs.

I suck in a deep, deep breath and nod my head. "Yes. My safe word is wallflower."

CHAPTER TWENTY-FOUR

"So... What do you want to know?" she asks.

"Well, a lot, I suppose. But suddenly I just kind of want to know the etymology of 'wallflower.' Weird expression. Wall. Flower. Where does that come from?"

"I dunno. I think it means a woman who kind of sits by a wall waiting for a suitor to come ask her to dance or something."

"Oh. Yeah, I get that. Huh. That's actually nicer than how it's always sounded to me.

"How so?"

"Your version presumes that the woman is, in fact, a flower."

"Yeah, I suppose."

"I mean, it makes her sound as though she's a flower that can't thrive in her current habitat, but that perhaps the suitor is the kind gardener who helps her find the light and soil and allows her to bloom and flourish. That's nice. I like that."

She stares out the window for a moment, considering. The way the sun is shining through, I can see her reflection in the glass. "So," she says, "In your version, the flower is incapable of thriving on its own and needs the help of a man to reach its potential?"

I bite at my bottom lip. "So! Let's talk about you, then!"

She laughs, and I feel something like relief.

"Sure," she says. "Shoot."

"Um…" I don't actually know what I want to ask all of a sudden. I go with an obvious one. "Do you have any siblings?" She shakes her head 'no.' It's such a guarded head shake that I decide I'm going to have to give a little to get a little. Maybe opening up to her will cause her to feel easier doing the same. So…

"Hey, did you know I had a sister?" I ask.

"Yes, of course I did."

"Really? You did? How? Did I tell you?"

She shakes her head again, "Your mother."

"Paulette told you that?" She nods. "When?"

"Two Thanksgivings ago, at your house when you hosted the orphans' ball."

"No shit?"

"No shit."

"… Was she drunk?"

"Maybe a bit. Not sloppy."

I'll be damned. "What did she tell you, exactly?"

She twists her head to half look at me and half not. "That you had an older sister who died when you were three."

"Yep. That's accurate. She say any more than that?"

"Um. That she was eight. That she drowned. That she liked to read. That she used to make you wear dresses."

"Well... OK, let's all just... I'd call them 'frocks,' but... what do you want? We lived in France."

She smiles. Then she says, "Do you remember her at all?"

"Who? My sister?"

She nods.

Without a moment's hesitation, I say, "Oh, yeah. Hundred percent."

"Really?"

"Yup. I remember everything about her. I remember the way she laughed. I remember the way she ran. I remember how she ate her poulet... that means chicken."

"I know what it means. How? How did she eat it?"

"Like this." I put the Escalade on Super Cruise and let autopilot take over while I illustrate the dainty way Michelle would cut her meat, using only her thumb and index finger. And how, instead of transferring the fork into her dominant hand, like I do, she'd keep it in the same hand she braced it with to cut it and lift it carefully to her mouth. And then she'd bite it playfully free from the tines as if to let you know that the whole process was just a show.

Myrtle laughs at the sight of me emulating an eight-year-old girl eating her supper. I'll choose to believe that she's laughing because she can't believe how goddamn good my impression is rather than because she thinks I look silly. Because—and there's no way for her to know this, but it's true—it is a goddamn good impression.

"What else do you remember?" she asks.

"Shit, I don't know. My memories of her only span probably about six months. Before that I don't remember anything. Because I was, you know, an infant."

"Fair."

"And then, as you've already been made aware by my mom, she died. So..." I pause for a moment. I haven't thought about Michelle in a long time. "I wish I had gotten to know her better, but... ah, well. C'est la vie."

I take the control of the car back into my hands and turn on the stereo. Que Sera Sera as recorded by Sly and the Family Stone begins playing from my phone through the speakers.

"Well, that's a coincidence," I say. And smile.

Feels like she's relaxing now. I see her legs uncross and slide forward as her ankles hook over one another. She kicks off her shoes. Good. I want her to feel comfortable. I have no interest in torturing her. Got a real 'been there, done that' attitude as far as that goes.

"How can you remember all that about your sister?" she asks.

"Whattayou mean?"

"I mean you don't remember anything. Like, ever."

"What? That's not true."

"Pierce... you couldn't remember Eden's name for a month."

"So?"

"So? She was dating your best friend."

"Yeah, but he's my best friend. She isn't. And I remember his name."

"So... so, are you saying you only bother to remember things that are important to you, personally?"

I nod. "Yeah. Pretty much. I try to devote as much of my brain power as possible to the things that matter to me, and that doesn't leave a lot of room for things that don't."

"That seems kind of—"

"Hey, what do you care? You're one of the things that

220

matter to me."

She gets a coy, sheepish grin. But then she says, "Things?"

"Oh, Jesus, it's a figure of speech. You're not a thing. Lighten up."

"I'm just fucking with you."

"I know. Me too." I grin at her and bounce my eyebrows. She giggles. It's a curious thing to hear her giggle. Giggly is not a quality I ever would've assigned to her before, but it seems to fit, somehow. I like it.

This is… surprising. Easy. Unexpectedly so. The little things. The casual conversation. The fact that I put my hand on her back as we left the office and then held her hand in the elevator. All these things seem just about as natural as anything I've done in a long time. On the one side, it shouldn't be a shock. We've known each other a long time. But on the other side, we haven't. And if we've learned anything in the last few months, it's how little we really do know about each other. Hell, if we've learned anything in the last few days.

This weekend was just supposed to be… I don't know what. When I demanded a renegotiation to the wacky contract she dropped on me, I had no idea if this would even come to fruition. I just felt overcome by a need not to lose. Not to give away the farm, as it were. I think maybe I was just swept up in the contract stuff with Derek about the Paris deal.

Ha. I should have let Derek look over the dom/sub paperwork. He's such a straight shooter. He probably would have said something like, "This part here should put clear limitations on how much spanking she gets to do."

But this Vail business was intended as a

counterattack. A way of showing force. A ploy. A decoy. An empty threat, almost. And now, somehow, it's turned into an actual date. A bona fide romantic weekend away.

Hell, Eden may have been right. Damn, Andrew may have been right.

I've always believed I know who I am.

But in this case, I may not have known what I actually felt. Maybe it took a couple of people who are already in love to see what was going on with me.

I may be falling in love with Myrtle. It's possible I've been in love with her for a while. Why was it so hard for me to see it, I wonder?

I dunno. It may have something to do with the fact that dating all the way back to some of my first memories, what I learned early on was that when you come to care about something, and enjoy it, and attach to it, somehow it always seems to get taken away. My sister. My father. My innocence.

Oh, boo fucking hoo. Poor Pierce.

Hell, it doesn't take a neuroscientist to figure out that my issues with control, and my issues with intimacy, and my issues with loss, are all pretty inexorably bound up together. Good thing it doesn't, because I am definitely no neuroscientist. I'm just a guy who owns a men's magazine and seems to have fallen in love with his former executive assistant without meaning to.

Jesus.

I sound like one of the dopes in Myrtle's dirty books.

"Pierce?"

"Hm? Sorry? What?"

"I said… did you want to ask me some questions?"

Oh. Right. I did say I wanted to. And I do.

"Oh, yeah, uh, so… Myrtle?"

She waits for more. There isn't any. That's it. Finally, she says, "Yeah. That's my name."

"I know." I get a little smirk that I can't conceal. "What's that about?"

CHAPTER TWENTY-FIVE

It's a fairly safe question so I'm not nervous about answering it. "My mother," I say, then stop.

"Yes?" Pierce takes his eyes off the road to look at me, then puts them back where they belong. We're on I-70 now, climbing that first hill up into the foothills. I always feel like my car doesn't handle it very well. Like I have to really press my foot down to feel like I'm making progress. And it's a really steep hill too, so you're always like... leaning back, like you're taking off in a plane, wondering if you're gonna make it up the mountain. Or if you're me, imagining what happens when a car stalls out and everyone else around you has their foot on the gas too... which never ends well in my imagination.

But he's got the Escalade on cruise and the engine is taking it all in stride—kinda like Pierce and this whole game I started with him—so that whole Am I gonna make it up this mountain? worry doesn't seem to be there.

"Her name is Ethel," I finally say, focusing on the

gray clouds ahead. Because we're almost at the top now.

"So she's what? Old-fashioned?" And he kinda chuckles.

"I guess. She's a librarian so—"

"She is not!" He laughs.

"She is." Then I sigh. "She one hundred percent is."

"Like... stereotypical?"

"Yup."

"How did that happen? I mean, your father is... well, not stereotypical."

"You know. The old I-went-to-the-circus-once-and-came-home-pregnant-by-a-lion-tamer thing."

"Oh, that." He laughs again. "Happens all the time." He's in a pretty good mood. I am too, if I'm being honest. "Did they like... date? Or was it a one-time thing?'

"One-time thing that ended in marriage. That's how things are done in her family. And my father is a stand-up guy so they gave it a try."

"How old were you when they separated?"

"Five," I say.

"So not long after that picture of you sitting on the lion?"

"Yes, that was the last time she ever went on location with him for work."

"Maybe I'm just not seeing the whole picture here, but... doesn't sound very romantic."

"Romance?" I chuckle. "My mother doesn't even know the meaning of the word. She's not a Wuthering Heights kind of woman. More of a Scarlet Letter kinda woman."

"Hmmm. And you?"

I think about this for a moment. "I'm more of a... Tell-Tale Heart kinda woman."

"I can see that."

"Maybe a little Frankenstein too."

"Oh."

"With some Dracula thrown in."

He laughs. "Come on."

"For real. I like horror. My mother was appalled when I was young because I'd sneak books from the library."

"Like what?"

"You know. Pet Sematary. Carrie. Shit like that."

"She thinks Stephen King is a hack?"

"Pretty much. But in her defense, she's just one of those... serious people. Ya know? Not very experimental."

"Except for that time she banged a lion-tamer on a whim at the circus?"

I guffaw. "Yup. I guess she learned her lesson, right?"

Pierce doesn't laugh. Just kinda mulls that last outburst over for several seconds. Then he looks at me and says, "Is that what she learned? That you were punishment for behavior outside the norm?"

"I... she... no," I stammer.

Silence. Then, a few moments later he says, "OK. So then what? You left her house and—"

"No, I grew up in a school."

He furrows his brow. "Boarding school?"

"Yeah, but she was there. She was the librarian. We lived in an apartment above the library."

"Huh," he says. "And then you left for college. I know you went to the University of Colorado. I remember that from your résumé."

"You... remember my résumé?"

"Of course," he says. "You were applying to be my number one. I memorized that thing. And I thought it was weird that you left your high school off, but I just assumed it was a regular high school, not worth mentioning. But that's not true, is it?"

I shake my head. Say, "No," very quietly.

"What was it called?"

"Philadelphia Friends School," I whisper.

"Jesus Christ. And you left that off your resume? Why?"

I shrug. I don't know which answer to give. Because it was for kids like you, not me? And I didn't go on to Princeton or Yale. Which is true. People see that school on a kid's résumé and they expect big things out of them. Or I could say, I was only there as the librarian's weird daughter, my education was part of her benefits package. Also true.

Or I could just tell him the truth.

"I think I get it now," he says.

"Get what?"

"You left that behind, right? You left her behind and you came to Colorado to be close to your father."

For a second I don't understand the pronoun her. Because I mistake it for me, but then quickly realize he's talking about my mother. "Yes. I... guess you could say that."

"I did say that, but I want to hear it from you."

"Fine," I say, suddenly feeling agitated. I look out the window. We're at that part of the drive up to Vail where the scenery takes your breath away. Most of the aspens are bare this late in October. The time to really come see them change color was two weeks ago. But there are still some patches of gold on the side of the mountain. And anyway, you don't need to see the aspens to see the beauty. "I left her behind. I didn't fit in there. I was the lion-tamer's daughter. They made fun of me, OK? I was…"

I deflate a little.

"I get it," he says. And then his hand is on my knee, squeezing. "I totally get it."

"I don't want to talk about that part of my life."

"OK." He pauses. "So then what happened?"

Jesus Christ. I should've seen that coming.

"You left Philadelphia and came to Colorado. And I'm gonna go out on a limb here and say you weren't the Myrtle I know now when you arrived. So things got better?"

"They… did," I say, hesitantly.

"So how did you become this woman? The one with the dungeon in her basement?"

I turn in my seat to face him. Because I need to make this very clear. "I'm not her," I say. "I put the dungeon away years ago. It was all packed up in boxes before you came over. I left her behind too."

"How many years ago did you put it away?"

"Seven," I say.

"So… when you came to work for me?"

I sigh and turn my whole body to the window. I feel like I've led him down this path and now I'm stuck in the middle of nowhere, defenseless.

"Myrtle?" he asks. Quietly. "What happened when you got to Colorado?"

I glance at him. He's looking at me. So I avert my gaze and stare at my feet. I suck in a deep breath of air. Slowly, so he can't hear it. Then on the exhale I say, "Wallflower."

There is a long silence after that. Both of us pretend to admire the view as we make our way up the last mountain before the tunnel and then the darkness inside feels like it deserves silence. When we come out the other side, heading down into Silverthorne, the sun is shining brightly, reflecting off the snow on the ground, so we both go fishing for our sunglasses. The weather difference from one side of the mountain to the other never ceases to amaze me, but I'm relieved to put the sunglasses on.

"So…" I say, once we're past the small towns and back in the wilderness, desperate to break our standstill. "Where are we staying this weekend? You have a house here?"

"No. I mean, yes. Le Man does have a house here. But we're not staying there. It's for corporate retreats and it feels like it's for corporate retreats, so… Four Seasons."

"Nice."

"Yes. Much better than a corporate cabin. At least we'll have room service. And they have a nice restaurant. And we can walk into the Village and… do stuff." He glances at me for the first time since I used my stupid safe word. "Better than being stuck on the side of a mountain, don't you think?"

I'm trying to figure out if he'd be nervous stuck with me in the corporate cabin or if he just put a lot of thought into this weekend, when the first sign for Vail whips by on the side of the freeway.

It's an odd town, Vail. Because if you've never been here you picture one thing and that's so not what you get. Oh, it has the view, and the ski slopes, and the golf courses. But it's a small valley with a lot of high-priced real estate packed between the mountains, which are always towering over you in a pressing way, so the whole place feels claustrophobic in a car. You don't ever get that mountain feeling until you get out and walk around. And if you don't know your way around Vail, it's hopeless. Because there are many narrow, winding streets and no large, gaudy signs announcing entrances to anything, and all the buildings seem to run together. But Pierce has obviously been up here many times because he knows where the Four Seasons is, even though you can't see the small, unobtrusive sign until you're turning in to the valet.

We walk into the lobby together. We approach the desk together. We are led up to the suite together. We do everything together. But I can't shake the feeling that I'm not in charge anymore.

After he tips the bellman and closes the door, he turns to face me. "So…"

"So," I say, turning away and walking through the cozy living room and over to the window. There's a nice view of Vail Mountain.

"So," he says. And somehow he's right behind me.

"What do you think you're going to get out of this, Pierce?" I ask. My tone is slightly defensive. Maybe even a little accusatory. I turn to face him. Because I'm not a coward and I feel like my vulnerable moment back in the car is giving him the wrong impression of me. "Because there's only one bed in here."

He winces a little. No playful eyebrow lift for this question, that's for sure. He looks very nice today, I decide. This is a suit he wears, but not all the time. It's not in the normal rotation. He's worn it maybe three times, and all of those times have been for evening functions. So why today? Why this suit on this day?

"What do you want?" I ask.

"Just… you."

"Me? How? Me as… your girlfriend? Your assistant? Your VP? Your friend? Which of these versions of me are you after?"

"All of them?" he asks, doubtfully.

"You can't have all of them," I say, crossing my arms as I quickly run that list back in my head. Because I said girlfriend and he didn't deny it.

"Why not?"

"Well, that's a typical reply, I suppose. From you. Because getting what you want is typical too."

"Too rich," he says.

"What?"

"That's another one of my toos. Too rich."

"Can a person be too rich?" I ask.

He shrugs, walks over to the bar on the far side of the living room, and says, "Would you like a drink?"

"I would, actually."

He holds up a bottle of Scharzhofberger Trockenbeerenauslese from an ice bucket. "Will this do?"

I walk toward him, almost against my will. "Where the hell did you get that? And don't tell me that the Four Seasons keeps that in stock, it's just not possible."

He smiles a little. Like this is a good story. But it's not a proud smile. It might even be a sad smile. "Remember that weekend trip to Germany I took last month? I went to the Trier wine auction."

"Why? You don't drink."

"No, but you do. This is your favorite sweet wine, correct?"

I place my hand over my heart. "I mean, yes. I've tasted it a few times and I love it. But it's not like I buy it regularly."

"You wouldn't. Unless you're in Trier, Germany, the

third week of September for the auction, you can't get it."

"You... planned a weekend trip to Germany to get me this bottle?"

He presses his lips together and then lets out a long sigh. "I've been saving it for the day you forgave me. I didn't want to use it as a bribe. You made it pretty clear that's how you felt about the promotion. And the office. And the furniture. So... Yeah. I felt like we were in a good place last night so I had a messenger drop it off here this morning so it would be chilled when we arrived."

I just stare at him, open-mouthed. This bottle is worth somewhere in the neighborhood of five to six thousand dollars. And the trip. A private jet. A car service to get him to Trier. A hotel. Then backtracking two days later.

"I hope it wasn't presumptuous," he says, drawing in a deep breath.

"Jesus Christ, Pierce," I say.

"See," he says. "There is such a thing as too rich."

It would be ridiculous of me to unbutton one more button on my underbuttoned white button-down blouse right now, but that's what I feel like doing. I'm flushed all over with... I don't know. Not desire, because Myrtle Rothschild does not get hot over gifts. Not even one like this.

But... something else. Gratitude isn't the right word either. I don't want to thank him with a boob shot, for fuck's sake.

But I am hot for him right now. And I do want to thank him for being... thoughtful. And for being my friend. And invested in me the way he is. And something else too. But I'm not quite sure what that is.

"I... I don't know what to say," I stammer. "But...

thank you." It's so not enough. These words are not enough words to make him understand what I'm feeling right now.

He pours me a glass, hands it to me, and then holds up his own bottle of Perrier. His beverage of choice. And so very Pierce. I touch my glass to his bottle and he says, "To something new. I think what we had is gone. And I truly, truly regret that. It's all my fault and I'm so, so sorry. But we're not done yet. We can't be done yet."

I take a sip. And he sips his water. And then we just stare at each other. Eye to eye. Soul-searching, I think.

"Can I ask you a question?" I ask.

"Of course."

"Why don't you drink?"

"Partially just because of Paulette." He has always tended to call his mother by her first name. He shrugs. "And partially because of control."

"Control?" He nods. "How so?"

"I don't like being out of it."

"That's funny."

"Isn't it just?"

We both take another sip of our preferred drinks.

"When I came to Colorado I met a man." I don't even understand how that came out of my mouth, but it did. And now, just half a second later, I want to take it back.

He must see the panic in my expression, because he takes my hand and leads me over to the sofa in front of the fireplace. "Let's sit down. I know we're been driving and you might be anxious to go outside and shop—"

Shop? I almost laugh. Because shopping is the farthest thing from my mind right now.

"—but let's just relax and have a nice conversation. Sound good?"

I nod, then sit down like I'm on autopilot. I hold my glass in my lap with both hands, staring down at it.

"You don't have to tell me," he says. "But if you do, you should know it won't matter. Not that it won't matter. Everything you say matters. But that it won't change the way I feel about you."

I look up at him. "How do you feel about me?"

"Honestly, I have no idea. No," he says, putting a hand up. "That's not true. I do know one thing. I... like you. Like that. You know. I like you like that."

I smile, feeling better than I have in months as I look back down at my glass. "It was just a really weird time."

"What was weird about it?"

"Well,' I say, looking up at him again. "I was weird. I wanted to be someone else. I didn't want to be the shy, quiet, librarian's daughter anymore. And I didn't quite know how to go about that, but I met this man one night in a bar. I didn't realize it was a kink bar. It was up in Boulder and all the girls in my English Lit class were talking about going there. But... they were not my friends. I just overheard, ya know?"

He nods at me.

"So I talked myself into going alone. And it was all this dungeon stuff, right? Mostly men dominating women, but there were a few dominatrix ladies there too. And somehow..." I shake my head as I remember that night. "I was a little bit drunk, and a lot less inhibited, and the guy asked for a volunteer from the audience and... he picked me. The rest is history, as they say. I went home with him and pretty soon I was spending weekends at his house—"

"As his... submissive?" Pierce interrupts.

"Yes." I nod. "But for months after that I kept asking

myself, why me? Why in the world did he choose me? And do you know what I figured out?"

"You were a submissive?" he asks.

"No." I laugh. "Well, yes. Because I am." I hold up a finger real quick. "Just a little bit. Just enough. But that's not why he chose me. He picked me because I was... alone. I was shy. I was quiet. He picked me because I was a wallflower."

"And he wanted to open you up?" Pierce asks, trying really hard not to go down the path I'm leading him.

"No," I say. "He wanted someone easy."

"He told you that?"

I nod. "He did. He wanted someone easy. Someone who would just do as she was told. He didn't want the drama, or the challenge, or the stress of training a difficult sub."

"And what did you think of that?"

"I thought it was bullshit." I laugh. "I threw plates at him until his cupboard was bare, I was so angry. And I was ashamed too. That I fell for his bullshit so easily. So I packed my shit up, and two months later I entered the dungeon club again, but as a top. And I liked it. I lived it. One hundred percent lived it. I mean, I had men in cages in my apartment."

"There were there willingly?"

"Of course." I laugh. "I know I didn't show you my professional side this week, but I'm a professional. Or I was. I'm sorry about that."

"You already apologized."

"I know. But it should be said again." I shrug. "I'm not proud of who I was back then. I'm not ashamed of her, but I don't want to be her. I don't want to be wallflower Myrtle, either. I just want to be me, and I

thought that's who I was with you, but it turns out, I just...
fell into another kind of top/bottom relationship. I never
really moved on, I guess."

"Please don't move on," he says quickly. "Please
don't go. Whatever it is you need, I want to give it to you."

And then, very abruptly, he leans in and kisses me
hard.

And I let him. And then, maybe because I'm done
being a top, or a bottom, or anything else having to do
with power... I meet him on shared ground. And I kiss
him back.

CHAPTER TWENTY-SIX

Once, about five years ago, Myrtle came with me to a conference in Bern. I wasn't seeing anyone at the time and I didn't want to go to this event alone. I knew there would be a bevy of Swiss companions from whom to choose, but I just wasn't in the mood for whatever reason. So I asked her to attend for the simple reason that when Myrtle is around, she takes up a lot of space in the room. She draws attention. And she also scares people.

She has the ability to be both seductive and repellent all at once. And that is power. A power that is very nearly inimitable. Because I have only ever seen it successfully at play in one other person.

Myself.

There was a moment, on that trip to Bern, when I walked her to her suite after dinner, that I thought we might… kiss. Fuck. Whatever. I don't know.

But we didn't. And until about a hundred or so hours ago, I thought that was going to be the only opportunity I

239

would ever have to see if there was something more between us.

Missed opportunities are very most often just that. One does not usually get second chances to do the things one wishes one had done in the first place. I will not allow the chance to find out what there could be between me and Myrtle to slip away again.

My plan for this weekend was vague, but definite. If that isn't too much of an oxymoron. It began as a power play, morphed into a seduction design, and as of about ten seconds ago has become the intention to get her into bed for the next two days and not let her out. For someone who has a lot of feelings a lot of the time, I sure don't understand mine very well.

I lean into the kiss, pushing her back on the sofa. She counters, pushing equally hard into me. We lock somewhere in the middle, rigid, and hungry, and wanting. A smile finds its way into my kiss and it is equaled by the smile on her lips.

We stand, still kissing, neither one of us willing to give an inch but at the same time not wanting to disappoint the other. Making our way to the bedroom, I pop loose the remaining buttons on her shirt that cling to their cotton/silk blended holds. She strips me of my jacket and does the same type of unencumbering of me from my own top.

I find the fastener on the back of her bra and remove that as well. And now our chests are pressed into each other. Flesh on flesh. My skin on hers, hers on mine.

Zip. Her skirt in the back.

The clang of a belt buckle and another zip. My pants in the front.

We step back from each other. She gets an impish

grin and I feel myself matching it. And then, as if a starter pistol had been fired, we now race to get the rest of our clothes off. Truly. A race. It's as though we're competing to see who can strip naked first.

It winds up as a tie. (Technically, I think I won, but I don't want to make a big deal out of it.)

And we stand, nude, facing each other.

This week, she has seen me naked. This week, I have seen her naked. But for the first time ever we are naked together. At the same time. In the same place. With the same reason for being so.

My eye is drawn down to her crotch. I can't help it. It has a lot to do with the astonishing fitness of her body and the inherent sexuality she possesses, but it also has a fair amount to do with the tiny, metal barbell adorned with sapphires on the ends that crosses the hood of her clitoris.

Seeing me stare, she bends her head to find my eyes and says, "Hey."

"Oh. Hi. Sorry. It's different than… the other one you had on."

She shrugs. "Weekend jewelry."

"Sure."

I step into her, take her around the waist, and press her to me so that I can feel the whole of her naked body against mine. My mouth finds hers once more and my hardening cock can feel the metal bar between her legs as it continues to fill itself up, readying for what's next.

She lets out a moan and throws her head back when my dick pulses against the silver pressing into her skin. My tongue trails down her neck and lands at her collar bone, which I bite out of impulse.

"Ow!" she says. "Fucker!" She slaps at me.

"Sorry! Shit. Did it really hurt?"

"Uh, yeah." Then she grins and says, "Do it again."

The smile that blooms on my face can probably be seen back at the TDH. I oblige. I nibble at her again. Around her neck, across her collar bone, down her breasts, making sure that they both get their due. Once my tongue traces down her stomach and reaches the mound of flesh just above her piercing—the double entendre of which simply fills me with joy—I pause for a moment to decide what I want to do next.

Everything. Everything is the answer. So I better get started.

I grab her ass and toss her onto the bed. She lands with a bounce and props herself up on her elbows. Her hair has released from any semblance of being composed or put together and for the first time in seven years, I am getting a look at a completely unmanicured version of her. Wild, and reckless, and feral. It is a side of her that I never thought I'd see. It is a side of her that pretty much no one on earth gets to see, I imagine.

She stares at me with an intensity that, if I were not me, I imagine would be pretty intimidating. Truth be told, it's still pretty intimidating, I just don't get intimidated all that easily. I smirk at her and I suppose she takes it as a challenge of some kind because she lowers her chin, looks at me with a lancing gaze, and spreads her legs open. Wide.

I nod at her, slowly and certainly, say, "Mistress," and brace my hands on her knees as I bring my mouth forward and place it around the jeweled metal bar that feels to me like a velvet rope at an exclusive club where, inside, dark and dangerous things are happening. Things that don't get talked about in polite company. Like a place in Denver some old acquaintances once told me about, but to which I declined to go. I'm glad now that I waited. This exclusive club seems much, much better. And even more exclusive.

When my lips and teeth tug on the bar, her entire body tightens and shivers. She moans a guttural sound from somewhere deep in the back of her throat and falls back onto the bed, letting her elbows give way.

Funny thing about the bar she's got in… it's like a divining rod leading me directly to the most tender and sensitive part of her. It's a road sign. A guidance device. A lightning rod.

I feel so tickled that it is my namesake.

After a few moments of allowing my tongue to stroke the swollen flesh of her clit, just as I'm about to really go to work, she grabs me by the hair and pulls my head up.

"Ow. Ow, ow, ow. Hi. What's up?" I say as she jerks my neck backward.

"Fuck me. Now," she says.

"Oh. OK. I was going to—"

"Now!" she commands.

"Oui, oui, mademoiselle," I say, as I lift to my feet, my cock now completely on high alert. She pushes herself up the bed, widening her legs into almost a full side split as she does.

"Holy shit. I knew you were agile from back when I saw you climb the rock wall, but—"

"Now!"

I place my knees on the bed, line my body up with hers, and lean over, allowing my palms to land on either side of her head. Her hair is even wilder now. Her lipstick is almost gone. I assume most of it is on my mouth. And looking into her eyes… I see it all.

I see the librarian.

I see the lioness.

I see the submissive.

I see the dominatrix.

The assistant, the VP, the girl in the castle, the woman in the office, I see it all.

And without losing eye contact with any one of them, I slide myself slowly inside her.

"Oh, God," she moans out.

The feel of her walls closing in on me is unreal. The hard metal of the bar pressing into the top of my pelvis is like... I don't know. I have no words. It's like nothing I've felt before.

"Shit," I say.

"Yeah." She sighs.

"No... Sorry," I admit. I mean... ugh. Just so you know, I'm clean, and... and I hope you don't mind me asking, but you have an IUD or...?"

"I'm clean, I'm on the pill, please shut up and fuck me."

"As you wish," I say.

The metal rubbing between us as I stroke in and out of her creates a friction that I didn't know was possible. The long, slow strokes... the short, frantic stabs... all of it is magnified by the piercing.

And all of it is magnified by the Piercing.

Or at least I'd like to think so.

When she finally explodes, the vise-like clamp of her thighs around my waist very nearly cracks my ribs. I come inside her at the same time because if I try to hold out and keep going, I'm concerned I really will get a bone fracture.

We lie there for a long few moments, me collapsed

on top of her and her holding tight, not seeming to want to let go. I give her a minute to catch her breath, and if I'm being honest, I give myself a minute to do the same.

And after a long sigh, I give her a small kiss and say, "And you wanted to shove my dick in a tiny box…"

She smiles and says, "Well, I kinda did."

I laugh a bit and then say, "I'm gonna pull out now. K?"

"Don't go far."

"I won't."

I wink at her. She winks back. And then I slowly draw my semi-softening cock from inside her. A tiny bit of my pubic hair gets caught in the metal and pulls out of me as I pull out of her. It hurts in a beautiful way. I roll over on my side and lie next to her on the king-size bed. I glance out the window briefly to see the mountain in the mid-afternoon, almost autumn sunlight. Incredible place I live. Every time I look out a window I see something beautiful.

That was even more true when Myrtle sat at the desk just outside my office.

Well… this more than makes up for that.

I lean onto my side, prop my head on my elbow and look at her. She counters, mirroring me exactly. What an adorable pair we fucking make.

"Hi," I say.

"Hello," she says back.

"Um… do you want to go shopping?"

"Not even a little bit."

"Good. Me either."

"What do you want to do?" she asks.

"I kind of think I'm doing it."

"Good. Me too."

Quiet settles in the suite. We stare at each other. After

several long moments, she breaks the silence.

"I don't need to work for you, you know."

"Uh… yeah. I get that. I mean, I guess I get that now. What made you—?"

"It was about wanting to start a normal life. Be a, whatever, traditional girl. Get a job. All the stuff people do."

"Uh-huh."

"And then, when I met you… I mean… you're you. So."

I nod. "Well, yeah." I blow out some air. "And now?"

She puts her finger on my chest and traces it around the area where my heart lives. "Now? I don't know. "

"What don't you know, exactly?"

"I don't know."

OK. Redundant, but I don't want to push.

"I don't trust very easily."

"Yeah, no, I… I get that."

"The thing that happened with the whole Sexpert…" She sighs. "Something like that can never happen again."

"It won't."

"Ever."

"It won't. Hey, look at me." She does. "It. Will. Not. OK? Look, I don't care if you quit at the magazine, or if you don't, or if you want to do weird things to my dick, or whatever… seriously. I just… I just want you around. Me, I mean. I want you around me. The promotion, all the other stuff—yes, it was an apology, obviously it was an apology, but—the real reason I've been working so hard to get your forgiveness is this."

"What? So I'd fuck you?"

"Yes, Myrtle, that's exactly what I'm saying. No! Jesus. So that you'd be here. So that you'd be around. So that the one person that I feel like, honestly? That I feel like is my equal would be there when I needed them. That probably sounds pretentious."

"It doesn't sound pretentious."

"It doesn't?"

"It is pretentious."

"Fine. The point is…" Oh, boy. Are we really doing this? Um… yeah. I think we may be doing this. "The point is that our pals Eden and Andrew may be right about something."

"Yeah? What?"

I suck at my teeth. Which is gross and a terrible habit. But can't be helped just now. "Uh. It may be within the realm of possibility that… uh. Je… t'aime. Myrtle. J'aime motherfucking vous. It would seem."

Telling someone you love them in a language that is not the native tongue with which you're used to speaking to them doesn't make it any less difficult, turns out.

Her eyes widen just fractionally. "Yeah?" she asks.

"Yeah. I mean, maybe? I mean, yeah. I think so. Yes."

Silence. Which is always what one wants to hear, after…

"OK. Well," she says, "I…" I lift an eyebrow at her. "I think…"

"Yeah?"

"I think you're pretty cool too."

And then she leans in and kisses me. On the fucking nose.

Holy shit.

I think I just got Pierce-d.

CHAPTER TWENTY-SEVEN

The weekend was perfect. Candlelit dinners, and soft music, and walks through Vail Village. Sexy, but not overly so. Except for the sushi, which was… kinky. Or almost kinky. Turns out Pierce and I both love sushi and he kept tasting the rolls as he was placing them on my body, then holding them up to my lips for me to try. He'd take a bite. I'd take a bite. And pretty soon we were too full to play the rest of the game.

I stop to smile here. Because it was fun. And maybe a little bit romantic. And also quite ridiculous. Which is sorta who Pierce and I are, in a nonconforming kind of way.

We also had sex. A lot. I feel a little bit like Goldilocks right now. Smack in the middle of who I am and what I'm supposed to be doing.

I think about this as I drive into work, not minding the traffic. I don't even mind the thought of work—which is a big deal. Because I've dreaded going into the office for months and today is the very first day where I feel like I know my place.

And I don't care if other women hate this idea. That a man—not just any man, but this particular man—is what makes my world feel complete. I do not care. Every woman is allowed to be her own woman. And if, to some, that means that they must feel complete without a man in their life, cool. Good for them.

But I'm not one of those women. I like this feeling and I'm not going to make excuses for it.

I like him. I like being near him. I like sharing things with him. And I like working for him.

I have spent my whole life before finding Pierce defining myself with sharp lines and clear rules and you know what? I'm done.

I'm gonna be whoever the fuck I want. And I want to be Myrtle, Pierce's right-hand man. Woman, whatever. I'm going to tell him that today. I'm going to tell him I want my old job back. That I do not come into work for money, or accolades, or obligation.

I come into work for him.

That's it. That's all there is to it.

Just him.

His McLaren is already parked in his spot when I pull in next to it. And it occurs to me that he must, on some level, feel the same about me. We didn't discuss work at all over the weekend, so I'm guessing now. But he gave me this parking space the very first day I was hired. Right next to his. Literally, because my space is to the right of his.

So he must've felt this... thing we have right from the beginning because my space supersedes all the other VPs as far as parking accommodations go. And I know it's dumb, but work hierarchy is a real thing. It's telling and I should've noticed this before today.

I should've noticed a lot of things before today. That I am happy serving him. Not as his subordinate, because he's never asked me to submit at work. But as his partner.

No, we're not equals. He is the boss. But I have never felt a power struggle in our relationship.

We are in this together.

I truly believe that and this calm I feel—for the first time since the whole Sexpert debacle last summer—this satisfaction, well, that just proves it.

I gather my black, leather, studded work bag, get out of my car, and make my way up to the fiftieth floor somewhat in a daze. Still thinking about our weekend. What a nice couple we make. How we complement each other. He is one hundred percent the king and I am the queen who stands beside him.

People are looking at me funny in the elevator and for a moment I wonder why. But then I realize… I'm smiling.

I get off with the other fiftieth-floor people and see Pierce in his glass-walled office, talking on the phone. I slow my walk, waiting for his eyes to catch mine. And it's like we're playing out some scene in a movie, because they do. And he stops talking. Just locks his gaze to mine, then lets it travel down to take me all in. And when his eyes reach mine again, he smiles at me.

Me, and only me.

And sure, I'm dressed super sexy today. I mean, I pulled no punches when I chose this outfit. But I didn't do it for him, I did it for me. A tight red pencil skirt with a black silk camisole top that has a softly drooping collar that bares the curve of my breasts and shows off the silver choker I'm wearing. A matching red, perfectly-tailored, cropped jacket. My legs are luxuriously covered up by sheer, black silk stockings attached to a red garter belt. My bra is red with black lace. And even though I'm not expecting to show him any of my undergarments today, it makes me feel powerful to wear them. To put on this outfit and just be myself. Knowing he understands.

It feels like me.

I finally know who I am.

And he gets me.

"Good morning!" Valerie calls from her desk as I approach my office. "A package came for you on Friday after you left. I put it on your desk."

"Thanks, Valerie," I chirp, opening my office door. And I don't even mind Valerie today. I'm just too... satisfied.

I drop my bag in my desk and look at the box, reading the card taped to the top.

Oh, shit! The party invitations! I totally forgot! I was planning on having Valerie print me out labels on Friday and then drop them in the mail room on my way out, but... shit!

There's no time to mail them now. I'll have to just suck it up and go hand-deliver them. I mean, this party is important. I realize that now. Pierce has trusted me with the fate of this magazine. We need millions of dollars in new advertising and I'm going to make sure that happens. Because no one, and I do mean no one, wants to be laid off right after they spent more than they should during the holidays.

That would be a disaster.

"Knock-knock."

I look up to see Pierce standing in my doorway, smiling... what is that? Coyly? Sheepishly? I don't care what it is, he looks delicious.

"Good morning, Mr. Chevalier," I say smiling back.

He walks in, plops down in the chair in front of my desk and says, "Did you have a nice weekend, Ms. Rothschild?"

"Very nice," I purr, leaning over the desk.

We get lost in each other's eyes for a few moments. Like a couple of junior-high kids the morning after a perfect Valentine's Day dance.

It's such a sugary-sweet moment, I'm sure if anyone saw us right now they'd want to throw up, but I don't care.

"Ummm," he says, looking at my outfit. "I like that."

I sit down and allow myself a silly giggle. "Well, I wore it for you, so... good."

"Hey," he says. "So, I was just on the phone with my father."

"How is the patriarch doing this morning?"

"He wants me in New York this week."

"Oh," I say, deflating a little.

"I know. I don't want to go, but you can handle things here, right?"

"Sure," I say, perking up a little. "For sure. Go. Don't worry about a thing. And then when you get back you'll have the party to look forward to."

"Party?"

"Yeah, the Halloween party." I point to the box and say, "The invitations got dropped off on Friday while we were..." I waggle my eyebrows at him and he chuckles.

"Well, let's have a look." He opens the box, removes an invitation and studies it for a moment.

It looks like a door. If a door was made of silver lace. And the background is black, so it looks like a magical portal to another world. One that's sexy and mysterious.

He opens it up and reads the engraved silver calligraphy, then closes it and looks at me. "Jesus, this makes me hot for you. I don't know anyone else in this world who could pull off turning a Halloween party into a sexy black-tie affair. You're definitely in charge of all our parties from now on."

"Well… OK," I say. Because I've made peace with things. And hey, if Pierce wants me to be the official party-thrower, I do not care. I'm in.

"So hey, I really do have to leave now. The jet is waiting. But… Can we get together next weekend when I'm back? Aside from the party, I mean?"

I nod my head, lean all the way across my desk so one leg has to lift up and bend like I'm one of those sex kittens right out of a noir movie from the Forties, grab him by the tie, pull him towards me and say, "It's a date," as I give him a proper kiss goodbye.

And if it bothers him that we're doing this at work, he doesn't show it. Because he stands up, grips my shoulders with his large, strong hands, and kisses me back.

I'm ready to rip his clothes off and let him take me right here on this desk when my phone rings.

Fucking phone. Thing hardly ever rings so you'd think it would just give me this moment, but there it is. Interrupting.

"I'll see you when I get back," Pierce says, breaking away.

"OK," I say. Dreamily. "Have a great trip! Tell your father hello for me!"

"OK, but he remembers fewer names than I do." He smiles one last time, then disappears.

I grab the handset and purr, "Ms. Rothschild, how can I help you?"

"Myrtle? It's Pearl."

Oh, shit. I forgot all about Pearl.

"I just wanted to make sure we're on to discuss your class at lunch today."

"Umm... look, Pearl. I'm gonna be honest with you. I just can't swing it."

"Oh, no!" she moans. "Please don't bow out. Please reconsider, Myrtle. We really need you."

"I'm really sorry, but I can't make lunch today. I have this big party to save the magazine, and these invitations sitting on my desk that need to go out, and—"

"Tomorrow! We can do it tomorrow!"

"Well..." I try to come up with an excuse, but who am I kidding? I'm lucky I have invitations to keep me busy today. It's practically my only purpose at work right now. So tomorrow I'll be back to normal, twiddling my thumbs at my desk, anxiously waiting for my next erotic novel to drop. "OK. Lunch tomorrow."

"Thank you, thank you, thank you!"

"No problem. Same place, same time. See you then." And I hang up, anxious to make the rounds and personally invite everyone to a Halloween party they will never forget. If I chat everyone up, I might be able to stretch this out all day.

I empty my work bag and stack as many invitations as I can inside, because I am not hand-delivering these beautiful works of art from a cardboard box, and head straight to Josh Washburn's office as my first stop.

I find him eating a banana.

"Josh," I say, leaning on the door. "Do you have a moment for Myrtle?"

"Myrtle," he says, mouth still full. He chews hastily, swallows, and tosses the banana peel into the trash as he makes his way toward me. "What brings you here?"

You know, I have to give Josh credit. He didn't seemed pissed off that I took his office. He didn't bad-mouth me, accuse me of sleeping my way to the top, or become passive aggressive. So I am extra sweet to him right now. "I don't know if you heard," I say in my normal Myrtle-is-here-to-drive-Josh-crazy voice. "But we're having a party this coming weekend and I have your invitation." I pluck one out of my bag, and slowly wave it in front of his face.

"What kind of party?" he asks, transfixed.

"A very special one," I purr. I reach for his suit coat, opening it up just a little bit so I can slip the invitation into that secret pocket all suit coats have. I drop his jacket, pat his chest, and say, "And I expect you to be there in your finest tuxedo and a mask appropriate for the occasion." I make my tone stern, so he understands what I say next. "If I see one Dracula, one zombie, one rubber Nixon mask, you're getting my boot. Understand?"

I smile, place my hand on his cheek, then turn away, heading to the next VP's office just as Josh calls out, "I will! I mean, I do! I mean... I'll be there!"

I repeat that little act, complete with the warning about the masks, for each VP, then start on their underlings, changing up my delivery, when appropriate, to make sure there will be no Little Bo-Peeps, no sexy maid outfits, and no Disney princesses. This is strictly little-black-dress/black-tie attire.

I know the chain of command here at Le Man better than anyone, and it's a way to keep track of who I visit, so I use the hierarchy as my delivery guide. I'm just heading back to my office to refill my bag when Valerie comes rushing towards me. "Myrtle! Oh, thank God! I've been looking for you everywhere."

"What's going on?" I ask, pushing past her. Because it's almost lunch time and I want to finish the lower floor before everyone leaves.

"DogCo pulled their advertising for this month and we're left with a huge gap. The pages need to be at the printer by Friday and Pierce is in the air, so he's unreachable!"

I turn to face her. "DogCo? Why in Heaven's good name are we accepting advertising from DogCo?"

And then it hits me.

We're really scraping the bottom of the barrel if we can't even get DogCo to advertise.

"Something about hunting season?" Valerie offers. "I don't really know. But they pulled out."

"Did you inform Josh?"

"Yes, but he says it's too late to get someone new. We won't be able to get the spread ready by Friday morning."

"So what's he gonna do?"

"Just run the ad anyway," she says, then shrugs. "They had a front inside cover ad. I guess they get it for free now."

"Oh, hell no, they don't. Hell. No."

"But we can't—"

"Oh, yes, we can. I want all the VPs in my office. Right now. There is no way Pierce would let this go to print, and since he's not here, I will make sure we have a new advertiser on that inside front cover, or I will die trying."

"Oh... uh, OK," she says.

"Follow me, Valerie. I'm going to need you to deliver the rest of these envelopes, but I have a script you must say, so that everyone is perfectly clear on my dress code for the Halloween party."

"Sure, yes! I'll take care of it!"

At four o'clock I've got three more crises on my hands. The photographer has pulled out for the Halloween party shoot, the caterer is 'in between' bakers and can't provide a dessert, and one more advertiser has decided Le Man is not where they want to spend their advertising dollars this month but will probably be back in December.

"December?" I say, glaring at Josh. "December isn't going to help us in November."

"They'll be back," Josh says. "I mean, we typically shuffle advertisers like this a lot. We just credit them and roll it over—"

"Do we?" I ask, irritated. No wonder we're losing money! I might have to revoke Josh's party invitation.

"Pierce doesn't usually sweat it, Myrtle. He's been kinda chill about things since last summer when—"

"Enough," I say, holding up a hand to stop the inevitable when the whole Sexpert debacle happened comes out of Josh's mouth. "We. Will. Get. Two. New. Advertisers. By. Friday. Am I clear, Josh? Pierce is counting on us to keep things running this week while he's out and we will not disappoint him upon return."

He shrugs. "OK. We will. Get advertisers, I mean. Not disappoint Pierce."

"Perfect. On your way out, can you send in Valerie?"

"Sure thing."

I look down at my desk. There are now eight neat

stacks of paper and sixteen open tabs in my browser and for some reason this feels… really good.

"Yes, Myrtle?" Valerie says, coming into my office.

"Did you take care of the invitations?" I ask, smiling at her.

"Yes. And I read them the script you wrote. Black tie. Little black dress. No Nixon masks."

"Perfect, thank you, Valerie. I really appreciate it."

"But there's one problem."

"What?"

"I'm behind on my work now. Pierce left me a million things to do while he was gone and—"

"Say no more. I apologize for monopolizing you today. I'll make sure he knows that. In fact," I say, standing up. "I have an idea."

I walk out, go down to the forty-ninth floor, head into the intern pool, and look around. "You," I say, pointing to a blond young man who looks like he should be a starting quarterback for the Broncos and not pecking away at a keyboard at a men's magazine. Which, now that I think about it, might actually be the perfect place for him.

He looks up at me. Points to himself.

"Yes, you. What's your name?"

"Uh…." He stands. "Bryce, ma'am?"

"Bryce, you have now been promoted to executive assistant intern to the VP of Social Media. Come with me."

CHAPTER TWENTY-EIGHT

Whoever came up with the expression "New York minute" completely nailed it. Everything in New York moves faster than anywhere else. I know. I've been everywhere else.

I mean, I move pretty damn fast, but New York laps me. And my dad, even at his age, he laps me too. So being with him for a week to discuss taking over a newspaper felt like being a rocket shoved into a Cuisinart or some damn thing.

But it was exciting. It was awesome, actually. For the first time in maybe ever he treated me like an equal. Every meeting we walked into, every dinner we attended, he really allowed me to speak. He allowed my voice to have purchase. About halfway through the trip I actually had the thought, Oh, shit, he's dying. That was the only rational explanation I could come up with for why he was being so cool with me.

And then, just this morning, right before I got on the

plane...

Fils, je suis très fier de ce que tu as fait avec ton entreprise. Je suis très impressionné.

He's never told me that he's proud of me before. Or impressed. And then he said both in two sentences. Back to back. That was... unexpected.

He went on to talk about the excellent marketing decisions I've made and how he now feels I'm ready to start taking on other parts of his empire myself. He noted the Paris deal as something he's particularly excited to have me run point on.

And then I thought, Oh, shit, he really is dying!

I asked him if he was. He just laughed and got on his plane, headed the opposite direction.

But here's the really, really weird part about the whole thing: As cool as it was for that to happen, and as long as I've waited for my father to show me anything resembling pride, the only thing I could think was, I wish he'd just take off so I can get back and see Myrtle.

That realization both excited me and freaked me out. Because I've been so focused on earning my dad's approval for so long that to get it was awesome, and to place it in second position below the idea of seeing my VP of social media was friggin' bizarre.

It's heightened by the fact that I haven't been able to connect with her all week. Every time I tried to call she was busy with a meeting or doing something. And the one time she tried to FaceTime me, I was at a dinner I couldn't break free from. Long distance sucks. I don't know how people do it.

We texted a few times. Mostly dirty GIFs. The seventy-year-old wife of a guy we were at dinner with saw one of them and kind of gave me the eye. I couldn't tell if

it was judgement or if she was hitting on me. Either way…
awkward.

It's so wild. I've known Myrtle for the better part of
the last decade, but suddenly, in what feels like a New
York minute, everything is different. It's tough to start
something new with a person and then immediately get
pulled away from them. As usually secure as I am about
things, I have to admit that I have allowed myself to
entertain certain unhelpful and anxious thoughts. What if
she somehow has regrets? What if she doesn't feel the
same way I do when I get back? What if she starts really
reflecting on 'us' and concludes it's a bad idea?

I suppose that's a thing people do. Consider negative
outcomes in order to prepare themselves for the
possibility of being disappointed. I just never realized
before that I was "people." I don't love feeling vulnerable
like this, but oh, well. Even Achilles had a bad heel, I
suppose.

In any case, I'll find out what's what soon enough,
because I'm replaying all this in my mind as the elevator
approaches the fiftieth floor of the TDH.

The doors open and I step out to see Valerie on the
move.

"Oh, hey, Val."

"Hello, Mr. Chevalier. Welcome back."

"Where you headed?"

"I just have to run and handle something for Ms.
Rothschild."

"Really? What?"

"It's for the party. She's really taken over since you've
been gone, sir."

"She has?"

"Oh, yes. She has."

And then she's gone. K. That was... odd. But then again, Valerie is odd, so...

I stroll down the line of executive offices, nodding and saying hello. I pass by Josh Washington's office, wave hello and he jumps up from his desk. "Oh, Pierce?"

"Washington! What's up?" He looks at me curiously. Which is when I glance at the name plate outside his door. Goddammit. "Washburn! What's up?" Sometimes the best cover is just to pretend the fuckup didn't happen. Ugh. I really gotta get better with names.

"Uh," he starts, as he reaches me in the hall, "hey, I just wanted to check... we're fine. Right?"

"Uh, you and me? Yeah. We're great. You're my guy, Washburn!"

"No, no. Well, I mean that's awesome, thanks. But, no, I mean Le Man. Myrtle's really been busting my ass to sell space to two new advertisers by day's end, and—"

"She what?"

"Yeah. She seems to think it's pretty crucial. And I know you were in New York all week with your dad, so... the magazine's not in trouble, is it?"

I'm genuinely stupefied by this line of questioning. "Uh, no, man. Everything's great. So, wait, so Myrtle, my VP of social media, told you that it's crucial we get two new advertisers by today?"

"Yeah."

"And—and forgive me, but—you're the VP of..."

"Ad sales."

"Right."

"So, y'know, I just assumed that was a direct order from you because, y'know..." He wags his head back and forth. Here we go. Now that Myrtle and I are together, I'm gonna get this 'afraid to talk to the boss about the fact that he's seeing an employee' head wag all the time.

"Because...?"

"No, nothing. Just... you're saying the magazine's good though, right?"

I feel totally challenged answering the same question multiple times. "Yeah, Josh. Everything's great. I'll ask Myrtle why... just don't worry about it. Everything's great."

"OK. OK, good. Thanks, Pierce." He smiles. And as I move a few feet away from him he adds, "Hey! Really looking forward to the party this weekend. Really." And he winks at me.

What an odd guy. Man, I have some weirdos working here.

When I landed, I texted Myrtle that I'd be here soon, but she didn't text back. As I'm almost at her office, I grab my phone and check to see if I missed a message from her when I hear a deep, husky, man's voice say, "May I help you?"

I look up from my phone to see... well, basically John Elway at twenty-three.

The guy stands up from behind the custom desk and chair that I bought for Myrtle and which, when I left last week, was still sitting in her office, but now is placed in front of her office, just outside her closed office door. Rising to his full height, he must be about three inches taller than I am and about twice my horizontal depth. Guy has a really well-developed chest, is what I'm saying.

But, for whatever reason, seems like he accidentally bought his shirt in my size because it clings to every muscle on his torso and looks like it wants to weep from being stretched so tight. It's possible that I notice it more because his tie is very, very skinny. Don't get me started on his pants. And he's sitting in front of Myrtle's office. K.

I've been gone for three and a half days. What the hell is going on?

"Uh, yeah," I say. "I'm going in to see Myrtle."

I start to walk past him and he puts a bear-claw-sized palm out to stop me. Wait. No. That can't be right. Lemme say that to myself again.

He stops me. From going into Myrtle's office. At the magazine I own.

OK. Yeah. No, that's right.

What the fuck?

"I'm sorry, sir. Ms. Rothschild is on a call. She asked not to be disturbed."

"I—She—OK, well. Thanks." I start past him again. This time he moves his whole body in front of me. I look around for hidden cameras for the second time in two weeks. Then...

"What's your name?" I ask him.

"I'm Bryce," he says. "Ms. Rothschild's executive assistant."

When I was running through the list of what ifs in my mind, this was definitely not in there.

I look around again. Valerie's still away from her desk and no one else seems to be in sight, so I have to use a phrase that I absolutely deplore, and resist at every occasion, but...

"OK, Bryce... do you know who I am?"

He stares at me, his expression unchanging. Then he lifts his other giant paw, in which is what appears to be a miniature note pad. I think it's actually regular sized, but in his hand... he picks up a pen off the desk, holds it above the pad, and says, "No, sir. I don't. Who may I tell her is waiting?"

I—This guy—What the—?

I bow my head, close my eyes, swallow, take a breath and say, "Pierce Chevalier." And then I look at him for something resembling, if not ignominy, at least acknowledgement.

"Can you spell that, sir?"

Nope!

But now, fuck it, I just wanna see how this plays out...

"P-I-E-R-C-E..."

"And Chevalier like Maurice?"

Gobsmacked. Seriously. Gob. Smacked.

"Big Maurice Chevalier fan, are ya?" I ask.

"Thank heaven for little girls," he says, and smiles. This guy is... probably exactly the kind of guy who should be working here. I'll admit it. "I'll be right back."

And then he opens Myrtle's office door. I get a glimpse of her, wearing a headset, and in the middle of what looks like a very animated phone conversation. Bryce closes the door behind him and I feel my eyes go wide. I do that thing people do when they look around for anyone at all to share a "can you believe this shit?" look with. Still no one.

And then, from inside Myrtle's office, I hear what can only be described as an uproarious cackle. Oh, good. I'm glad everyone's enjoying this.

A second later, the door opens again and Bryce squeezes his way out. Not because he doesn't open the door all the way, but because the guy can barely clear the frame.

"Ms. Rothschild will see you now," he says.

My jaw tightens around a tense smile. I nod, and as I

walk past him, I think, Fifty Shades of Go Fuck Yourself, pal.

When I get inside her office, the first thing I see is Myrtle with her hand over her mouth, suppressing a laugh. I can feel the WHAT THE FUCK IS GOING ON bellow working its way up in my lungs. But that gets quashed by the next thing I see.

Photos. Family photos. Myrtle's family photos. All over the walls. Some of the same ones that adorned the foyer of her house. And a desk that looks very... Myrtle. Same with the chair. The whole office feels like... her. And my shoulders drop, the tension falling right out of them.

She brought part of herself here. Her actual self. The life she's lived before and the life she's living now, with me, here, all in the same place. What the fuck is in my throat? It's hard to swallow. Where did that weird lump come from?

She pulls her hand away from her smirking mouth, shakes her head and says, "Shit, I'm so sorry."

"Um, who? The fuck? Is—?"

"Bryce?"

"Yeah, Bryce. Who the fuck is Bryce?"

"I pulled him from the intern pool. I just kind of assumed he'd know the owner of the company. But I'm starting to get the feeling he didn't get a gig here because of his attention to detail. Hi." She runs over to me and throws her arms around my neck. She gives me a kiss, which I gladly reciprocate. "I'm sorry that we've been playing tag this week," she says. "It's been crazy. How was New York?"

"Um, fine. Good. I missed you."

"You did?"

"I really, very did."

She smiles. "Was it OK with your dad?"

"Surprisingly so, yeah."

"I'm so glad!" She kisses me again. I'm thrilled, but at the same time, I have to ask...

"So what's going on here?" I gesture to nowhere in particular.

"Oh," she says, stepping behind her desk with a calculated cool. "Not much. I just hung up with the Perrier people."

"You did?" I ask, thoroughly confused.

"Uh-huh," she says, giddily. "Guess what?"

"Oh, shit. It's not had another benzene contamination, has it? That happened when I was a kid and I couldn't drink it for months."

"No," she says, grinning, "they want to buy ad space in the magazine for the next... year!"

"What?"

"Yep!"

"Guess what else?"

"Free bottles in the café?"

"They're actually going to sponsor the party!"

"Which party? The Halloween party?"

"Yep!"

"On such short notice?"

"Whatever. It's a banner outside and a bunch of free bottles at the bar. It's perfect."

I feel my jaw go slack. I don't know what to say. I manage, "That's... amazing."

"Uh-huh," she says, nodding and bouncing her eyebrows.

"You did all this?" She continues nodding. "Why?" I ask.

She cocks her head to the side and says, "Whatayou mean?"

"I mean why are you handling ad sales? That's Washington's job."

"Washburn."

"Sure."

"He wasn't taking it seriously. We lost two ad buyers this week. And why were we selling space to DogCo?"

"What's DogCo?"

"I don't know. I thought you'd know."

"Are they the ones that make hunting jackets for dogs?"

"Hunting jackets for dogs? Who wants that?"

"I dunno. People who buy stuff from DogCo, I guess."

"Whatever!" she says. "That's my point. Washburn was acting like losing advertisers and selling space to doggy hunting jacket makers was just business as usual."

"Well, I think they're like the Burberry of dog jackets, but whatever. And, I mean, it is business as usual. We lose ad buys all the time. And then we make them up. No big deal."

She looks at me with a confused expression. Crosses to me. "But... but you said that the magazine needed the party and the spread and the ad dollars because... because we're in trouble. And then when your dad had you come to New York this week, I assumed..."

Oh, fuck me. Jesus Christ. I did. I told her all that shit. Why did I tell her all that shit? Forget that, why didn't I tell her it was all bullshit? Because. Because it was just something I said, and I didn't think about it again. Because I'm selfish. Like Andrew said. And I was getting things I wanted from all this and neglected to remember...

"Pierce?"

The look in her eyes is so vulnerable and hopeful and proud. Goddammit.

It's OK. It's OK. It doesn't hurt anything. It helps, actually. Nothing wrong with getting more money. Never a bad thing. And, y'know, if she winds up thinking that it was her who made it all happen and she 'saved my magazine,' well, so much the better.

Yeah. Because it's always dynamite to start a relationship on a foundation of lies.

"Pierce?" she says again, this time placing her hand on my chest.

"Yeah?"

"Is everything OK?"

"Yeah," I say. I look in her eyes and I can't risk hurting her. I just can't. Not again. Not now. I'll explain everything later, but not now. "Yeah, everything's great." Besides, she looks so good that... I take her face in my hands and kiss her on her beautiful mouth.

We stumble back into her new desk. Her desk that she placed here for herself. To do the work that she wanted to do. The work that she did for this company. Because she loves it. The work she did for me. Because... because she thinks I'm pretty cool. That's OK. That's enough for now.

I place her on the desk, push her skirt up, and spread her thighs.

"Wait," she says.

"What?"

"Here? Now?"

"Here is where I am now, so... yeah. It's my company! I can do what I want!"

And what I want right now is to be inside my VP of

271

Social Media.

I slip her panties to the side and look down to see a tiny diamond stud. I meet her eye.

"Friday is bling day." She shrugs.

I unzip my pants and pull my cock out. It has no accessories, so I'll just have to accessorize it with Myrtle. When I slide inside her, her stomach tenses and she looks over my shoulder.

"What is it?"

"I want to make sure no one can see."

"Fuck 'em."

"Are you an exhibitionist and forgot to tell me?" she moans out between slow strokes of my cock sliding in and out of her.

"Dunno," I groan. "I'm learning a lot about myself."

But just because I'm curious now, and also because I don't have any great desire for Bryce to come bursting in and get the idea that this is an office perk, I glance through the slender, vertical window to make sure no one is, in fact, looking in.

Nope. Bryce has his back to us.

Myrtle moans.

Oh. Huh..

I feel my balls tighten.

He appears to be chatting up the handsome FedEx guy.

I turn my attention back to Myrtle.

Well...

Myrtle's mouth opens in a silent scream.

Good for him.

And in what has to be world record time...

You go, Bryce.

She comes.

Do you, man.
And so do I.
Do you.

CHAPTER TWENTY-NINE

It was exhilarating, and satisfying, and empowering to be busy at work all week. I'd almost forgotten what it was like. The crises, the stress, the energy... God, I've missed it. But everything about Pierce's return feels right. I don't want this VP job, I don't want to be in charge of people. The only reason I was so aggressive this week is because Pierce wasn't here to handle things himself. If he had been, I'd just have been back-up support.

I like being back-up, I decide. Much more than I do being the boss. I like being part of the team.

Well, Pierce's team. That's the only team I want to play on.

Anyway. It's party night and I'm dressed like a Halloween goddess. If a Halloween goddess looks like the Myrtle Rothschild version of Breakfast at Tiffany's. I decided that if every woman at this party will be wearing the little black dress, then I'm going to be wearing the floor-length gown version.

I'm the first to arrive at the Le Man building because I need to double-check the details with Maggie. We played phone tag all week and I finally just told her to make decisions herself because I was too busy saving the magazine.

But I want it to be perfect. It is, after all, my first foray into the world of glossy magazine photoshoot parties. Speaking of which, that was one of the details I ended up dropping into Maggie's lap last week after the first photographer canceled. And the dessert. I assumed Maggie is clever enough to hire Eden's father to provide the baked goods, but I haven't seen Eden all week either, so I'm not even clear on what the dessert table will look like.

I'm just going to assume it will be spectacular and delicious.

When I enter the building I am pleased to see the security staff dressed in tuxedos. So far, so good.

"Good evening, Ms. Rothschild," one greets me as he checks my badge and collects my invitation. "Maggie is waiting for you in the second floor lobby."

I thank him, hand my coat off to a woman in the coat check who is wearing a perfectly acceptable little black dress, and then head for the escalator, feeling pret-ty good that this party is gonna go off without a hitch.

The first thing I notice is the music. A string quartet being piped through speakers.

Nice touch, Maggie. Nice touch.

And there she is! "Maggie!" I call. She's talking to the catering staff—all of whom pass my dress-code requirements—but turns when she hears her name.

"Myrtle," she says, coming towards me with both hands outstretched. She is done up right.

"Wow," I say, letting her clasp her hands into mine and give me a squeeze. "Love the dress."

"Yours too. This is"—she puts a hand on her heart and blinks her eyes three times fast—"the most spectacular Halloween party I've ever planned. Such a vision, Myrtle. Such a vision."

"Thank you," I say, beaming with happiness. "But the hard work was all you, Maggie. I love it."

"The photographer is here and he's just great. He even threw in a photo booth at no charge. How fun is that?" She giggles.

My brow furrows. "A photo booth?" I ask.

"Yeah, you know. Those old-fashioned things you see in the mall? Where guests can go inside and make funny faces." She leans in, cups a hand to her mouth, and whispers, "Or, you know. Do other things."

I tap my perfectly manicured fingernail to my chin, trying to think if I've ever seen a photo booth at a cocktail party before. "Hmmm," I hum.

"What? What's wrong?" she asks. "You don't like the idea?"

"Well," I say, cringing. "I'm not certain it fits with the theme, that's all." Her face falls. "But I'm sure it will be great. And I'll love it," I say, giving her a boost. She did pull this whole thing together in less than two weeks. And I really appreciate her picking up the slack while I was busy this week. So we had one miscommunication. No big deal.

"Good," she says, relieved. "I think you'll like it." Then she glances down to the main lobby below and she says, "People are arriving. Do you want me to give you a quick tour before everyone comes up?"

"Yes," I say, my excitement back. "Lead on."

She walks over to the nearest set of double doors, pauses, then opens them with a flourish like she's turning letters on Wheel of Fortune.

Inside I see… a cage. With a girl inside wearing…

"What the…" I step into the auditorium, which has been transformed from top to bottom. Literally, top to bottom. Because tables have replaced the chairs, but they're not dining tables where people sit. Unless the people want to get a good long look up a girl's little black dress, that is. And from the ceiling hangs yards and yards of thick strips of black satin fabric, creating… peekaboo rooms, I guess.

There must be a fan somewhere, because the thick satin strips are flowing back and forth, giving me little glimpses of women and men doing… what the fuck are they doing in those peekaboo rooms?

"Ta-da!" Maggie says. "Don't you love it?"

Love it? I'm not even sure there's a word to describe what I'm feeling. Or seeing, for that matter. Oh, every woman in a cage is certainly wearing a little black dress, that's not the problem. The problem is that they're wearing undergarments I can see and they look like they just walked out of my dungeon. Or have plans to visit it later. Take your pick.

"Ummm… what the hell is this?" I ask, trying not to freak out, because the first guests are now opening other sets of double doors and entering the… the… sex club? Because… "Holy shit, what are they wearing? Why are they all dressed like that?"

And then I look at Maggie, and her mouth is moving, and she's forcing a smile because she can see this was not my vision, but I can't hear her, because, yes, there's Josh Washburn cracking a whip in the direction of a woman, who I hope is his date, because I think he actually touches her ass with that thing. She whirls around, hand covering her giggling mouth. Wearing a dress cut so low I can clearly see her red and black bra. She has on stockings and thigh-high boots. And then Josh—"Jesus Christ," I mutter. "Is he going to handcuff her to that cage?" I whirl, turning back to Maggie. "What the hell is going on? This was supposed to be a black-tie affair! This looks like... like a succubus sex club!"

"Oh, my God, Myrtle. I'm so sorry. I thought—"

"I said," I say, gritting my teeth so I don't fly off in a rage, "I didn't want it to feel like Halloween. How in the world did you think this was my vision?"

"I came by several times this week to run all this by you, but your assistant told me you were too busy, so I just asked your co-workers and they all agreed I was on the right track, so..." She stops, realizing there is no good way past this fuckup.

"Which co-workers?" I growl.

"Well, all the ones around your office who had time to talk to me."

"So the other VPs," I say, looking around. There are dozens of people in here now, all of whom are wearing one version or another of what Josh and his sex demon have on. "They told you I'd like girls in cages?"

"Yes," Maggie says. "They did. They were sure of it."

"Great party, Myrtle!" I whirl around, find Josh standing in front of me. To his credit, he did get the mask right. Because it's just a simple black thing with eyeholes. But he's still holding the whip. And his little demon is still handcuffed to the cage. She's doing a damn good impression of a stripper as she sways and bends to the beat of string quartet music. How that's even possible, I'm not sure. I might have to chalk it up to talent.

I open my mouth to say something but I'm blinded by flash photography. "Perfect," a tall, gruff man coos. "I'm going to call this one Mistress Myrtle," he whispers, then moves on to take pictures of a crowd of people entering the auditorium.

I'm about to follow him so I can steal that camera and drop it into a punch bowl, when Valerie walks up wearing her version of the little black dress.

This isn't happening.

Because her version is something I'm gonna call Demon Black Swan. "What is this dress?" I ask.

She laughs, leaning forward to whisper, "No one will mistake me for Little Bo-Peep."

"They certainly won't," I say, turning back to Josh. "Did you tell Maggie that I wanted girls in cages?"

"I love them, Myrtle. So great. This is the best party ever. I mean, I knew you'd throw something fabulous when you stopped by my office to lecture me about the dress code in that sexy outfit, but this? Wow!" He holds up his whip, cracks it, nearly hitting Gretchen, Eden's old boss, who is wearing… what the fuck is she wearing?

"This is amazing!" she yells over the music and conversation. "Best costume party ever!"

I wonder how long she's had that Elvira costume in her closet, just waiting for Myrtle Rothschild to throw a Halloween party.

Another flash as the photographer catches Josh and Gretchen mid-jubilation.

I just stand there, turning in a slow circle, as people file in wearing every version of black suit and black dress their Halloween imaginations could come up with.

Witches. So many witches.

And to be fair, my perfectly-worded dress-code warning did not include no witches.

Or sex demons. So much worse than Josh's girlfriend could think up.

Most of the men are in regular tuxedos, but some of them, like Ryan in accounting who has spruced his up with stab wounds, and Dave, the VP of media relations, who appears to be an undertaker leading a girl by a leash, just decided the only real requirement was that they be dressed in black.

What is happening?

How did this go so wrong?

Another flash, then another. And with that my nightmare manifests in perfect clarity.

This is who they think I am.

All of them.

I am not just that weird woman who gets paid more than Josh Washburn and took his office.

I am Myrtle. Dungeon mistress. The kind of woman who cracks a whip while wearing black lingerie. The kind of woman who locks her boss in a cage and blindfolds him as she spanks his ass and then threatens him with a cock cage.

Hands slip around my waist as lips press up against my neck. "Great party," Pierce coos. "This is perfect."

I take a deep, deep breath, remove his hands from my waist, then turn to face him. "This," I say, looking around. "This was not my vision."

"No?" Pierce says, taking a step back as he looks around the party. "Well, I love it. And the photographs," he says, shaking his head. "Wow. I mean, this is gonna be some spread. No one will ever accuse Le Man of being boring, that's for sure."

"They thought—" But I don't want to say it out loud. I don't want to admit it, especially to Pierce.

"They thought what?"

"They think this is me, Pierce. That this is the kind of party I'd throw."

He looks around again, then shrugs. "So? I mean, it kinda is." He laughs, then abruptly stops when he sees I'm not. Laughing, that is. "Come on. It's just fun. And you actually have a bona fide dungeon in your basement, right? Not to mention you dress like—"

"Hey, Myrtle!" Josh calls out.

"I dress like what?" I ask Pierce, ignoring Josh.

Josh comes towards us, two-fisting cups of blood-red punch. "Sorry I gave you such a hard time about the advertising at first. I just knew the magazine wasn't in trouble, that's all. And you were getting a little carried away, which is my cue to just go with it, right, Pierce?" Josh elbows Pierce in the ribs, spilling punch on the floor.

"What?" I ask, confused. But when I turn to Pierce, he's making one of those slashing motions across his throat. Telling Josh to shut up. "What's he talking about? What's he mean he knew we weren't in trouble?"

"Oops," Josh says, elbowing Pierce again, spilling more punch on the floor. "My bad, man. I thought you told her."

"Told me what?" I growl.

"Thanks," Pierce says, taking Josh by the arm and turning him around. "See you later, Washington. Enjoy the party."

"What is going on?" I ask.

Pierce rubs a hand across his jaw, then sighs. "I might've... misrepresented the financial situation of the magazine."

I clench my jaw and say, "Explain."

"You felt... adrift to me, Myrtle. And I was afraid that one day I'd come into work and you wouldn't be there. I mean, you were refusing to forgive me, OK? I had to do something to make you... stay, I guess. Be the woman to me you always were."

"And you thought lying to me and giving me a fake job to do was the answer you were looking for? So this whole party..." I stop. Look around at the joke I've been turned into. "Was for nothing? We don't even need—"

"We're doing the spread, Myrtle. That part's not fake."

I laugh. And he laughs with me. But then he stops, because he can see that this is not a real laugh. "OK. So it's just everything else that's fake?"

"Myrtle, you're overreacting. Just listen—"

"Do we need advertisers, Pierce?"

"We always need advertisers, so yeah, of course."

"You weren't going to lay anyone off in the new year, were you?"

"Myrtle, listen—"

"Answer me."

"No." He sighs. "No. The magazine is fine."

I take another deep, deep breath. "So this is... just a joke to you."

"What? No! Of course not!"

"'Plan a Halloween party for me, Myrtle. You're into that, right?'"

"I didn't mean it that way."

"'We're counting on you, Myrtle. To save the magazine. To keep people from being laid off after the holidays.'"

"Listen to me," he says, taking my arm.

I shrug it off and shake my head. "I am a joke to you people."

"You're not a joke, I swear. No one thinks you're a joke."

"Fucking Myrtle," Janet, the lobby receptionist says, coming up to me dressed in what everyone will be calling Myrtle-wear by Monday. "I always knew." She laughs.

"Knew what?" I say, eyeballing Pierce to see what he's going to do about this interruption that has no possibility of being productive to his cause.

"If I ever got invited to one of your parties, this is exactly what it would look like."

"Is that so?" I ask, still waiting for Pierce to put a stop to this.

But he just stands there. Looking at her, then me, then back to her. Like he has no idea what to do.

"Say something," I snap.

"Can we just… go upstairs and have a conversation?"

"That's your reply to this?" I hold my hands up to indicate the entire fucking mess. "Let's go upstairs? So you can what? Stop being embarrassed for me?"

"I'm not embarrassed for you—"

"Well, you should be," I say. "Because…" I just shake my head. "I thought there was no way I'd ever feel as humiliated as that moment you had me hauled out of this room by security last summer. But you know what? I was wrong."

I lift up my long skirt with my gloved fingertips, and start to make my way down to the coat-check girl to gather my things.

I feel Pierce's hand on my arm.

"Hey, no, wait," he says.

I look at his hand and then up at his face. "You know what's really ironic?"

"… What?"

"Of all the things I may be—and God knows I'm a lot of things—I'm not a liar. I didn't lie to you when you thought I was lying. I didn't lie to you about the things I wanted from you. I didn't lie to you… ever."

"Myrtle… I didn't lie. I mean I did, but not intentionally. It's not that I lied exactly, I just…"

"You just… what?" His mouth contorts. He looks away. "You just… forgot?" I say.

"Yeah. I just kind of forgot about it is all."

I nod slowly. "Right. Right. And as you told me… you only forget about things that aren't important to you. So…"

I let it hang in the air, giving him ample opportunity to respond. But he doesn't. I suppose he can't. It's not possible to defend against the indefensible.

I say, "I told you that something like what happened last summer can never happen again."

"This isn't like last summer."

"Isn't it?"

His expression changes. Pierce the ball-busting deal-maker emerges. I know what it looks like. I've seen it before. Just never directed right at me.

"Jesus, Myrtle," he says. "I mean, look, I'm sorry. I really am. But… fuck."

"Nice. Nice apology. Thanks."

"Y'know, I've tried to… Jesus Christ. I've apologized for last summer. I've paid penance. I've, literally, prostrated myself. And this was, y'know, an accident. And it's not my fault that you handed this party off to someone else and they misinterpreted what you wanted. I mean, to be fair…" He trails off.

I can feel my eyebrow arch. "To be fair, what?"

"Nothing."

"No. What?"

He sighs and says, "To be fair… this"—he gestures around him—"is the impression you've given off for pretty much the whole time I've known you. That this is the kind of thing you'd be into. And—and let's be real—it's not unfounded, so…"

My eyes go wide and my mouth falls agape. Not in shock, but in anger.

"I'm just saying," he says. "Stop taking it so seriously. Just let it go. I mean, goddamn, how many times are we going to wind up back here again?"

"Where? Exactly?"

"You pissed at me and me begging for your forgiveness?"

"You are fucking unreal."

"Look, what's it gonna take? You wanna have another contract? Some more 'dominate Pierce' time? Is that it? Hey! You wanna do it now? Here? How about we just go right over there, stick me in a cage, and you can pour candle wax on me or have a tiger lick my nuts or something. How about that? Let's do it in front of everybody. Would that make you feel better? I mean, I've already told you that I love you and you've told me that you think I'm 'pretty cool,' so, you know, what difference does it make to put myself out there for you one more time just to wind up looking like an asshole?"

His hand is still on my arm, I realize. I look at it again, then I look at him once more, take a breath, and say, "Fuck you."

And pulling away from his grasp, I go ahead and make my way down to coat-check.

I glance up at the second-story lobby, hoping. Hoping that he will come flying down those stairs, trying to make me understand. Trying to make me see it from another perspective. Trying to say anything that offsets everything he just said.

But he doesn't.

So I feel like I have no other choice.

I walk out.

He doesn't call. Not on Saturday night. Not on Sunday.

And on Monday morning I call in, leave a message for human resources that I've had a family emergency and I'm taking my two weeks' vacation, then hang up and wait.

I wait for that call.

The one with Pierce's voice on the other end, asking me to give him a chance to explain. Or asking to come over. But he doesn't come over. I leave strict instructions at the guard house that no one be let in, but... I expect him to try.

When Samantha gets to work on Monday evening I call up there and ask her if there's anything in the logs about Pierce coming by, but she says no.

Nothing. No call, no visit. Nothing but my own last impression.

And then, on Tuesday night, while watching the election results, I see that Chad whatshisface won and realize... I blew off Pearl's very real save-the-community-center plan a second time because I was too busy with my very fake save-the-magazine plan that week.

I think that's what does it for me.

I'm pretty sure that's what does it.

The realization that I am:

A) That weird woman who used to sit in front of Pierce's office, but now has one of her own because he accused her of having a secret sex identity last summer, and oh, hey, turns out she does have a secret sex identity, because she only has one job at Le Man now. Throwing a Halloween party. Which, turns out, had a sex club theme.

B) The kind of person who blows off a commitment, twice, ruining any hope some perfectly sweet do-gooder named Pearl had of saving the TDH community center.

And C) a woman who waits around for a man to call and make her whole again, even though he lied to her and made her feel like a complete fool in front of two hundred people. Twice.

It's all three of those things. But C), in particular, bothers me the most.

And there is only one way to fix that.

Just one.

I pack up all six pieces of my Tiffany luggage, call a car service, and go to the airport.

Because I need a do-over. I need a reset.

I am the tiger who woke up, realized I've been living content, fat, and happy in a cage, and decided... I've had enough.

Because this is not me.
This is not who I am.

CHAPTER THIRTY

"Saturday night!?" That's Eden. I'm in the kitchen of her and Andrew's apartment. Local election results are on in the background in the other room.

"Yeah," I say.

"Dude!" That's Andrew. "Why are you just telling us now? And why are you telling us? Why aren't you at Myrtle's right now?"

"She said, very clearly, that it could never happen again. So, y'know, I figure that's that."

"What the fuck is wrong with you?" Andrew asks.

"What the fuck is wrong with me?" I don't feel super supported by my old pal right now.

"Yeah, Pierce! What the fuck is wrong with you?" Eden pretty well shouts at me. I feel even less supported by his girlfriend.

"Why are you both yelling at me?"

289

"Because you need to be yelled at!" says Eden. "You tell a woman you love her and then you let her feel humiliated and embarrassed and just walk away?"

"She's right, man. That's messed up," Andrew says.

"Um, no offense, but do I need to remind you two about what you went through with each other just a few months ago? Pot? Kettle?"

"Don't change the subject!" Eden squeals at me.

"Let's all just…" Andrew takes a breath and presses his palms toward the floor, encouraging us all to calm down, I guess.

"Listen," I say, "Has she, y'know, called you at all?" I ask it of Eden.

"Me? No. No, she hasn't. And even if she had, it's not my job to play go-between for you. If you want to talk with her, talk with her yourself."

"How come you were never this assertive when you worked for me?" I ask her.

"Rock climbing," she says.

"What?"

"Rock climbing. I've gotten really good at rock climbing. And you have to be definite and resolute. I think it's maybe spilled over into my everyday me."

Fucking rock climbers. Bunch of assholes.

I take a breath. "Jesus. Look… I'm not just being stubborn—"

"You so are," she says.

"You really kind of are, dude," Andrew chimes in.

My fists clench. I try my hardest to stay calm. "I. So. Am. Not!" Whatever. I tried.

And at that, Eden shakes her head at me and storms out of the kitchen. We watch her go and then Andrew turns to me.

"You know that somehow this is now going to become about some shit I did wrong, right?"

"Sorry, man," I say, taking a swig of my Perrier.

He blows out a breath. Shit, I still have to set up that pulmonologist appointment for him. "On the bright side—"

"There's a bright side?"

"Well, Eden said that the buzz she and Zoey have generated about the event was huge. I guess photos on Le Man's Instagram have been viewed more than the Met Gala?"

"Yeah?"

"Yeah. You didn't know that?"

"No. Didn't ask."

"Oh... oh. Well. Yeah. Apparently, the whole event was a huge success."

"Guess it depends on how you measure success."

"Um... I suppose I thought you measure success the same way you've always measured success. Money and... attention. And... money."

I gulp down the rest of my water and toss the bottle in recycling. "I suppose."

"Man," Andrew says, slowly. "Why haven't you called Myrtle?"

I rub at my jaw for a moment and then say, "You know what my dad said to me in New York?"

"No."

"He said that the reason he feels like he can trust me now is that he sees me having come into my power. He said that he thought what happened this past summer was me not reacting, but seizing control of a situation. He said that even though the whole thing was a shit-show—"

"He called it a shit-show?"

291

"A 'spectacle de merde,' yeah. That he thought the way I maneuvered around it and used it all to my advantage was capable and forward-thinking and all that shit."

Andrew stares at me for a moment. I oblige his silence by going on.

"Remember when you first got to town and I told you that if I didn't do something to turn the magazine around that he and I would be done?"

"Of course, I do."

"I've waited my whole life for him to believe in me the way he is now."

"What does that have to do with—?"

"My father is the man he is because he doesn't bow to anyone. He doesn't prostrate himself. Ever. Ever. To anyone. Ever."

I open the fridge and grab another Perrier. I pop the cap and drink. After another few long moments, Andrew says, "Can I ask you a question?"

"Yeah."

"Since when have you wanted to be your dad?"

"Don't—"

"I dunno, man. Just seems to me that part of being in your own power is being in your own power. Not the shadow of someone else's."

I nod, taking this in.

"Can I ask you something else?"

"You realize that asking if you can ask something is asking something?"

He ignores me and says, "When you came into my office and got all excited about what happened with Myrtle that first time you were in her, uh…"

"Dungeon."

"I know, it just weirds me out. But that next day, you came into my office all excited. Why?"

I think back to just a couple of weeks ago. How it felt when Myrtle came into my office and demanded a Fifty Shades of Chevalier type contract. And how it felt when I showed up at her place and submitted to her.

"I guess because, for the first time in my life, I let someone else have some power over me. And it felt really amazing to be able to give over to someone and trust them and shit. I guess."

"Someone? Or Myrtle?"

I rub both hands down my face and my palms land, pressed together, in front of my lips in what might look like a tiny prayer. "Yeah," I say.

"Shit!" That's Eden from the other room.

"What?" asks Andrew. "What's wrong?"

"Chad Walter is gonna be the new mayor!" she shouts to us.

"I didn't know you were so invested in local politics," Andrew says.

"I'm not. I just hate seeing dickheads get what they want." It's possible that I'm being overly sensitive, but I could swear that's a veiled swipe at me.

"Hey," Andrew says, pulling my attention back.

"Yeah?"

"What's Myrtle's middle name?"

"What?"

"What's her middle name, man?"

"Astrid. Why?"

"What's my middle name?"

"Dude—"

"Pierce, what's my middle name?"

I stare at him and he raises his eyebrows and smiles.

After a moment, I nod. "Yeah..." I say.

"Go," he says, putting his hand on my shoulder.

"It's been three whole days. I don't know if I can walk this one back."

"I hear there's a seventy-two-hour grace period. You've got"—he bends my wrist and looks at my watch—"about an hour. Just go."

I twist my neck because... fuck me. Then I nod, pat him on the arm and head for the exit that leads straight from the kitchen to the back hallway. I'll have to take the service elevator down, but I really don't feel like getting more abuse from Eden on my way out.

Just as the door is about to close behind me, I turn back to Andrew. "Hey..."

"Yeah?" he says.

"What is your middle name?"

He smiles. "It was a trick question. I don't have one. But I'm thinking of having something added, legally. The frontrunner at the moment is Cransfandimmelberg."

While I am aware there is no seventy-two-hour grace period, I keep looking at the clock on my dashboard anyway. It's now in my head that I have to make it to Myrtle's within the hour as if she's Cinderella and if I don't get the shoe on her pumpkin in time, she turns into a broom. Or whatever. Nobody really read me that stuff as a kid.

When I pull up to the edge of the long driveway that leads down to the wrought iron gates, I pause and let the car idle for a moment. I think about the first time I came here and how I didn't know what to expect. I have a similar set of feelings now. Just for very different reasons.

I roll down to the guard gate and find my old friend Samantha reading the same novel I've seen in her hand every time I've been here.

"Hey, Sam. Still reading the same book?"

"No. This is a different one."

"Really?" She nods. I twist my neck to see it better. "It looks the same. Shirtless dude on the cover."

"It's a Scarlett Savannah erotic novel. They all have shirtless dudes on the cover. Can I help you?"

"Yeah. I need to see Myrtle. Can you let me in?"

She looks down at her clipboard. "I'm sorry. Your name is not on the list."

Are you fucking...? "Samantha? Don't do this, okay? Please. Just call inside and tell her that Pierce is here."

"I'm sorry. There is no Pierce on the list."

"Goddam—!" I take a breath. Then, slowly, "OK... Anastasia—"

"There is no Anastasia Steele on this list either. There are no names on the list. Nor do I imagine there will be for the foreseeable future."

"Fuck does that mean?"

"I'll welcome you not to swear."

I slam my head back into the headrest. Samantha places her hand on her night stick.

"OK. OK. Fine." I grab up my cell and ring Myrtle's number. Or I try to ring her number. It goes straight to voicemail. I try again. Same thing.

"Where's Myrtle, Samantha?"

"I have instructions—"

"Can I tell you something?"

She pauses, looks at me, then says, "OK."

"I'm in love with Myrtle Rothschild. Hear what I'm saying? I'm in love with her. I've been in love with her for a long, long time and I just didn't know it. Or I did, but I wouldn't let myself admit it. Because, because—I dunno. Because I have weird daddy issues and because I'm super selfish and self-involved, and quite honestly, I'm not particularly good at dealing with actual emotions. It may have something to do with my sister dying when I was a kid, I have no idea, but I'm not. So I peacock and deflect using bombast and artifice, and when shit gets too real, I push it away. I did that to Myrtle this past summer. I think I could tell that something was brewing up between us and it scared me a little bit, I think, and that happened to dovetail with this stuff I had going on at work—you may have seen it on local news, whatever, doesn't matter—and I wound up kind of pushing Myrtle away by accident. And, frankly, I just kind of did it again, and look, as somebody who reads those"—I point at her paperback—"you must see how ridiculously romantic everything I'm saying is. Or, at least, has the potential to be. And you have a chance right now to play a major, important role in a real-life love story. So, please, please, don't be that character in the story who acts as an obstacle to true love. Be that character who shows up out the blue, when everyone is least expecting it, and becomes the accidental Cupid. Because I know we don't know each other that well, but the way I am right now? It isn't me. And if I'm willing to lay myself on the line in front of a virtual stranger… well, if you did know me, you'd know what a big deal that is, so please… will you help me?"

I'm spent after my unexpected soliloquy. I huff out a massive breath. Samantha stares at me for a long, long time. Finally, after what feels like a minute, she says,

"Cool. Probably should tell her all that, though."

Jesus.

"Look, just tell me—"

"I dunno where she went. Can't help you. Sorry."

And then she slams shut the door of the guard house and goes back to reading her book.

The next several weeks are exceedingly strange.

Actually, the weeks themselves are kind of cool. It's just that I feel strange inside of them. The combination of the press we got from the Halloween thing coupled with our new ad partnership with Perrier has done something most unexpected. It has made me, not the magazine, but me, the "New Face of the Modern Man."

In truth, a lot of things that have done that.

It really started with the whole Sexpert debacle, ironically. That definitely began attention flowing in the direction of Le Man. And all the work that Eden and Zoey have done since then has been fantastic. Even in the wake of this blow-up with Myrtle, Eden has been on top of things. She still kind of hates me, but she's a pro.

Also, I pay her an exorbitant consulting fee.

The fact that my father (and therefore, I) owns twenty-five of the most major publications in the world doesn't hurt. One hand washes the other. Press begets press, and so on and so forth. I'll be the first to admit that it's gross. But it's also business.

All of that stuff is somewhat unexpected and surreal, but the thing that makes it the most odd is that Myrtle isn't here to be part of it. And not just because of our recent history. But because of our ancient history.

She has been by my side, one way or another, for every success, failure, and everything in between that I've had for the last seven years. And now… she's gone. And I have no idea where.

Her phone continues to stay off. Her only email is her Le Man email and it comes back with a message saying that she's away on holiday and will respond when she returns. She's not on social media, so I can't find her there.

In this day and age, it is awfully, awfully hard to just up and disappear. But she's done it. It's not that shocking, I suppose. She is a woman who changed who she was at least twice and is better at keeping her secrets secret than anyone I've known.

I sit in my office, spinning a pen around the base of my thumb and catching it with my forefinger, when a voice comes over my intercom.

"Mr. Chevalier?"

"Yeah, Bryce?"

Bryce is my new assistant. Turns out that Valerie did such a great job helping Myrtle while I was gone that week before Halloween that I decided to give her a promotion. She's now Josh Washington's… shit, Washburn's (trying to get better about that) AVP of ad sales. They're a couple of weirdos, so they seem to complement each other. But that left me with an assistant spot to fill.

As it started to become clear that Myrtle doesn't plan on coming back…

Which is something that dawned on me with painful clarity when I remembered that first night I was in Myrtle's house and thought: This is it. I'm here. I'm doing this crazy shit. And I have to make a choice right this second. Stay and go through with this insanity. Or risk pissing off

Myrtle again, fully endowed with the understanding that if I do, she is gone. In the wind. Vapor. I will never see her again. In my gut, I know that it's either go through with this or face the wrath of a Myrtle scorned.

... I pulled Bryce off Myrtle's desk and put him on mine. He's actually not bad. And more importantly, I just didn't think I could look outside my wall and see anyone who might even smack of being a replica of Myrtle, and Bryce is about as far from that as you can get. So. I'm trying to keep moving ahead.

But I'm not even sure what day it is anymore. I think it's close to Christmas. I know Thanksgiving came and went. I ordered Chinese food and read a Scarlett Savannah novel. It wasn't terrible. Lots of sex on motorcycles. Which was hot but wildly reckless, I thought.

In any case...

"Derek is on the phone for you," Bryce says.

"Yeah. Thanks."

"Hey, Pierce."

"Derek! What's up?"

"Well... I hesitate to tell you this, but the Paris deal looks like it's falling through."

"What? Why?"

"I don't know. They're being very French about the whole thing. I'm going to fly over there this week and see if we can save it."

"No... no. Don't do that."

"What? Really? Why?"

"I'll go and talk to them myself."

"Pierce. I'm not sure—"

"Derek, I got it. I won't freak out. These are my people. I know how to deal with them."

There's a long, long pause. Followed by, "Pierce?"

JA HUSS and JOHNATHAN McCLAIN

"Yeah?"

"Are you okay? You're not... sick or anything, are you?"

I laugh. Because I get it. I remember when my dad was nice to me back in New York, back when the fuse to the bomb that blew everything up got lit and I didn't know it; I wondered if the guy was dying. Just because he was being nice to me.

When not being an asshole is the exception in your personality and not the rule, that's something one really should take a hard look at.

"No, man, I'm fine. Just... I'll go. K?"

"OK. If you're sure..."

And then I decide that there's only one way to make Derek realize everything's OK...

"Derek, I said I'm sure! Jesus! Do you need me to have someone translate it for you? What the fuck?"

I hear a smile in his voice as he says, "OK. Great. Have a good trip."

When people think of London around the holidays, what they're actually thinking is Paris. Paris around the end of the year feels very Dickensian. Christmas villages, lights, trees... People fawn over La Tour de Eiffel, but L'arc de Triomphe is my favorite. They used to have the Christmas Market right on the Champs Elysées, but after some bullshit city ordinance dispute—it happens everywhere, it seems—they moved it to the Tuileries Gardens. Which is where I am right now. Strolling along, taking it all in. Andrew was right a few months back when he suggested

I should come for a visit. It is grounding for me. I feel…
I feel OK.

The situation with the building contract was no big deal to hammer out, after all. It came down to money, which so many things do. But in this case, I decided it would be easier to just give them what they wanted. In the past, I would've fought and been intractable and pushed and pulled until something broke or someone gave in.

But something I'm learning is that not all hills are worth dying on. Sometimes, to get the thing you want, you have to give up some control. Not completely. But enough so that, in the long run, you wind up getting the thing that actually, really matters to you.

Another way to say it is: Compromise.

Walking along, nursing my coffee, looking at all the gifts in the market, I catch a glimpse of something that draws my attention. A sign that reads: Joyeux noel de la maison de Sade!

Merry Christmas from the house of de Sade. As in: the Marquis de Sade.

I have to admit, I'm intrigued.

Landing at the joyfully decorated table, I see…

Whips. Handcuffs. Slings.

Cock cages…

All beautifully designed and all decorated with a distinctly holiday motif.

My God, I really do love Paris.

A smile comes over my lips and I can't help but chuckle. I pick up one of the cock cages and my chuckle turns into a laugh. And then my laugh fades and I get unexpectedly forlorn. Which is not the usual reaction one has to a cock cage. Or maybe it is. I dunno. Could go either way, I suppose.

The woman working the tent—a woman who has multiple piercings in her ears, nose, eyebrows, and, I presume, elsewhere—asks if she can show me anything in particular. I'm just about to answer, "Non, je vais bien," when off to my side I hear, in English...

"He'll take one of everything."

CHAPTER THIRTY-ONE

I'd be lying if I said that Paris was a random choice when I decided to leave town and try to start over.

I'd be lying if I said I haven't imagined a chance meeting with Pierce while I was here.

I'd be lying if I said my heart isn't beating irrationally fast in this moment.

Because all those things are true.

When I got to the airport I looked up at the departures board and saw many possibilities. Most of which would've never ended with me staring straight into the eyes of Pierce Chevalier. I saw Anchorage. I saw Maui. I saw Orlando.

But Paris was on that board too. A non-stop to London with a layover, then on to France a few hours later. So I booked the one remaining first-class ticket and left. Telling myself the whole time that this was it. I was walking away for good. The end.

But inside I had this little dream. Little fantasy, if you

will. That I'd be walking out of a classic Parisian coffeehouse, glance across the street through traffic, and our eyes would meet.

Not quite like this. I never imagined we'd both be standing in front of a house de Sade table admiring their dungeon wares. But it feels close enough to fate to justify my galloping heart rate.

"Myrtle," he says.

"Pierce," I say back.

I want to say so much more. Things like, You hurt me. I expected more from you. You remember my middle name but you forgot that you lied about the magazine? And the entire party was just a way to keep me busy?

But all that has been in said in some way or another. And it feels sad. It feels like it would lead to an argument and I don't want to fight with him.

Because I have lost my fight. I am the tamed tiger, after all. And what I really want to say is, You hurt me and I'm sorry I walked out, because in doing so, I just ended up hurting myself. I want to tell him I've been miserable. Sad. Maybe even a little bit depressed. I want to tell him that I'd like to come home. I'd like my old job back. Not the VP job, but my job. The one he chose for me. The one I did better than anyone else. The one that made me whole. The one I looked forward to every day because it involved being on his team.

I want to tell him that he looks good. And ask him if he's happy. And say congratulations on the booming success that Le Man has turned into under his leadership.

I want to tell him I'm sorry I didn't give him a chance to explain. That was wrong. He deserves to be heard just as much as I do.

I want to tell him I miss him. Terribly.

I want to tell him I love him. Because I do. And there's no way to deny it anymore. I feel this in my heart. I feel like we were meant for something bigger than this little string of misunderstandings.

But when I open my mouth none of that comes out.

Why, Myrtle? Why can't you just say what you feel?

Some might blame past experiences. I was in a relationship once when I first got to Colorado that didn't involve feelings like this. Or open communication. And even though I didn't enjoy being that man's submissive, I did enjoy his… detachment. So much so that when I left, I started up my own string of detached relationships.

It felt like the right way forward for me back then. And I was smart enough to know when it stopped feeling like the right thing to do and then I walked away.

And I've been thinking about this whole walking away thing since I got here to Paris. How I have done it several times now. How I have reshaped myself. Remade myself into a new woman.

That's all I thought I wanted when I left but… turns out that's not what I want.

Not even close.

I want him. I like me, with him. I want us to be a team again.

"Say something," he says, swallowing hard.

The woman in charge of the table looks at me, then at Pierce, then back at me. And she's just about to open her mouth and save us both from this terrible, awkward moment when a patron comes up and distracts her.

Fate, it seems, will not intervene again. Once is enough, says fate. Now you're on your own.

"Love is stupid," I say.

"Is it?"

305

I nod. "Because…" I swallow hard now. "It's so messy."

The corners of his lips lift up, just a little. He nods. "It is pretty messy."

And then all the messy things that have happened since last summer come rushing back. All the stupid feelings. All the stupid reactions to those feelings. All the wrong words that could come flying out of my mouth are there, hanging in the air in front of me. Whole paragraphs of wrong words strung out in long sentences flow out and shimmer in the cold December air.

All the ways to make this worse present themselves.

And I lose my nerve.

I am not the woman I thought I was.

I have never been that woman. Ever.

I am the wallflower. I am someone who fades into the background. I am the one who turns away and never looks back because I am too afraid to step forward and be seen.

That is what fate is trying to tell me now. That is the final chance I've been given.

Proof that people don't change no matter how many costumes they put on. No matter how many blindfolds they wear. No matter how many cages they put themselves in.

I am just… a tiger, I guess. But in all the wrong ways.

"Well," I say, wringing my gloved hands together. "It was nice seeing you again, Pierce."

And then I just accept this fact and turn away.

CHAPTER THIRTY-TWO

"It was nice seeing you again, Pierce? Are you kidding?" I reach for her gloved hand. I catch it. She looks down at me holding her wrist and says...

"Let go of me, please."

"No, thanks. Already did that. Didn't like it much."

With a knowing smile, the woman working the Christmas present sex toy table asks, in her Parisianated English, "Ah, you two are married?"

"No, we're not," Myrtle says.

"You talk like married people. Here. This, you should try." She holds up a full latex suit, complete with a face mask that has only a breathing tube where the mouth hole should be.

I walk away, pulling Myrtle with me.

"What are you doing?" she asks.

"I don't want to have this conversation in front of Catherine Robbe-Grillet."

"How do you know who Catherine Robbe-Grillet is?"

"How do I not? She's like the most famous dominatrix in France."

"That wasn't her."

"Yes. I know that wasn't her."

"Catherine Robbe-Grillet is almost ninety."

"I know! I was making a joke!"

"Oh, right. I forgot. You're hilarious."

I pull her off to the side, away from noisy children and meandering tourists.

"What?" she asks, huffily, as I let her arm go and she faces up to me.

"You've been in Paris?"

"Wow. How'd you puzzle that out?"

"OK—"

"You're a real sleuth."

"Jesus! Will you fucking stop for a second?"

I guess that was a little loud because a handful of people stop to stare.

"Alló, alló. Joyeuses fêtes," I say as I smile and wave. Then I turn back to face her. The look on her face is as chilly as the winter wind.

"What?" she asks. "What do you want?"

"What do I want? Y'know, I didn't see you. You saw me. You're the one who came up and engaged me just now."

"Yeah, well. Serendipity," she says.

"OK, I don't even know what that means."

"It's like coincidence, but—"

"I know what the word means! I don't know what… look. Let's just… can we start over?"

The look that meets me is one of near confusion.

"Start over?" she asks. "From when? Exactly which starting over point would you like to pick? From before you lied to me? Or from before you humiliated me? Although I guess those are technically related. So how about just before we met? How about we get in our wayback machine about seven years and maybe you just hire Valerie from the start? How about that?"

"What. The fuck. Are you talking about?"

"I gotta go," she says and starts off.

"Myrtle, I'm sorry," I call after her. "I'm sorry, please. Please, come on. Please let me try to apologize."

She stops walking. She doesn't turn around. Just stands there with her back to me. Her black hair blending into the black cashmere of her ankle-length winter coat. Then, after a moment, she turns slowly to face me again.

"How do you want to apologize?" She says it quietly. I have to step to her and ask her to repeat.

"What?"

"How do you want to apologize? Do you want to give me another raise? Make me CFO? COO? How about your job? You think that'll be a good apology? What are you doing in Paris?"

"What?"

"Are you here about the building that you're going to scoop up? Since the magazine is not only not failing, but doing so well that you can apparently buy a Paris headquarters?"

"Yeah…" I say, sheepishly. "That's why I'm here."

"Well, then. Just offer me that. I'm in Paris. I have no plans to go back. Why don't you just offer me the job of running the Paris office? You think that'd make it all OK?"

I pause for a second. Then… "I—Would it?"

"Oh, my God! You are the stupidest smart person I've ever met!"

"Yeah, I've heard that before."

"Goodbye, Pierce."

She takes off again. Faster this time. I chase.

"Please, Myrtle, wait. Wait! Please! I love you!"

She doesn't stop before she turns around this time. She just whips on me.

"Well, that's great for you. That's great that you get to feel that way. But that doesn't really have anything to do with me, does it?"

"What are you talking about?"

"Do you know why I came up with the idea of making you my submissive? Even if it was just going to be for a minute?"

I look at my feet. Nod. "Because you wanted me to feel humiliated like you felt humiliated. I know. I get it. I—"

"No," she says, sadly. "You don't get it. I mean, look, it's partially on me. There's no way that you could learn how to submit to me in the way I wanted in the time that we were going to have. It can take years to really understand. But, in short, being a submissive means that you learn to rely on me. To trust me. To trust me. And to know that I will never abuse that trust. That I will never hurt you. In return, I accept your submission and do not take for granted the gift of you giving your trust over to me."

She looks into my eyes, searching for something.

"I'm saying the whole dom/sub relationship is about trust, Pierce. That's it. That's the deal. And it's about considering someone else instead of just your own wants and desires. The problem? You can trust me, but I can't trust you. And I've shown for years that I can put your needs above mine, but you can't put me above you in any way. And to even consider trying anything with you again, I'd need something shared. Something we agree on. That's why I wanted you to sign a contract, an agreement. Because for a long time, this has been a one-way street that travels in a direction I'm just not willing to go down by myself anymore."

"That's not fair."

"Isn't it?"

I think for a moment. Because you rarely get a second chance. And you really don't get a third. Or a fourth. Or what the fuck ever number I'm on now.

"OK, it is fair. You're right. But you just said it can take years. And I'm assuming that's when you're dealing with someone who isn't so totally on the other end of the spectrum as I am. So, y'know, it'll take me a little longer. But... is there any way you can try to give me that chance? Any way at all?"

She folds her arms and tucks her gloved hands against her chest. "How can you expect me to try when you didn't even try a little?"

"Try a little what?"

"To come after me. To call or to come by or anything."

"Yeah, I know." What I don't know is if she can hear the requisite shame in my voice. But it's there. "I know. That was... I know. I'm sorry. I can try to explain, but... it doesn't matter."

"It does to me."

"Right. OK. Well, I thought I was doing what you wanted. You made it very clear that we were on a zero-tolerance kind of a deal, and so... I just wanted to honor that. To submit to what I thought your wishes would be, if you will."

311

"Don't get cute."

"I'm not trying to. I swear."

I've known Myrtle for a long time. I've not known Myrtle for a long time. Both things are true. So I can't be certain if what I'm sensing in her energy is a slight thawing, or if she's just a sleeping tiger that's about to wake up and rip my face off. But this is it. This is one hundred percent it. This game of cat and mouse stops here. I will have no more chances. I have to do something. And I have to do it now. So...

"What are you doing?" she asks as I put my coffee cup down, pull off my gloves and strip off my overcoat. "Pierce?" I don't say a word. Competing voices volley in my brain. My father. Andrew. Eden. My own.

Myrtle. Hers is the one that's the loudest. And it's the only one that matters.

"Seriously, Pierce. What are you doing?" Her voice is a little more urgent. But that's only because my shoes are off now, and I'm unbuckling my trousers.

"Oh, my God," she says. "You're not—?"

I am.

My pants come down and the cold winter air hits my legs like an icy scythe. What I wouldn't give for some hot candle wax right now.

"Pierce..." Her voice goes up at the end of my name.

Off comes the sweater and the shirt underneath.

And now I'm standing in the middle of the Tuileries Gardens Christmas Market clad only in a pair of black boxer briefs. Oh, my nipples are hating me right now. But it also feels kinda good. Pleasure and pain. Kissing cousins.

People have noticed. This being Paris, no one seems all that shocked. For the most part they just kind of glance over and move on. A couple of kids do gawk.

Well, kids, it's about to get a whole lot more gawk-worthy in about five seconds.

I put my hands on the waistband of my underwear and go to tug when Myrtle's hands land on mine.

"No! Don't. This is insane."

"I know."

"This is not going to help anything."

"Maybe not. But lying down naked in front of you in the middle of a French park in winter sure would put you above me. Literally. And metaphorically. It would show submission, I'm trying to say. I mean, I think it would."

"Jesus. You're all about the grand gesture, aren't you?"

"Is there any other kind?"

"All the toos. Every last one."

"Yeah. I know. Look, if this isn't what you want, I won't do it. If it is, I will. I'll do whatever. I can learn. I swear I can. Because I love you. I love you, Myrtle Astrid Rothschild, lion-taming librarian. I love you and everything that you are. And I don't need you to be anything for me. You're everything I could want. And I just want the chance to be that for you. To be what you need. To be what you want. And to think about what that is and serve that before I serve myself. I swear. Please, just give me the chance to start over."

"Monsieur! Monsieur!"

Two gendarmes are making their way toward me.

"Please, Myrtle. Just give me a chance. Because the cops are coming over here and before I get hauled off to jail, I'd just like to know if I should plan on it being the last cage anyone ever throws me in again. Because I'd really like that to not be the case."

And then… a Christmas miracle happens.

She bows her head, covers her face with her hands, and I hear her say, "I love you."

"Monsieur!"

"What did you say?" I ask

"What?" she says.

"Monsieur!" They're about five meters away now.

"Did you just say you love me?"

"Love you? No. I said, 'I can't believe you.'"

My shoulders drop. "Oh. I thought you said—"

"No, no, no, no, monsieur!" The cops are on me now. One is grabbing up my discarded clothes while the other takes me by the arm and starts to pull me away.

"I'm staying at La Réserve!" I shout to her. "I'm checked in under Anastasia Steele!"

"Why?"

"Mona said that now that I'm kind of famous, I should start keeping a low profile!"

"Great job!"

"Just please… if I'm not in prison later, come find me! I think we should keep talking!"

And as one of the gendarmes throws my coat over me and the other leads me to a waiting police car, I look back at her over my shoulder, and I can't be sure, but I think I see her smile.

Or it may be a grimace as she spots the tree branch that hits me in the face seconds later as I'm staring back at her rather than watching where I'm walking.

Could go either way.

CHAPTER THIRTY-THREE

You know those moments that stop time and you have a bazillion thoughts running through your head and somehow a whole other lifetime happens in the span of two or three seconds?

I'm having one of those as I watch Pierce be led away by the police.

I'm seeing weird things. Old things. My mother in the library, reading to my class that first year we moved onto campus. And the girl sitting next to me telling me her name and I just looked at her. Like… what was I supposed to do with that information? I mean, the obvious answer is tell her my name back and say, "Let's be friends!" But I didn't understand that back then. No one gave me a rule book and wouldn't life be so much easier if it came with a fucking rule book?

But there are no spare moments to ponder that because I'm back in time. That first summer I went to stay with my father, he gave me a kitten. Not an exotic one or anything. Just a plain old kitten. He said I could train it and take it home with me. But I said, "It doesn't want to be trained and I don't want to train it." So it didn't come home with me. It stayed with him.

And then that first day I met the man who would later become my dom and I just kinda went along with it. Too afraid to respond, I guess. That was always my problem. It wasn't that I was scared. Not the way people think, anyway.

I just don't know how to respond when these small things that have big-event potential happen unexpectedly, so my default reaction is to say nothing, or reject the offer, or just... play along. Let fate sort it out.

But something happens as Pierce waits for the police to open the door and shove him inside.

He's talking, I can see that much. And then one of the gendarmes—a young woman probably not much older than Eden—throws her head back and laughs.

And Pierce laughs. And then he's talking again, and then they're all laughing.

None of them are looking back at me, so it's not me they're laughing at. In fact, I don't think they're laughing at anyone. I think Pierce just said something really funny. Or blurted out something really inappropriate.

Just being... Pierce. He's always just being Pierce. So comfortable in his own shoes. So sure of himself. So damn funny, and ridiculous, and over the top.

Pierce walks through life telling everyone to take him or leave him.

And sure, some people leave him, but that never sets him back. He just... goes for it. Every single time. One hundred percent.

So even though he didn't come to Paris to see me, when that moment came and he saw his opportunity, he didn't settle for the default option.

I realize I'm still in that altered state where time has stopped and the world is on pause. Because I log every one of their faces. Eyes bright. Happy and in the moment. Laughing. Probably thinking this guy isn't worth the paperwork.

I hold my breath, hoping that they'll just let him get dressed and tell him to be on his way.

But the spell breaks, everyone is moving, the door opens, the woman places her hand on his head so he doesn't hit it when he gets in the back seat, and less than a minute later he's… gone.

Just gone.

Just as quick as he appeared, he disappears.

I realize then that I did it again.

I just let fate sort it out.

And this is what happens when you do nothing. When you choose the default option.

You get stuck with a default life.

You don't make a friend that first year of school. You don't take a kitten home from your summer vacation. You end up being something you're not. And you let the only man who matters to you get hauled off in a police car for just being himself.

And himself is actually a genuine, caring, funny, quirky man who lets you drip candle wax on his balls, and puts up with your weird bullshit, and lives every day like it's just another opportunity for a grand gesture.

He is the polar opposite of you and you love it.

It's this realization, this witnessing of Pierce just being Pierce that wakes me up. Makes me yell, "Wait!"

But I am a lifetime of eternal moments too late.
Because he's gone.

I think time stops again because I don't know how I even get to the police station they took Pierce to. I don't even remember pulling out my phone to find the nearest one or getting into a cab.

I just know that I'm standing outside when he comes through the doors hours later, shrugging on his coat with one hand while simultaneously shuffling his phone into the other as he looks down at the screen.

He's so busy with that phone, he walks past me.

And for a second I think, Well, there you have it.

I am the wallflower after all.

But then I hear myself say, "Hey."

Which makes him turn. Confused. "Myrtle?" he says. "What are you doing here?"

"I bailed you out."

"Oh," he says. "That was you? I thought it was Derek, but I should've known better. He was laughing when I called him earlier. Like burbling giggles. I figured I'd be in here all week." Then he looks at me, serious, and says, "But I should've known it was you. Because you have always had my back. No matter what scheme I have cooking, or what ridiculous antics I get into. You've always been there through every single 'too.' Of course it was you who got me out of a cage. Thank you."

I shrug. "Turns out… there's room for improvement. So this is me. Improving. I said I never lied to you and that's true. But I'm going to lie to you now and apologize for this." I wave my hand at the police station. "Because I should've lied the first time and I didn't. So... it's all my fault. "

"What?" He runs his fingers through his mussed-up hair. He looks uncharacteristically frazzled. His collar is crooked under his sweater, his shirt untucked, his normal clean-shaven jaw showing a hint of a shadow. "What are you talking about?"

"I said some things that... I actually love the idea of a New Year's kiss. And I think candles are good for more than just dripping hot wax."

He looks thoroughly confused. "You do?"

I nod. "And..." I hesitate. The same way I did when that girl told me her name in the library. But it's a do—or-die moment for me. So I press on. "And you know what?"

He smiles at me. "What?"

"I did say I love you." I nod my head in some random direction. "Back there at the market."

"You did?" I nod. "But... oh. I see. You just told me you're going to lie to me, so..."

"So, yeah. I didn't say it. But I should've. So I'm going to erase that moment and ask for a do-over. That's what this is. Myrtle's do-over. And so... I love you. I love you, Pierce Constantine Chevalier. I absolutely do. You're a lot, yes. You're too much for most, in fact, but you're just the right amount of everything for me."

My heart is beating irrationally fast again but I don't care. In fact, I decide to embrace it.

I decide to embrace him. Literally. I step forward, wrap my arms around his waist, press my lips into his neck and just... sigh. Like I've been away from home for a long, long time but now I'm back.

We stay like that for a few moments. Just enjoying this new thing we are.

Himself. Herself.

I smile at that.

Because that's when I realize.

I've been Pierce-d.

I like to win. Always have. Probably always will. Winning makes my blood pump. Gets my motor revving. Keeps me feeling sharp.

I know who I am.

But there is no part of me that feels like I "won" with Myrtle.

I mean, she is a prize. One that I'm lucky to have standing by my side here on the sidewalk of Rue Amelot in Paris's Eleventh Arrondissement at almost midnight on New Year's Eve. But I don't feel like a winner in the way I have traditionally. Because, if I did, that would mean there would have to be a loser. And there isn't. We both won. I mean, my prize is a little better than hers, but she seems relatively happy being here with me, so I won't disabuse her of the notion that she's getting something awesome in this bargain.

Because it's not my place to tell her how she should feel.

We're leaving tomorrow. Heading back to the TDH. New year, new us.

Or old us, in some ways. Myrtle's coming back to her old life. Not her old, old life. And not her old life after that. And not even her old life after her old, old life and her old life after that, but her old life that she had before I screwed it up.

That train of thought seems unclear. I'm a little nervous right now.

What I mean is, she's going back to being my assistant.

I tried to offer her the job running the Paris office but she said something like, "I was being sarcastic when I said that. Pierce…" And then she sighed. But the sigh sounded different than her usual sigh. There was a smile in it.

So I asked her what she wants. What she wants. And she said that she wants to revisit what it means to be my direct subordinate. That she feels like that's the role where she's most comfortable. Because, she says, she likes knowing that she can be of service but also knowing that she has influence.

I tried to say, "No, no, no. That's not right. You should…"

But I stopped myself. Because telling her what she should do is some non-listening, mansplaining bullshit of the highest order. So I shut up and said, "Great."

I made the choice to submit myself to her decision and trust that she's doing the thing that gives her the greatest satisfaction. It's the most balanced contract negotiation I think I've ever been a part of. In exchange, we have agreed that when we're not in the office, we'll continue my… training. I'll keep learning how to submit to her. Properly.

Seems like a fair deal.

As for her current job, I suggested that we bring Eden in full-time again as the director of social media, but Myrtle said she'd never do it, and then went on to describe the phenomenal job Valerie did of helping take care of things while I was in New York. So, when we get back, Valerie will be surprised to find that she now has a private office with a two-thousand-dollar desk chair, an assistant called Bryce, and a fifty-thousand dollar raise. (I'm giving Josh Washington a twenty-one-thousand-dollar raise so he doesn't get freaked out that people keep getting promoted over him. He did go back and convince DogCo to keep advertising with us, so...)

And that brings us to now.

New Year's in Paris. One of the most romantic places in the world and one of the most romantic times to be in that place. For someone like Myrtle, who has previously claimed to be inured to the idea of romance, it might be uncomfortable. But she's coming around. As we both now know, confronting things that make you uncomfortable can sometimes make you feel good in a way you didn't expect.

So, as the clock strikes midnight, I lean into her and give her the softest kiss on the mouth I think I've ever offered anyone. She accepts, nervously. But willingly.

"How was that?" I ask, pulling away.

She smiles, her eyes still closed, and says, "I didn't hate it."

"Yeah?" She nods. "Does that mean you're suddenly going to be into Halloween and all the other holidays too?"

"No. I still hate holidays. I just like the kissing part. But we can do that any time."

Parisian revelers all around us cheer and fire off streamers. We're not in front of L'arc de Triomphe, or at the Moulin Rouge, or any of the traditional places one might look to find lovers on New Year's Eve. We're on a lesser-known street in front of a lesser-known place, about to enjoy a less conventional way of celebrating the new year. Or, at least, it's less conventional to me.

Which is why I'm nervous.

"You ready?" she says.

I half-nod. "Mm-hm," I sound out, not at all convincingly.

"We don't have to do this," she says.

"Yeah, we do."

"No, we really don't."

"Yeah, we really do. I paid the guy a shit ton of money to stay open."

She sniffs in a laugh and shakes her head. "Grand gesture," she mutters. "Okay. Then let's go!" She takes my hand and begins pulling me across the street toward the glowing neon sign.

And then, totally unexpectedly, I hear a syllable leave my lips.

"Sac—" I get out before stopping myself.

"What?" she says. "What was that?"

"Nothing."

"No, what did you start to say?" She arches an eyebrow.

"Nothing. I didn't start to say anything."

"You started to say 'sacapuntas,' didn't you?"

"No."

"Yes. You did."

"No… I started to say… sock… Puppet." That's the best I can come up with?

"Sock puppet..."

"Mm-hm."

"...Why?"

I shrug. "Dunno. I hear there's a great sock puppet show we should check out when we get home." She eyes me with deep skepticism. "What? I like puppets."

She closes her eyes and shakes her head as I now take her by the hand and charge ahead.

We enter the place and it's more well-lit than I think I was imagining. It's not very dungeon-like at all. It's as sterile-looking as a doctor's office.

A massive, hulking fellow called Jean-Luc is waiting for us. The only part of his body that is not covered with tattoos is his face. There is a tiny rose just below his left eye, but comparatively, his face is clean. Everywhere else though... I can only imagine the hours it took.

He shakes Myrtle's hand, then mine, and when I glance at his forearm, I see "De douleur, de plaisir."

Out of pain, pleasure.

Yep. That's what they tell me.

"Monsieur. Mademoiselle. Bon année," Jean-Luc says. Then, in English, he adds, "So. What are we doing?"

I describe to him what it is we want. He looks at me with slight reservation.

"And this will be your first?" he asks. I nod. He follows up with, "I have to ask... Have you been drinking this evening?"

"Me? No." I laugh. "Nope, I'm completely sober."

"And this is what you would like..."

"New Year, new Pierce," I say. He squints. "Oh. No. That's not—That's my name. Pierce."

"Ton nom est Pierce...?" I shrug and nod. "Ca c'est drôle," he says.

Yeah. I guess it is kind of funny.

He leads me over to the chair that looks like a dentist's chair. I take off my coat and settle in. A couple of kids stumble into the shop and Jean-Luc excuses himself for a moment to toss them out and lock the door.

"Pierce?" Myrtle says.

"Mmm?" I say, absently.

"You. Do not. Have to do this."

I take her hand, smile at her, struck by just how much I feel for this woman. For how important she has been in my life. For how important she will be. For how much she has taught me. For how much she has forgiven me. For how much she trusts me. And I say...

"No. But I want to." I add, "Besides, my father is moving me more and more in the direction of taking over everything."

"Yeah?"

"So... I really will be king someday. I'll need a prince."

She chuckles. "There are other ways of making a prince," she says. "Super fun ones." She strokes my cock through my trousers.

"Stop, stop," I whisper earnestly. "Jean-Luc's gonna have it in his hands in a few seconds and I don't want him to get the wrong idea."

I wink. She smiles again. And then she says, "OK. But just know that one day, when we do have our little prince, I'm not naming him Albert."

"Oh, God, of course not. That'd be weird." She nods. "We're already gonna have a Prince Albert."

Jean-Luc returns, sits next to me, puts on a pair of surprisingly nerdy reading glasses, looks to me for permission, I nod, and then he unzips my pants and pulls out my cock. There's a moment where he regards me with a very French pressing of his lips and nod of his head as if to say, "Très bon." I nod back with a, "Merci."

He lifts up the piercing gun and adjusts the light. I look over at Myrtle one last time and she mouths, Are you sure?

I just smirk—in a way that I, throughout my life, have been told is, "so Pierce"—and say...

"Definitely. Let's crown this prince."

And off everyone's joyous laughter...

THE MOST INTENSE FUCKING PAIN I HAVE EVER FELT COURSES THROUGH ME.

And it feels amazing.

Welcome to the End of Book Shit where Johnathan and I get to say anything we want about the book. These are always done last minute and never edited so excuse our typos. :)

Was this your favorite BDSM rom-com set in a fictional suburb of Denver and subsequently Paris that you read this year?

We hope so.

When we set out to craft this story and realized that this was the direction we wanted to take it, one of the conversations we had to have was how do we utilize an underlying subject matter that has plenty of opportunity for being funny without making fun of it? How do we honor the fact that the dom/sub relationship is a real one that matters to people while simultaneously being jokey about it? Is this the direction we should go? How do we direct the story? How do we control the events?

And, as with everything we now do together, we decided there was only one answer. Stop controlling the story and just submit to what the story wanted us to tell about it. Because these two people, Pierce and Myrtle, have strong, defiant personalities, and there's no way we could have forced them into anything without their explicit permission. They were in control. Not us.

Julie once said to me, "The reason Fifty Shades was a success wasn't because of a goddamn red room or some "kinky" sex. It was because of the contract." (And let's go ahead and abandon the notion that such a thing as "kink" exists, shall we? That's a judgement. And it's relative. One person's kink is another's Sunday brunch.) She noted that the real appeal of those books, conceptually, was that Anastasia Steele was agreeing to her dynamic with Christian Grey.

And look, there have been myriad articles written about the success of the series and the whys and wherefores and what it says about the male/female relationship and female empowerment... And even though I'm a man writing romance with a woman and I do have things to say on the matter, I doubt I have anything new or particularly bright to add to the subject today. We can have that conversation another time. Suffice to say, given Julie Huss's achievements in the world of erotic/romantic fiction, her thoughts about what makes a book like Fifty Shades work can be considered just about as close to expert as anyone's.

Here's why I bring it up ...

Let's assume for the purposes of this essay that hers is an accurate assessing. That at least part of the reason that so much attention has been given to the world of Fifty Shades and the sexual culture contained therein owes to the front facing way those books examine the nature of the relationship between Ana and Chrissy (as I have just decided to start calling him). And not just because it's hot, or sexy, or taboo, or whatever else it might be. Although, if that's the thing about it that draws you in, more power to you. Hell, maybe you just like the suits. I know I do. Custom suits and shoes are my metaphorical red room of pain. It hurts my wallet so badly, but it's worth the agony. (As I say, we all have our fetishes. #NoJudgements)

Since being invited into the romance writing universe just about eighteen months ago, I have learned a lot. A lot about what romance writing is, what it isn't; about what romance readers respond to, what they don't; about the kind of people who read romance (spoiler: there is no one kind of person who reads romance – you are a wide, wonderful, diverse group of humans); and about myself and how I view erotic fiction and its place in the zeitgeist. In other words, I've learned a lot about my own relationship to the world writ large.

And one of the many things I've discovered is that as much as I know about control being an illusion and that giving over to the power of the cosmos is always liberating, it can still be a hard action to practice.

331

I have long had a complicated relationship with the ideas of power and control. I have always believed that no one can take power from you. That power is not about dominion over someone else (or someone else's dominion over you) but about your own engine; how you fuel it and where it takes you. But that notion has frequently butted against certain realities. As an actor, I have spent many years of my life walking into rooms filled with "powerful" people in order to ask them for things. In premise, those "things" have been jobs. (That is the actor's actual job. To audition for jobs. The "job," if you book it, is the reward for having done your actual job well.)

But, in reality, what you are asking for (or what I know I was asking for for a long time), is validation. Am I good enough? Am I deserving? Am I worth something to you? Am I desirable? Y'know... Ego shit.

It is a curious dynamic. On the one hand, you must be self-possessed, and self-reliant, and confident, and poised, and all the rest of it, while on the other hand you are asking for someone else's validation and stamp of approval. There is a reason actors go crazy. (Also, the field attracts a lot of people who have a natural craziness about them. Let's not blame the profession entirely.)

And then at some point many years ago I came to realize that the only way I could get the things I wanted from other people was to learn to give them to myself first and then not care if anyone else noticed. This is the well-known paradox that seems to be proven true time and again: As soon as you stop wanting the elusive thing, the elusive thing shows up. The trick, of course, is that you have to actually stop wanting it. And then, when you get it, it's like, "Eh. I didn't really need it. But thanks."

Another way to say all this is: When you let go of your ego and stop trying to control everything, stuff somehow has a way of working out.

That may mean that it works out exactly like you wanted or it may mean it doesn't but you don't care because you're already fine without it, but either way... You win.

And your win doesn't have to come at the expense of anyone else's loss. You just feel that victory from within. It is frequently unexpected, always unlike what you planned for it to be, and if you're present and honest, it is welcome.

Last week, for a few days, I was ranked inside the top 100 authors of romantic suspense on Amazon. Julie told me that this is something that would happen. That people would read the books we write together and would enjoy them and eventually it would result in some kind of validation that would be measurable.

I didn't necessarily believe her. I couldn't put my finger on why, but I think I have an idea now. It was because I wanted to control things that aren't mine to control.

At first I was very much like, "No. I want to write such and such kind of thing. I want to do this. I want to do that. I want to be able to control the reader's experience in x, y, z kind of way." Julie would say, "Okay, but trust me, this will work. Or that will work. Or just ... trust me. I know what I'm doing."

It was tough for me to give up control. It was difficult for me to try not to bend the work to my will. Hard for me to give over to that kind of trust and believe that I would be safe inside this new experience. Because it was uncomfortable. It was intimidating. It was another way in which I was going to be putting myself up for judgement and asking people to like what I was doing.

But somewhere along the line, I started feeling differently. Not that I didn't care what people would think, but that by trusting my instincts about what we were doing along with submitting to the proven truths of what works in this type of storytelling, I could feel safe. I could believe that my own, sincere giving over of myself to the work might still be scary, or sometimes painful, or sometimes invigorating, but it would always be honest and that the reward I would gain would be growth. Both as an artist and as a person. I learned to trust my collaborator completely. I learned to trust the reader completely. I learned that by becoming submissive to the process, I could let go of the burden of perfection. Or ... whatever the fuck I was chasing on a given day.

It's an odd thing to spend a lifetime in pursuit of personal liberation on a variety of fronts only to discover that when you come face to face with a new experience, you have to learn to liberate your mind all over again. It never ceases to amaze me how much individual power I gain from the act of giving over. I guess it's as simple as ... you can't know how good it feels to stand tall until you've experienced the pain of growing.

Any success I'm having in my life right now owes to the relationships I have. The relationships I have with my writing partner. With the readers. With myself. I have made a contract with all of us.

To Julie, I have made a contract to work as hard as I can, be as invested as I can, and be as honorable as I can to our partnership.

To you, the reader, I have made a contract to give you something worthy of your time, to tell the truth in the stories I write, and – whether funny, serious, suspenseful, or all of the above – to take you on a journey that comes from a place of wanting to serve the work. And by serving the work, serve you.

And with myself, I have made a contract to give over to this incredible journey and enjoy the ride.

It is still challenging sometimes. It is still intimidating sometimes. It is still painful sometimes. But when I get to the end of a new journey (like this one, right now) it always feels so very good.

My never-ending love and gratitude to Julie Huss, for bringing me into her crazy dungeon, my wife, Laura, for coming along with me and holding my hand in the dark, and to you, as ever and always, for being curious enough to peek behind the curtain.

Until next time...

Submissively,
-JM

24 October 2018

As usual I am fashionably late with this EOBS. I am literally down to the wire in must-get-this-thing-written and what-the-hell-do-I-talk-about mode.

Well, I don't think I can top Johnathan's eloquent essay so I'm not even gonna try.

So I'm gonna talk about our 2018. Both the one I shared with you, the reader, and the one I shared with Johnathan, the partner. It's been a helluva year. We began 2018 with a pretty crazy writing schedule (and reading schedule for you guys, right!). Sin With Me was done by the time January 2018 rolled around but that was only book one. We still had three more books to write and not very much time to do it. And in between all that I was writing and releasing the Jordan's Game series.

I think as we were finishing up Passion Rising, which is the last book in the Original Sin Series, Johnathan and I were looking forward to the break. We'd worked hard and now it was time to take it down a notch.

And that lasted… oh, maybe two weeks. Because we were going to be signing at Book Bonanza in July and we really (like REALLY) wanted The Sexpert to be available for it. So we doubled down. And during this time Johnathan was super busy recording audiobooks and acting, but writing a book is a lot like giving birth. It sucks a whole bunch while you're in the whole gestation part and becomes almost unbearable in the week leading up to release, but when it's all said an done and release day is over and you're holding that pretty paperback in your hand you kinda forget that you hated everything and everyone around you just a few weeks ago.

So even though we REALLY thought (for sure this time) that we're gonna take a break after Sexpert was born, along came The Triangle. And hell, let's just stop pretending, OK? Let's just knock this second TDH book out because Myrtle and Pierce are super cool and funny and bigger than life in every way imaginable.

So let's just face the facts.

Johnathan and I just aren't "down-time" people.

:)

I think that part of the reason we work well together. We love to work.

When we finish a book and there's no words owed to each other the next day it feels weird. I wake up and think—"What is this day that has no deadline attached to it? I must start a book!"

And maybe some of my workaholic nature rubbed off on Johnathan, but I don't think so. I think this is just who we are.

So good news for you! More books coming! Because we can't stop writing! lol

As far as this books goes—hell, Myrtle was one fun character to be for seventy-five thousand words. I respect the hell out of her. When I decided to make her come from "circus people" it was a little bit because I sorta come from circus people too. (If you knew that already, you get a cookie for being one of my superfans.)

I wanted to make her outrageous, but believable. And I wanted people to relate to her. Maybe your father isn't a lion tamer and maybe your mother isn't a librarian, but most people can relate to the idea that you don't want to end up like your parents.

If you did want to end up like your parents, well you're a very lucky person. That's all I can say. Because my father was a professional golfer and I hated golf. To this day I can't stand the idea of golf. And my mother was always pretty satisfied with her lot in life, pretty content to just do her job and let things happen as they will, and I'm just one of those people who likes to create my own future. I am always on the lookout for another opportunity to change.

So I relate to Myrtle a lot. She is a woman who has remade herself several times. She started out in the shadow of her mother, the simple librarian, and her father, who courted danger every hour of his working life. And when it came time to step out of those shadows she didn't know who the hell she was.

But my favorite thing about Myrtle is that she wasn't looking for anything. She was very happy, very content, and she probably wasn't even thinking about her future. She was just... comfortable.

And comfortable is a dangerous thing to be when you're a person who craves change. So most of her conflict in this book mirrors my 2018 conflict in real life. Because I decided to reroute my career and become part of a writing TEAM, it felt a lot like starting over. And even though starting over was something I've done many, many times and been very successful, if I do say so myself, it was pretty scary. But you know what they say—what doesn't kill you makes you stronger.

I think that's Myrtle's take home from this experience.

The other cool thing I loved about this story is that Myrtle's perception of herself isn't the same as how other people saw her. Which is probably true for almost everyone. But the way they saw her, though horrifying to Myrtle, was really kinda validating. Because whether she knew it or not, she was projecting that image. No doubt about it, no one was missing the fact that Myrtle was one wild woman. No lions or tigers necessary. If Myrtle is in the room, she is at the top of the food chain.

Some people are just like that.

And I am in love with this crazy guy called Pierce. He stole the show in The Sexpert and I think we knew, almost from day one, that Myrtle and Pierce were destined to be together.

I hope you enjoyed the second book in the Tall, Dark, and Handsome series. I hope the TDH is starting to feel like your neighborhood. I hope you enjoyed meeting some characters in this story—Pearl will be back at some point. And I'm pretty sure, by the time Johnathan and I are done with this neighborhood, you'll be BFF's with just about everyone we'd mentioned so far.

Well, maybe not that weird artsy chick from the gallery because she kinda scares me.

(But there's one thing I've learned about this business is, "Never say never!")

I *think* the next time we revisit the TDH we'll be going back to see what Zoey and Baby Stevie are up to. So stay tuned for that.

Until then you can check out our other romantic suspense series The Shape of Love Book One, The Triangle. Or get my next solo book The Dirty Ones, which releases December 4, 2018 and is up for preorder now.

Until then, Unicorn Bitches.

Thanks for reading. Thanks for reviewing. And see you in the next book.

Julie
October 25, 2018

P.S.
If you enjoyed Pierced and haven't checked out THE SEXPERT it's now in Kindle Unlimited! Have a read to see where it all started...

If you want to try out another JA Huss book that's "sorta" rom com, give Mr. Perfect a go. I also have a to-book series called Social Media that is super cute and funny and a standalone book called Sexy that has some great LOL moments too. (All of those are available at Amazon, KOBO, Nook, and iBooks.

Julie & Johnathan
HussMcClain.com

Johnathan McClain's career as a writer and actor spans 25 years and covers the worlds of theatre, film, and television. At the age of 21, Johnathan moved to Chicago where he wrote and began performing his critically acclaimed one-man show, Like It Is. The Chicago Reader proclaimed, "If we're ever to return to a day when theatre matters, we'll need a few hundred more artists with McClain's vision and courage." On the heels of its critical and commercial success, the show subsequently moved to New York where Johnathan was compared favorably to solo performance visionaries such as Eric Bogosian, John Leguizamo, and Anna Deavere Smith.

Johnathan lived for many years in New York, and his work there includes appearing Off-Broadway in the original cast of Jonathan Tolins' The Last Sunday In June at The Century Center, as well as at Lincoln Center Theatre and with the Lincoln Center Director's Lab. Around the country, he has been seen on stage at South Coast Repertory, The American Conservatory Theatre,

Florida Stage, Paper Mill Playhouse, and the National Jewish Theatre. Los Angeles stage credits are numerous and include the LA Weekly Award nominated world premiere of Cold/Tender at The Theatre @ Boston Court and the LA Times' Critic's Choice production of The Glass Menagerie at The Colony Theatre for which Johnathan received a Garland Award for his portrayal of Jim O'Connor.

On television, he appeared in a notable turn as Megan Draper's LA agent, Alan Silver, on the final season of AMC's critically acclaimed drama Mad Men, and as the lead of the TV Land comedy series, Retired at 35, starring alongside Hollywood icons George Segal and Jessica Walter. He has also had Series Regular roles on The Bad Girl's Guide starring Jenny McCarthy and Jessica Simpson's sitcom pilot for ABC. His additional television work includes recurring roles on the CBS drama SEAL TEAM and Fox's long-running 24, as well as appearances on Grey's Anatomy, NCIS: Los Angeles, Trial and Error, The Exorcist, Major Crimes, The Glades, Scoundrels, Medium, CSI, Law & Order: SVU, Without a Trace, CSI: Miami, and Happy Family with John Larroquette and Christine Baranski, amongst others. On film, he appeared in the Academy Award nominated Far from Heaven and several independent features.

As an audiobook narrator, he has recorded almost 100 titles. Favorites include the Audie Award winning Illuminae by Amie Kaufman and Jay Kristoff and The Last Days of Night, by Academy Winning Screenwriter Graham Moore (who is also Johnathan's close friend and occasional collaborator). As well as multiple titles by his dear friend and writing partner, JA Huss, with whom he is hard at work making the world a little more romantic.

He lives in Los Angeles with his wife Laura.

JA Huss never wanted to be a writer and she still dreams of that elusive career as an astronaut. She originally went to school to become an equine veterinarian but soon figured out they keep horrible hours and decided to go to grad school instead. That Ph.D wasn't all it was cracked up to be (and she really sucked at the whole scientist thing), so she dropped out and got a M.S. in forensic toxicology just to get the whole thing over with as soon as possible.

After graduation she got a job with the state of Colorado as their one and only hog farm inspector and spent her days wandering the Eastern Plains shooting the shit with farmers.

After a few years of that, she got bored. And since she was a homeschool mom and actually does love science, she decided to write science textbooks and make online classes for other homeschool moms.

She wrote more than two hundred of those workbooks and was the number one publisher at the online homeschool store many times, but eventually she covered every science topic she could think of and ran out of shit to say.

So in 2012 she decided to write fiction instead. That year she released her first three books and started a career that would make her a New York Times bestseller and land her on the USA Today Bestseller's List twenty-one times in the next four years.

Her books have sold millions of copies all over the

world, the audio version of her semi-autobiographical book, Eighteen, was nominated for an Audie award in 2016, her audiobook, Mr. Perfect, was nominated for a Voice Arts Award in 2017, and her audiobook, Taking Turns, was nominated for an Audie award in 2018.

Johnathan McClain is her first (and only) writing partner and even though they are worlds apart in just about every way imaginable, it works.

She lives on a ranch in Central Colorado with her family.

If you'd like to learn more about JA Huss and Johnathan McClain you can visit them on their website at www.HussMcClain.com.

You can also join their fan group, Shrike Bikes, on Facebook at www.facebook.com/groups/shrikebikes and you can follow them on Twitter at @JAHuss and @MisterJMcClain.

Printed in March 2019
by Rotomail Italia S.p.A., Vignate (MI) - Italy